LAND OF THE
HOOSIER DAWN

LAND
OF THE
HOOSIER DAWN

NICK YOUNKER

Cover Art:
Hand: © Can Stock Photo Inc. / andreykuzmin
Cliffside Town: © Can Stock Photo Inc. / anshar

Edited by
Laurel Black

Cover Design and Interior Formatting by
Will Overby/Black Cat Books

Published by
Fogstow Jamison Press

ISBN-13: 978-0692676196
ISBN-10: 0692676198

ACKNOWLEDGEMENTS

My Folks, for paving the road I walk down.

My Kids, for walking down the road with me.

Laurel Black, for her strong editing skills.

Will Overby, for his amazing knowledge of cover design, formatting and many other publishing skills.

-N.Y.

News Brief: Op-Ed from *Louisville-New Albany Metro/Regional Gazette*: Online edition, October 5, 2013. Article by Reina Petrow originally published in horror and sci-fi news magazine *Fogstow-Jamison Morgue*: Online and Print edition, October 2, 2013.

FOGSTOW: 20 YEARS LATER

Nothing says October quite as well as Fogstow, Indiana. And nothing says Fogstow, Indiana quite as well as disaster, tragedy, murder and intrigue. Dead bodies and coal mines. Creatures and the supernatural. Of course, those have been the running theories now for 20 years, ever since the real tragedy that took place in the small Indiana town just an hour's drive from here, in the Louisville metro area.

But nowadays, you can't just drive into Fogstow. The ghost town has been sealed off ever since the event that rocked the region and brought thrill seekers in from around the nation.

So how has the legend of Fogstow progressed over the last twenty years and what kind of "riverlore" has been attributed to it?

Well, before you start listening to those stories and what they mean to the people who tell them, let's start off with a few facts.

Fact #1: Fogstow was a fractured mining community. Although the coal mines had shut down years before the events of October 2, 1993, it was the deserted Oarshire Mines that played a major role in the day that would set a series of events into motion.

Fact #2: Izzy Brown! Yes, the leading lady from iconic goth-rock band *Izzy Lives* was actually from the small town, and legend has it that she went back there just before she disappeared.

In fact, this reporter was covering the story for the *Louisville-New Albany Metro/Regional Gazette* back in 1993, and I found out that she was in town on Oct. 2 of that year, which was the day the event took place. But she got out just before it reached critical mass.

For those of you who have been living under a rock for the past two decades, Izzy Brown went missing on June 23, 1994. At least, that was when she was last seen. This was just days before the release of her debut album, *Two-Ton Moon*, which went on to sell over 20 million copies. At the time, it was considered a posthumous release.

Fact #3: Disasters happen. This town is no different from any other town that has faced an industrial tragedy. You don't have to chalk that up to supernatural forces or mysterious creatures. These kinds of tragedies are real.

With that said, let's talk about the legacy Fogstow left behind. The legacy that has caught the nation's attention and vivid imagination. Even Hollywood has been chomping at the bit to take a bite out of this mysterious story.

Details from the devastation left behind have been a closely guarded secret by state and federal officials. Jamison County is still in litigation with parent mining company Oarshire Inc. regarding its former mining operation in the county. It has been cited for multiple violations against the terms of its lease and state reclamation mandates.

Although some accounts that emerged from ground zero have indicated there was more devastation there than just the disastrous mine incident, Oarshire representatives have been fighting the state and the feds for detailed reports that have been classified now for the past two decades.

Denial of access to these reports could ultimately get Oarshire off the hook for financial responsibility to the victims and their families. This Catch-22 has fueled independent investigations into the incident. People have gone missing over the course of these investigations, which occurred in the late '90s and early 2000s.

You might also say that what's taken place after that day is almost as interesting as what happened on that day.

Chapter 1

Opening Day

1

IT WASN'T ONLY THE SMELL of frying bacon and eggs that riled appetites in Fogstow, Indiana in the early morning hours. The sound of the food cooking was enough to bring everyone to the serving counter ready for a hearty breakfast and a good reason to start the day among people they knew and cared about.

Even though the Riverbend Deli and Grill was originally meant to be a lunch counter, it had grown over the years to bring in the breakfast and dinner crowds. As more time went by, the late night barge traffic and the recreational boaters on the Ohio River gave it a reason to expand to some overnight hours, and before long, it was the place to go for dinner in eastern Jamison county, with the exception of the Elk's Club on Saturday nights. There was also a Tastee Freeze out on Fischer Road just before the Highway 66 on-ramp, which was a quick in-and-out for ice cream and chili dogs.

But the Riverbend is where the community came together and ate dinner, laughed at each other's stories, arranged carpool plans for the school days and made PTO decisions. It was where they came to hold booster club meetings for their small high school and where the Tiger Scouts earned their merit badges. It was also where they all met to form a search party for the boy who went missing on the rolling pine hills and for the young female musician who went missing out on the river.

The Riverbend was right there in the heart of their nice little town of just over 1,200 residents. It sat next to the Co-op, which also had an A&W stand on the backside next to the hay bales and grain tanks, where trucks entered off Locust Street.

The Riverbend (or just the 'Bend, as the townsfolk liked to call it) and the Co-op both sat high on the bluff overlooking the Fogstow channel, which fed in from the Ohio River. They also overlooked the old Weyerbacher Coal Docks, which now host the Stow Tavern and various river recreational shops, including Anderson Bait and Tackle, Fogstow Marine Supply and a small gas terminal. The old docks still took in a lot of river commerce once the Weyerbacher Coal Yard and Docks closed down.

The coal docks were quite active in the '70s and early '80s, with the Ayrlobe coal quarry just a couple of miles to the northeast and the gigantic Oarshire coal quarry half a mile west of town, just before you get into the Hoosier National Forest. Oarhsire originally owned the stripping operation on the northeast end of town, but when talk about organizing into a labor union started in the late '70s, Oarshire split the leases and isolated the union agitators in the northeast quarry, then sold it off to Ayrlobe.

Ayrlobe came in and got the operation running again, but they never built a belt line to the coal docks because their grandfathered laborers were getting irritated by the $5.75 an hour pay rate. They brought the union talk back into the equation and Ayrlobe decided they would rather shut the operation down completely instead of paying their workers a living wage.

The Oarshire beltline fed the yard and sometimes even loaded the barges without the assistance of the dock cranes. Most of the time, the barges were fed by the belt. But when there was an overflow, the coal got deposited in the yard and the cranes loaded the barges. There were even a few times when they had to hold the belt line just to get more barges in for immediate loading because the yard was too full. That entire area had been blackened down to a coal dust wasteland before the mines were stripped clean and closed down back in '82. Workers voted a union in about 16 months before the mine closed, without much slack from the company. Most people thought Oarshire likely knew the operation was winding down due to a depletion of the natural resources, so they didn't put up much resistance to the union vote.

The Weyerbachers kept the Fogstow townsfolk working by leasing dock space to crushed stone companies for barge loading.

But once those companies started building their own yards back in '84 and running their rock straight out of the quarries onto the barges, they shut down permanently.

The people of Fogstow didn't exactly truck out of town, though. They found work in nearby Barrelton or they commuted to Louisville, even though it was over an hour's drive. Some also found work in the nearby Cape Sandy quarry, working the crushed stone mines and keeping the barges moving. When the New Amsterdam quarry opened up on the other side of the river bend, it created more avenues of income for the townspeople and Fogstow survived. Sure, a few might have left town after the docks closed, but most of them just settled in nearby Derbie because it was closer to Barrelton. Derbie was just a quick hop across the National Forest and most of the transplants frequently visited Fogstow.

The simple fact was, this town had something that most others had failed to accomplish in the early '90s; a sense of community. It was like their own little version of that TV show, *Where Everybody Knows Your Name*. 1993 was a time of trust, friendship, partnership and, most importantly, safety. No one locked their doors during the daytime when they shipped off to school or work. There was really no need. The people of this town were active; during the day, most people got out and did their business in town. Everyone was everyone else's neighbor and neighbors looked out for each other and their property. They locked their doors at night, though. Drifters from the Interstate would wander in to town, looking for a quick score.

Fogstow was a small town settled on the high bluffs of the Fogstow channel in Jamison County. The channel ran nearly a quarter mile inland from the Ohio River and terminated at the old coal docks. Although it was fairly deep inland, that didn't stop the river traffic from coming in. The county let them post a small wooden billboard on the edge of the river pointing into the channel for recreational supplies and necessities, which included the small business community that took over the Weyerbacher docks. The town invested a lot of tax dollars fixing them up and the business there prospered.

On most days, and all through the night, a johnboat, or a *johnny,* as the natives would call them, would roll in from the stone barges and pick up some takeout from the 'Bend. They always radioed in their orders from CBs because the deckhands could only be gone for 10 to 15 minutes at a time. The barges had to keep rolling to stay on delivery schedules, but a johnny motor could easily outrun the barges, so they were able to make the runs and catch back up to their barge. The 'Bend servers would always walk the orders down dockside and have them ready when they pulled up. They all ran charge accounts, so the deckhand would just scribble down a signature on a charge slip and take off with their food. The companies would come in every month and pay off their tabs. That's just how smooth things ran in their channel, driven by trust and respect.

The Weyerbacher docks sat at the bottom of the Fogstow bluff and a long set of concrete stairs led up to the main business district with the 'Bend, the Co-op and other various businesses including a hardware store and a funeral parlor. Adams Street led into the docks and most of the residential area circled around three rolling pine hills. The residential areas, although not considered subdivisions, were still separated into four main districts that divided them out.

One section was named Squaw Creek, which fed right up to the docks from Adams Street and was visible from the highland "uptown" area. It was always a part of the town and most of the people who lived there were multi-generational and had spent their entire lives in Fogstow.

Another was called Turkey Crossing, or the TC, which was settled on the west side of the tallest pine hill. This wasn't a part of Fogstow until the late '80s. A lot of the more affluent townsfolk built homes in this area to avoid paying local taxes in the early '80s. The town waited until the area filled up and annexed it in '89. But Fogstow never optioned to expand their sewer system underneath it due to fear of sinkholes collapsing the area. Most believed the original mine shafts and utility caves were never filled in, which violated the reclamation terms of the county lease and many other state and federal mandates.

There was another area generally referred to as Alcatraz Beach (or the Beach, by some) because if you stood in the middle of it, you couldn't tell if it was in the remote wilderness or part of a larger community. It was also an area that was level to the river and ideal for swimming, although no one dared swim in the polluted Ohio. The town of Fogstow annexed the Beach in 1989 along with the TC, then expanded their sewer system underneath it to collect town sewer fees. Even though it was part of Fogstow you cannot see the town from it because Pine 1 was blocking it. It fed into the bend on the river, so some people just came together and built a makeshift private dock and ran their boats over to the coal docks when they wanted to come downtown. The town built a small park around their dock area and a utility barn so they could give the Beach community a sense of belonging. Most of the people in Alcatraz Beach liked living in a more remote area of the town. But they were still close enough to do their business without having to drive all the way down to Barrelton.

The highland district, or uptown area, had a few older homes in and around it on the main level, but it was mostly older folk or town officials who resided there. They did build a town park over the western bluff that overlooked their large channel and they also built a trail (with Jamison County funds) all the way up to the Ohio River for hiking and exercise. The whole area there had been leveled decades earlier from the earliest Oarshire coal mines, but the reclaim land had been growing nicely over the past 40 years. Oarshire stripped all the western area and most of Jamison County leading into the National Forest over the course of about 75 years. Wild brush and trees grew in and put some fantastic shade on the trail. But a little further west of the trail, maybe half a mile, there was a sinkhole that swallowed up the area and the county had it off limits to the general public, with a lawsuit pending against Oarshire. Teens and children saw that as a challenge and spent a lot of time in the area exploring or just cutting loose and doing wild things. It was kind of like a magnet to youth of all ages, likely because there was a total absence of adult supervision.

Main Street ran north and south in front of the 'Bend and the Co-op, and then wrapped around heading due west toward Highway 66 and East Jamison High School. The 'Bend faced Main Street and the gravel parking lot came up on the wrap around, which sat adjacent to the park. Highway 66, heading west toward Derbie, had a few scattered homes that littered the area beside a lot of reclaim land with small brush and a few trees, and you could tell nature was struggling to reclaim the land once ravaged by the coal mines. The landscape looked like a semi-barren Serengeti. Bobcats and mountain lions even roamed it, but they were rarely seen, especially during the day.

Highway 66 was the express route to Interstate 64 heading north and Barrelton heading south. Barrelton was a much bigger city than Fogstow and was also the Jamison County seat, so there was a lot of business that most folk had to tend to there.

In the middle of Fogstow, leading north, Main Street came around and ran parallel to Squaw Creek. The area was much lower than the main district and that is where you could find the local supermarket, video store and various small businesses including Bev's Beauty Salon and Gil's Convenience Store and Gas Station. Gil's also doubled as a taxidermist and a deer meat processing shop.

In the fall, scores of trucks would line up in front of Gil's every

Saturday morning just before dawn, leave for several hours and then come back with deer strapped to their hoods or in the bed of their trucks. The kids would get out their three-wheel ATVs and make passes around the large rock parking lot shaking their strawberry soda bottles and spraying each other with them while their dads struck up racy conversations with each other and hauled their catches inside for tagging and processing. Their wives would usually wait until Saturday afternoon to come into the beauty salon because they certainly did not want to be around the primitive feeding frenzies that took place there with their husbands and children. That gave the men enough time when they got home to take their kids up on Pine Hill for a round of snipe hunting.

The Saturday snipe hunts were fully endorsed by the town, and they always wheeled the concession stand out and sold strawberry and cream sodas from the fountain along with Grippos Barbecue Chips. The kids would follow their dads' strict instructions to rustle up the brush on the side of the hill and scare the snipe out of hiding. They said the snipe all had one leg longer than the other so they could run along the hillside. The kids were all instructed to scare them out of the brush, chase them down and hogtie their legs, then bring them back down for inspection. Of course this was all a bogus trick on the youth, but it was a rite of passage for the younger generations and was carried down year after year. The men would sit at the bottom of the hill on their trucks, drinking beer and hosing the blood out of their beds while the kids would run all along the sides of Pine 2, rustling through the brush and screaming like banshees. Everyone always had a good time.

The supermarket was open every night until 8 p.m. and served the entire community, along with Derbie. It even got some Barrelton traffic. It was well known for having the freshest meat in the county. Their deli was also known for the best array of salads, which included German potato salad, deviled-egg salad, Coney Island spread and various other delicious small-town concoctions.

On the northern end of town, Main Street led all the way back out to Highway 66 because it formed an "L" shape running east and west before it got to town, then north and south when it ran through town. But before you got to the north end of Squaw Creek, it forked apart, with Main Street Baptist Church directly in the middle. This was by far the biggest church, and congregation, in town. The church building itself occupied a little more than an acre of land with two levels on the north end and a full vaulted ceiling sanctuary on the south end that rose two stories. The gigantic parking lot that occupied the northern and western sides of the building had a large picnic area on the north end accompanied by a soccer and baseball field that split in two.

The American Legion occupied the far north end of the block between the Main Street fork and spread all the way to the northern boundary of Squaw Creek at Spring Street. Members there routinely parked in the outfield and drank canned PBRs while watching the youth baseball games. Needless to say, more than one windshield had been shattered over the years from home runs, but they didn't mind. Deacon's Glass Service over in Derbie made a good living off the Fogstow Legionnaires.

Once October arrived in 1993, on a Friday nonetheless, the townspeople were gearing up for a great opening weekend with their bows. Opening day for deer season in Indiana was on October 1st, but in Fogstow, it was the first Saturday in October and most of the town was only working a half-day on Friday (if at all) so they could get ready.

Friday, October 1st, 1993 was a happy day and everyone embraced it with festive spirits. Early morning Friday at around 6 a.m., the windows and doors were open at the 'Bend because an unusual heat wave had caught them by surprise. At 6am the temperature was already at 68 degrees. The sounds of eggs cracking and frying, bacon sizzling and popping, mixers readying pancakes and toast popping out of the toaster filled the streets. Scores of townsfolk were up early and eating at the 'Bend. The room was filled by 6:30am and the mood was great. Everyone was truly happy with their lives in Fogstow.

What a difference a single day can make.

2

There certainly was no sleeping past 6 a.m. when you lived part-time on the second floor of the Co-op in a small town, especially next door to the 'Bend Deli. Breakfast was fired up early on that Friday. Everyone was on an October high, getting ready for the fall kickoff to deer season tomorrow. It was the first day of bow season, but the town didn't celebrate it until the first Saturday of the season, which was October 2nd in 1993. It was tradition.

By the time Police Chief Linton Derr got down to the 'Bend for breakfast, the place was already packed from wall to wall. You couldn't even find a seat at the serving counter on a day like that. The whole town treated it like a holiday and most people would only work a half-day and then come home early to get themselves and their kids ready for Saturday morning.

The Elks Club always cooked up a special dinner the Friday night before, which included brain sandwiches, burgoo with egg salad, Coney Island spread and Grippos Barbecue Chips for the kids. They also opened up their strawberry and cream soda fountain and gave the kids sparklers for after dinner. But most would be gone early so they could wake up at 4 a.m. and meet the scores of trucks down at Gil's at 4:30 a.m. to register for the half-pot contest. The morning check-in at 10:30 a.m. for processing and the half-pot winner did not get drawn from a bucket, but rather from whoever had the buck with the most points. The other half of the pot got donated to the Riley Hospital for Children Foundation up in Indy.

Linton did not like spending his nights on top of the Co-op, but if he had a prisoner in the cells, he had to stay. Last night, he got a call from Sheriff Marvin Kramer asking him to hold a prisoner due to a court scheduling conflict. But Linton knew the real reason was because he simply could not allow Bret Holder to be held at the county jail down in Barrelton. Bret had filed a complaint against one of his deputies. He accused Deputy Shane Aaron of stealing money out of his full-size Bronco after he arrested him for driving while intoxicated. Bret told them he would drop the complaint if they dropped the DWI charge.

Hell, the way I see it, Shane earned the cash by getting me off the road. Now he can keep it if you guys drop the charge and let me go. No questions asked, Bret had told Sheriff Kramer.

To be fair, he could have probably kept Holder at the jail in Barrelton overnight, but Deputy Aaron had a shift last night and he wanted to keep everything squeaky clean until after the internal investigation. Everyone knew that Holder was lying through his teeth, trying to get out of his DWI because that made three for him. He was just another rich kid who thought he could do whatever he wanted, but the law eventually caught up to him and now he was going to serve some time in the county lock up, or maybe in Terre Haute. But Linton didn't mind. He served as a deputy under Sheriff Kramer for seven years until he took the job up river in Fogstow. Kramer always treated him well and he was a good man. He didn't mind doing a few favors for him now and then.

The Fogstow town council voted unanimously almost two years before to hire Linton as the full-time chief of police, but he was chief only to himself. He didn't have anyone else to back him up from the town, the money simply wasn't there. Of course he always got the backup he needed from the county deputies and the sheriff. His job made him only a modest living, paying him just over $20,000 a year. Linton certainly wasn't in it for the pay. His family, especially on his mother's side (Weyerbacher), had enough money to tide them over for a few generations. But just like his mother had always told him, *if you have money then you can spend your life one of two ways: existing in the world, or making the world a better place.* Linton already saw what it was like to live a life wasted from watching his Uncle Kerry Weyerbacher and he was for damn sure not going to make the same mistake. He also saw the way it hurt his mother to watch Uncle Kerry day in and day out, drinking at the Mulberry Club in Barrelton and coming home to Linton's grandmother's house because he had no other place to go. He would sleep in the pool house and send the gardener or caretakers out for aspirin and food when he was hungover.

Linton's mother, Carolyn Weyerbacher-Derr, made sure he saw everything that his Uncle Kerry did, which included the constant boozing, doping and the misogynistic way he treated women around town. Although Kerry had spent a lot of nights behind the wheel with empty liquor bottles and a white mustache, it wasn't until he decided to feel up a young lady in the Mulberry that he finally got pinched for something.

Tisha Keethers was a 15-year-old Barrelton High School student who had sneaked into the Mulberry Club one day with her mischievous aunt. She may have looked a little older, but it was her aunt who had vouched for her with the club owners, so she was served drinks all afternoon and into the evening. Kerry came in early that evening and quickly sniffed her out. After several quick drinks and a few lines of cocaine, he took her into the VIP lounge for a more religious study of her body. She was passed out when they found him with her, but he claimed she was a very willing participant.

When he found out she was only fifteen, the shame of his actions caused him to attempt suicide with a broken glass bottle while he was out on bail. To Linton, it seemed that just about anyone under the influence of alcohol could reason his way into thinking his desires are acceptable and that they will not be held accountable for acting out on them. And it's *those days where we finally see that we are at the bottom of the barrel, the lowest we can go on the humanity scale . . . it's then and only then does our soul come awake to do its job.*

Of course, that was only Linton's take on the matter and after seeing his uncle locked up down in Evansville at the state hospital for two years, he was convinced everyone had a soul, and that some let their souls get lazy. They let it shut down and take long naps and what happens in between, that's what forces them to witness the evil mankind is *truly* capable of.

If you were to have asked the people of Fogstow what kind of evil they had around there, they wouldn't say any person in particular, with the exception of the Jeffries who lived high up in the plateau on the northeast side of Pine 2. Some people thought they were cannibals, but that was just riverlore and never proven.

The real source of evil in these parts, or so their superstitions would tell them, was the Ohio River. For starters, there was no one in the entire state, let alone in the town of Fogstow, who didn't know not to eat anything they caught out of the river. It was the most polluted river in the nation, and some people even sent their kids out with binoculars after a few campfire stories to see if they could find the glowing fish swimming around at night.

But people like Alice Konicke will swear to you that all of the bodies they pulled out of the Ohio River in these parts were dead before they went in. In her mind the river will never kill your victim for you, but it will hide your bodies. It was her belief that a truly evil man was not possessed by the devil. As a matter of fact, she did not believe the devil could force himself upon any human being. *But if he were to appear in the form of himself, clear as day, or in the form of an innocent human being, he would give you just enough information to make you believe he was your savior, because he cannot force you to do anything. He can only reason with you in a way that fits his agenda. He can only make suggestions. In the end, it was entirely up to you whether to heed his suggestion or to walk away from him and be a good person. In the end, it is only you who can make the world a better place. But at some point, you are going to face the devil and you're gonna have to choose. At some point, you're gonna come face to face with the true evil of the River, and when you do, be ready.*

Alice was not the only person who felt that way about the Ohio River. No one in town would let their kids swim in the calm Fogstow channel. But those feelings were a little different about ten years before. Back then, people knew the Ohio River was being polluted by the coal and stone quarries up and down it, but they also thought that nature would filter itself out and the water would be okay again. Unfortunately, they tended to dismiss the fact that the Ohio River stretched all way up to Pittsburgh and it flowed from there directly down to them. They were a little too tolerant of the fact that all the factories between here and there, which included the steel town itself, Cincinnati and Louisville, were also dumping their waste into the river. It was as if they thought the chemical and metallic pollution could not reach them, or that it would somehow be diluted before it got to them. At best, their naïve thinking cost one person his life.

After the coal docks closed down, they built a small beach on the eastern side of the channel and even cleared a path to walk to it. It was well away from the dock and there were also buoys that were marked with "CHILDREN'S SWIM AREA. NO BOATS OR WAKE PERMITTED." But sometimes, the bigger boats would pull through and dock and when the children were in their area swimming, they would wait for those big boats to leave and as they were pulling out, the children would yank their arms in the air and tug up and down on their imaginary air horns. The boaters would see them and set off their loud air horns, then kick it into high gear and send waves over to the kids. The deputies didn't say anything because the children loved it and their parents didn't raise a fuss. Nevertheless, they kept the signs on the buoys as an official rule in case they needed to detain someone who was out of control.

Back in '85, when the new beach was less than a year old, three teenage boys were swimming when the weather was just coming out of spring and the water was still moderately cold, 78 degrees maybe. It was on a dare, of course. They were the only ones brave enough to tough out the cool water, so off they went.

Later that day, those same teens landed in the hospital down in Barrelton. At first, it was just a severe ear infection. The next morning, emergency room doctors had them on an intravenous antibiotics and a morphine drip. The boys were in so much pain, they trembled when they slept. The antibiotic seemed to work for a while, but two days later, sepsis started to kick in. They were all three life-flighted to Louisville in helicopters and specialists were brought in from around the country. Although they were able to defeat the infection over the course of two weeks, the truly baffling nature of it was that they had never seen anything like it before, and never after. Those same boys went to college that fall and seemed to do fine. But one committed suicide after graduation. Student debt was a heavy load to carry and the boy graduated with a pre-law degree from UK. It was speculated that the debt was why, but he did not leave a note and no one could say for sure.

People like Alice Konicke and others around town said that the debt might be enough to drive someone to suicide, but they also pointed out that the river was directly responsible for his ailment in the beginning. *But just like with everyone, the river does not kill people. That kind of evil does not force itself upon human beings, so they survived. But once that boy gave in to the powerful suggestion he was exposed to, that's when the river had him.*

The town closed the beach after the boys were sent to Louisville. After the second week of their hospitalization, they came through and filled the beach in with rip-rap stones from the Cape Sandy quarry.

* * *

Linton walked into the 'Bend, flipped up the false-end on the counter and motioned for Kelly Doss. Kelly was an attractive lady in her late twenties. At about five and a half feet tall with brown hair, she could catch a man's eye fairly easily. She had one of those half smiles that Linton really loved. The kind where when she would smile, she only raised the right side of her cheek and you couldn't see it if you were standing on the left side of her. Kelly's grandmother said those kinds of smiles looked like *she was smarter than everyone around her. The half-smile was her way of condescending people without them ever knowing it.*

That always made Kelly self-conscious about her smile because she did not want to offend anyone, no matter how intelligent they were. But her grandmother just laughed and said, *Young lady, you are one of the smartest girls I've ever met. Don't you ever hold back! Don't you ever dumb yourself down for folks around you! When you have something to say and it's smart, then people in your life can only stand to benefit from it. But if you hold it back, then you cheat those around you.* Her grandmother died of natural causes when Kelly was 16 and less than a year later, her mother died of breast cancer. Her father had never been in Kelly's life, so she was on her own after that. Fogstow became her family and the people there loved her.

Kelly was filling coffee mugs at the breakfast counter. She

smiled at Linton and held up a finger: a signal for him to wait a minute. Linton had thought it would be a cool day so he wore his Chief jacket. But there it was, 6:30 in the morning and his chest was hot as an oven. The Bend was keeping its doors and windows open to let the breeze in, but that didn't help much with the stoves so close to the counter. He wanted to take it off but it was so packed inside that it would just be a hassle. He picked up a small, brown paper bag and filled it with hot peanuts from the warmer, then poured a glass of orange juice from the cool, sweaty pitcher on the back counter. Bob Stamps, one of Linton's closest friends and an old classmate, appeared from behind the dishing window, set an omelet plate on the window warmer then clanked the "order-ready" bell with a greasy spatula.

"Three-egg cheese omelet, burnt in ketchup and toast. Ready to go," Bob said.

Linton ducked down and looked through the window. "Bob? What are you doing back there?" Linton said.

Bob was turning away but he quickly looked back at Linton.

"Oh, hey Boss. I told Kelly last night that I would help them out on the back stoves. Pete has the front stoves today and I'm taking care of the specialties back here." Of course Bob was referring to Pete Brown, part owner of the 'Bend, alongside Kelly Doss.

Linton was a little embarrassed when Bob called him Boss. About a week ago, Bret Holder came into town with his dog Boner, an ashy black husky-hound mix, and stopped in at the A&W stand. Bob ran the forklift in the yard out back of the Co-op, and when people pulled up to buy a float, Bob would hop off and make it for them. Bret came in his father's new extended cab truck and ordered up 20 hay bales for a party. He also wanted a float while he was waiting, so Bob got off the forklift and made it for him.

Bret was passing the time by tossing lit matches at Boner in the truck bed and laughing while the poor dog jumped and yelped. His cruelty to all living things was equal in humans and canines. Boner was a shy and gentle dog. He had experienced a lot of cruelty at Bret's hands over the years, which included a branding of the NRA logo on his rear hind thigh. Boner had become skittish, but not aggressive toward humans.

Bob was the only one on the backlot taking care of the yard work, so it was taking awhile to get Bret loaded. Once Bret grew tired of teasing Boner, he started complaining about how long it was taking Bob to load his truck. He was really mouthing off to him, but Bob just kept on working as quickly as he could.

Linton was sitting on the bench out front of the Co-op, eating his peanuts, and he could hear Bret's mouthy insults. He came around back in just enough time to see Bret not just teasing Bob while he was on the forklift, but also forcing him to swerve. Fortunately, Bob missed Bret with the forklift, but knocked over a stack of hay bales and a shelf full of paint cans. Linton got so pissed off that he immediately shoved Bret against his truck and put the cuffs on him. He told Bret in his most disgusted tone that he had a choice: either clean up the mess and pay for the damages, or he was *going to arrest him for destruction of private property, endan-*

gering the safety of a citizen (he then peeked into the window of his truck and saw an open bottle of whiskey) . . . *annnnnd, whoo-wee!* He reached in, grabbed the bottle and held it up high. *An OPEN CONTAINER county violation!*

Well, that was enough to get Bret to shed his privileged attitude. Y*es sir Boss. I'm sorry Bob. I'll take care of it right now, sir.* Linton couldn't help but snicker at that. Even though Bret was from Barrelton, he had caused enough trouble all over the county that every law officer knew the next alcohol-related offense would give him jail time and a license suspension.

Bob could hardly believe what he saw and ever since then, he didn't call Linton chief, he called him Boss. The name stuck, and in less than a week, the whole town had heard about what happened and they, too, were calling him Boss. The truth is, Linton hated it. It not only embarrassed him, but it put him on a pedestal and now he would have to live up to the name in every situation that got thrown at him, then and in the future.

"Well, thank God she has you back there to help them. It's going to be a madhouse in here 'til 11 a.m.," Linton said.

"Sorry Boss. I'm only here until eight. I have to pick up my kids from Sandra by eight-thirty. I'm taking them to Patoka for the weekend."

Linton gave a sympathetic smile to this. He knew there was not a nicer man in all of Fogstow. Bob truly was a good person. He was always willing to help anyone in the town with anything, no matter who they were or how they treated him. His kids meant more to him than anything in his life, including his own life. It's just too bad that awful lady had primary custody of those kids.

Back in '85, Linton and Bob went up to Louisville for a night out, and they met a woman who said she was from Fogstow. Her name was Sandra Odair and although neither one of them had ever heard of her before, they believed her. She really came on to Bob, which was not typical for him. He was so taken with her that he brought her back with them to Fogstow and she stayed the night with him. Nine months later, Sebastian was born. Bob and Sandra got married a month later, then a year after that, Ellen was born. They all lived in Bob's house, which he had bought back in '84. A month after Ellen was born, Sandra kicked Bob out of the house, divorced him, took the kids, and then moved her mother, Candy Odair, into Bob's house.

But still, Bob saw the good in everyone. He never had anything bad to say about Sandra or her mother. That was always a major burning point for Linton because every chance those two women got, they shamelessly fed lies to those kids about Bob. They told them Bob had been in prison before they were born and that Bob used to beat Sandra. They even told Ellen that Bob wasn't her real father. Linton knew this because he overheard them talking one day when they were in Barrelton at the sheriffs office, which also had the prosecutor's office on the top floor, trying to enforce an alimony order by the Judge. Linton was a deputy under Kramer then and he was there that day dropping off a prisoner. He could see and hear them on the monitor in the control room.

Just remember, we're here because your father is a deadbeat. Just like I told you yesterday, he lived here in this prison for a while . . . before you two were born, Sandra's mother, Candy, said. He couldn't help but laugh at the fact that she didn't even know the difference between a sheriff's office and a prison.

Your father used to beat me and THAT is why we're here! He's going to pay for what he did before he getsta see YOU TWO again. But I wouldn't blame neither one of you if you didn't want to see him, Sandra said.

Linton could only think that this woman didn't just play Bob, but she played him as well. They had both fallen for her line back in Louisville. He checked around thoroughly and there never was a Sandra or Candy Odair in Fogstow. And that part about Bob beating Sandra? He wouldn't believe that for a second. She would have better luck trying to convince him that the government trains soldiers on Mars. Bob Stamps had never even been in a fight, never hurt anyone. She's talking about the same Bob that would go out with him on Halloween every year as a teenager and TP houses, then come back out after they went home and clean it up. He used to tell Linton, *Some of these folks are old with bad backs. If they get on a ladder and try to clean that stuff up, that could land them in the hospital.* Linton would just shake his head and smile. They would come back next year and TP these same people's homes and see them standing inside, eating candy corn and waving. They didn't mind because they knew Bob would be back to clean it up by morning. It sort of took the fun out of it.

The only reason Bob was behind on alimony was because he had gotten laid off at the Cape Sandy quarry. Bob had a run of bad luck with jobs over the previous decade. When he was with Oarshire mine, he was the newest and the first in the union to be laid off, just before they shut down. Then he came back to town to work the docks for the stone companies, but he got laid off when they closed the docks. He then went up to the Cape Sandy stone quarry and worked the belt line for a few years. But a couple of years ago, they shut down the central quarry about 40 miles north of the river and those guys took over at the Cape Sandy quarry, leaving Bob without a job again. He'd been with the Co-op ever since, and he was still the nicest person Linton had ever met.

If Bob Stamps was anything, he was empathetic. Linton truly believed Bob could feel the pain of everyone he came in contact with and he identified it as his own. As for those kids, he would have given them a heart, a liver, a lung or whatever they needed. But that Friday, he was just going to settle with fishing on Patoka.

Kelly finally walked over to Linton and gave him a tired look, like she was ready for a vacation. Linton and Kelly had been a couple for months and everyone in town pretty much knew it, although they had never really proclaimed it to anyone but themselves.

Kelly had a four-year-old daughter, Lucy, from a previous relationship that ended with the man (Dean Smith, but Kelly would never call him by his name so her daughter would not personalize him) skipping town. Lucy didn't really know about him yet. He was pretty much a transplant anyway. He came to town from Louisville when he got hired on with the stone barges as a deckhand and skipped town when Kelly got pregnant. He didn't leave any forwarding address, never talked about his family and left no clues that could help her find him. But she didn't mind; she enjoyed her personal time with her daughter. She lived in a town that took care of her, had a great deli she co-owned and worked at and she was always around for Lucy.

Kelly and Lucy lived above the deli, which was beside Linton's office and holding cells above the Co-op. Their balconies touched each other, which is how their relationship had blossomed. He would come over for dinner most nights just by hopping over the balcony and he would always bring her laundry in from the balcony line. Life for Kelly and Lucy couldn't have been any better. Throw Linton into the mix and everything just seemed perfect. She had very deep feelings for him and she was pretty sure he felt the same way about her.

"Where's Lucy?" Linton asked.

"She's in the back, cracking eggs for Bob," Kelly said.

Linton looked through the serving window and saw Lucy holding an egg up high, waiting for Bob to signal her.

"She couldn't be in better hands," Linton said. He smiled and kissed the side of her mouth, then turned her around and discreetly rubbed her shoulders for a moment. It was little things like this she fell in love with right away. He was so in tune with what she needed that he could probably finish her sentences. He was so patient with her and Lucy. She knew, actually she had known for a long time, that she wanted to spend the rest of her life with that man.

Pete turned from the stoves with a plate of hot pancakes and bacon and yelled into the crowd. "Okay, who ordered the pancakes and bacon, with syrup over the bacon?"

A precious little voice rose out from the backroom. "Mine! Mine! I ordered them, Pete!" Lucy could be heard jumping down from something, likely the freezer chest, and everyone could also hear her slipping around on the greasy floor in the backroom.

"Don't give them away Pete! I ordered them!" Lucy yelled. "I'm coming. I'm coming." Everyone heard a loud thud and saw the wall move. "I'm still coming."

Pete yelled again to the crowd, "Pancakes and bacon with syrup on the bacon! Going once . . ."

"Pete! No, Pete! They're mine! I ordered them! I told Momma and she told you!" The door slammed open and Lucy could barely maintain her footing as she slid out the door. Everyone at the lunch counter laughed heartily.

Pete yelled again to the crowd, "These are some the best bacon strips I have ever made with hot maple syrup oozing all over them. I'm gonna eat 'em if no one speaks up!"

Lucy slid right into Pete and yanked on his bib. "Don't eat 'em, Pete. I'll staaaarve!"

Pete grinned and handed the plate down to Lucy. Lucy quickly sat it down on the ice cream cooler, which was about a half a foot under the serving side of the bar. Everyone sitting at the counter leaned forward to watch her for a moment. She quickly shoved a fork and knife over her plate and was just about to go in when she suddenly stopped, took a deep breath, and slowly cut off a piece of sticky, syrupy bacon and put it in her mouth. She held her head down for a moment while she chewed, then she leaned her head back with her eyes closed, "Mmmmmm, so freaking good!"

Laughter erupted across the 'Bend and Kelly quickly covered her mouth with a gasp. She knew right away Lucy had heard those words from her, because that was what she had said when Linton stopped by late one night and she tasted the tuna noodle casserole he brought back from his mother's house in Derbie. It had the perfect blend of baked-in bread crumbs, peas, tuna, mashed potatoes and creamy gravy that just hit the spot that night. Kelly had thought Lucy was asleep.

Linton smiled at Kelly while he was flipping hot peanuts in his mouth and shrugged at her as if to say, *What can we do? She's just a kid and we're only human. Shit happens.*

Kelly would have spent more time laughing about it with Linton, but they were just too busy so she quickly grabbed a wet rag and wiped down a few areas of the bar. Pete kept turning out plates of pancakes, eggs and sausage. Four of them lined up alongside two bowls of oatmeal and three saucers of toast. Kelly looked at them a little bedazzled and tried to remember which plate went to whom. Linton put down his peanuts and grabbed a couple of them and Kelly pointed to the tables they went to.

"Make sure you also take the toast dishes to Herman and Nadine," Kelly said, then kissed Linton firmly on the mouth and whispered in his ear as she passed by. "I love you."

Linton made his way around the bar and almost pretended he didn't hear her. Several thoughts raced through his mind. He hadn't even had a chance to tell the town they're together yet, but she was already in love with him? They had been on several dates and he never had a dull moment with her. If they went to the theater, she was quick to analyze the movie on the car ride back from Barrelton. She said things that left him a little lost, even made him feel stupid because sometimes he didn't understand what she was saying. He knew she had six years at Indiana University and earned a bachelor's degree in journalism before she dropped out of the masters program to raise Lucy. He had spent two years at Vincennes University, but a career in law enforcement did not quite give you the well-rounded education a four-year university gave you. But still, every moment he spent with her was never a moment wasted. Was he in love with her also? He was always afraid that the day would come when he would be in love and not even know what it was. He was afraid he would somehow let that day pass him by and never even know it existed. Or even worse, that he would figure out what passed him by a few years too late, when she was happily married with children. When she was no longer interested in making up for lost time with him. There was one thing he was sure of – when he was with Kelly, he was a better man. When he was with her, he was . . . well, he was happy.

He dropped off Herman and Nadine's plates at their booth.

"I'll be right back with your toast, Herman," Linton said. "Did you get toast also, Nadine?"

"No, sweetie. But I got the oatmeal, not the pancakes," Nadine said in the kindest voice you could've ever heard. Herman and Nadine Smith were Fogstow Originals, or at least that is what they were called once the oldest generation in the town started dying out and they were next up for the title. Herman was 72, Nadine 68. They'd both been coming to the 'Bend for years and they could also be found at every home varsity game for the East Jamison Brainers, in both boys' and girls' sports. They donated regularly to the booster club and they also had honorary seats at the football and basketball stadiums.

"Oh, sorry about th . . ."

"Those pancakes are mine, Boss," Allen Morgan said as he turned around from the booth behind them and reached for the plate. Allen was also a "lifer" in Fogstow. He and his father before him had been running the Co-op for years, and now his son Russ Morgan ran it. Allen was in his 60s but he always made up a big story when people asked how old he was. *He likes to keep people guessing*, Russ would always say. Allen was on the city council and he was the one who made sure Linton got the job there in Fogstow, but he never told Linton that. He now drove a school bus part-time every morning and afternoon and he was enjoying his semi-retirement.

"Well hey there, Allen! I didn't see you come in," Linton said as he patted his back and reached over to shake his hand.

Burt Urnley, or Burnley as he was called, sat across from Allen. Burnley and Allen had been friends since they sparred over the love of Alice Konicke back in their East Jamison High School days. Burnley, the last black man in the town since the mines shut down, had swooped in and taken Alice out on a date the day after she broke it off with Allen. It was the one and only time Allen had ever called him a nigger. Later that week, Alice had already replaced Burnley with another. Allen came back around to Burnley and offered his apologies for the insult and ever since then, they'd both been best friends, going on 40 years.

Linton reached over to shake Burnley's hand as well. "How you doing, old-timer?"

"A lot better if someone would tell this old fart here to take a bath in the mornings," Burnley said, motioning his grinning head toward Allen.

Allen just grinned back and said, "We got here at quarter to six this morning. Russ and I are gonna eat, then go pick up tomorrow's load of hay bales so he can hunt with me in the morning."

"Oh, now, we both know you two just go out there to shoot your guns. Poor Russ don't have it in him to shoot an animal."

Burnley and Allen both laughed and agreed with him.

"Yeah, well, it's part of the festivities. Russ is in the bathroom. Make sure you stop back in and say hi before you head out to the bluff."

Russ was a couple of years younger than Linton and Bob, but they had always been friends and he was also the reason Bob had a job at the Co-op. Russ usually kept the Co-op open on Saturdays, but the next day Bob would be fishing with his kids up at Patoka, and Russ was going to be hunting with his dad. So he was going to have Burnley come in and tend to the register.

"Will do," Linton said and shook his hand again then turned back to Nadine. "I'll be right back with your oatmeal, Nadine."

Linton took Nadine her oatmeal then crossed back over the counter and picked up his peanuts and orange juice. He threw a few in his mouth when Kelly came up behind him.

"I'm sorry about what I said back there. That was stupid of me and I know it's all kind of new and I just got this stupid sudden feeling and . . . I don't know why I said that," Kelly told him, her words coming out like a confused mess.

Linton nervously tossed a few peanuts into his mouth because he was unsure what to say. He did know if his mouth was full, he was not required to say anything. But he smiled at her in a nervous way.

"Please don't think you have to say that back to me, I just . . ." She picked up her wet rag and started wiping part of the counter that she had already cleaned twice since Linton had delivered Herman, Nadine and Allen's food. Linton tossed back a few more peanuts and sipped his orange juice. Kelly walked away, a little embarrassed and disheartened.

Linton knew how she was feeling, but he was still speechless. There were a lot of things he wanted to say to her, but he was having trouble letting it out. It's just like with everyone in town calling him Boss. The fact was, he didn't mind taking a hard stance on Bret Holder, but the title stuck with him and now he had to do the job forever. Be the *"Boss"* forever. He never signed up for that. He just wanted to keep the peace. Enforce the law. But now it was going to be an expectation of him to go above and beyond to make sure everyone got justice, whether or not it was served by the county or by him.

The same thing applied to Kelly. There was no doubt in his mind that he needed her, that he was happy with her and he was happy with Lucy. But if he said it, if he responded to her in a way that will make her happy, then he would always have to be that to her. There would be no going back, no changing his mind, unless of course he wanted to be known as a misogynist. That's not who he was, nor who he wanted to be. It was just too early to make that kind of commitment.

But still, he was truly happy with her, so he did the best thing he could think of. The only thing he was capable of at the moment. As soon as she walked by him with a plate of hash browns, he held on to her arm and made her swing partially around with the plate held high. She was a little taken aback because she was not even looking at him when she was coming through. He held her arm gently, stood close to her and firmly planted a warm kiss directly on her lips. And when she pulled back and felt a little better about the whole situation he pressed against her lips again and this time held it a little longer. She closed her eyes and when the moment started to dissipate, he pulled back, still less than three inches from her face and her slightly watered eyes, and said, "There's one thing that's for sure. I'm a better man when I'm with you . . . and I like feeling happy like that."

He reached up and gently pulled her hair back behind her ear, then picked up his peanuts and left. Her brief moments of embarrassment and hopelessness earlier had weighed on her, but that moment defined her. Happiness and confidence slowly filled her face, and when Linton was leaving, a half-smile emerged. As she watched through the window, as he walked along the sidewalk up to the Co-op, the smile filled out her face. She was truly happy and now she knew he was to. Now she could call him her lover, her confidante, her best friend and when she was around people, she would call him *her* man.

3

Linton opened up the rusty, squeaking door on his Centurion Bronco and threw his jacket inside. The day had been getting progressively warmer and he was just going to overheat the longer he had it on. The weather was going to reach close to 73 degrees, and he was supposed to make a run down the bluff trail for patrol. He picked up his peanuts and closed the door while several more people came and went from the 'Bend.

Since he kept his office and holding cell above the Co-op, Russ just went ahead and gave him a key so he could come and go from the Main Street entrance whenever he wanted. Normally, he entered from Locust Street through his own stairwell in the alley, which reached up to Kelly's patio. Since Russ was in the 'Bend eating with his dad, Linton went ahead and opened up the Co-op and pulled the popcorn machine outside. Russ liked to make up a batch of popcorn for anyone who wanted a bag. He fired up the rotator and the kettle, then poured a cup of oil and a cup of popcorn into it.

He sat beside the popcorn machine in front of the Co-op on their welcome bench and ate from his bag of peanuts. The smell of fresh popcorn, an autumn breeze and warm peanuts outside on Main Street was his idea of a peaceful Indiana morning, at least until things around town got going. That morning was a little more fast-paced than others though. Bob came out front of the 'Bend and handed him a to-go box of eggs, biscuits and gravy.

"Take this and feed your animal," Bob said.

Linton smiled because somehow Bob knew he had Bret Holder upstairs in the holding cell. It was also funny to hear Bob refer to anyone in a derogatory manner because, well, he wasn't very good at it.

"I guess word travels fast in a small county," Linton said, scraping the bottom of his bag for every last peanut.

"I guess so. I'm taking off now and Kelly just got a barge order in for 9 a.m. She wants to know if you can run it down to the docks for her?"

"No problem. Have fun with those kids this weekend, bub."

Bob opened the door to his 1986 Jeep Wagoneer, hopped in and put on his light blue fly-fishing hat with all his lures attached to it.

He held up a tackle box and winked.

"There's never a bad time to do a little fishing. Especially with those two little roosters of mine."

Bob fired up the Wagoneer and backed out, giving Linton a couple of goodbye honks and a backwards wave. Linton waved, and as soon as Bob was out of sight, Sheriff Marvin Kramer pulled up. Linton knew this officially put a favor on the board for him down in Barrelton, so he was happy to see him. Kramer got out, removed his hat and wiped sweat off his forehead. Deputy Jeff Stark got out on the other side. Stark was a new recruit, fresh out of training. He was only five and half feet tall but he was a handsome young man and built like a brick shithouse. Linton knew him well because he had spent a lot of time in Fogstow in his youth, staying summers with his aunt and uncle in the Beach. Most of the young ladies around the area flocked to him with something as little as a finger snap, but he held them off pretty well, maybe even a little too well.

"Jesus Derr! Turn the damn oven off! It's October for Christ's sake!" Kramer said.

Linton smiled, turned his peanut bag inside out and tossed it in the trashcan. He got up, wiped his hands off on his pants and reached to shake the Sheriff's hand then they both sat down. Stark approached them and removed his jacket, which outlined his muscular physique, which also made Linton and Kramer a little uncomfortable.

"Stark! Can't you cut me and Derr a little slack here? No one wants to see you show off your extremities," Kramer said.

Stark smiled, inhaled deeply, stuck his chest out, rubbed it and buffed up a little before he sat down beside Linton and shook his hand.

"Whatdya know Boss?" Stark said.

"Too damn much, not sharing," Linton said.

They all three had a laugh and Linton handed Stark the breakfast bag for Bret.

"You sure are collecting the trash early this morning, Marv," Linton said.

Kramer stretched back on the bench and scowled a little at the notion.

"Well, about that. We need to leave him here another night, Linton."

Linton leaned over his knees and rubbed his head, a little irritated.

"Marv, if you absolutely have to, then I'll stick around. But you know Mom wants me down in Derbie for supper on Friday nights. She also has me bringing Kelly and Lucy every week."

Kramer gently held up his hands for calm measure. "No worries, no worries. That's why I brought Stark here with me. He's gonna babysit and give you the night off. You round up your girls and go on down. Tell Carolyn that Margie and I said hello and stay the night in the cabin while you're there. Just be here tomorrow by 10 a.m. so you can sign him out of your holding cell for me. Stark will be here the whole time."

Linton smiled, gave Stark a hefty pat on the back and said, "Well, I guess I can't argue with that." Even Kramer couldn't help but laugh at that because Derri Emmons was just walking by when he said it and she looked better than a pin-up photo on a mechanic's toolbox. She wore jean cut-offs with the front pockets popping out below the thigh line, complemented by a white tank top covered by an unbuttoned blue and gray checkered flannel shirt tied at the navel. Derri was a 16 year-old knockout beauty with a very protective father, namely Jack Emmons. Jack had raised her himself since she was two years old, after the disappearance of her mother, Lorie Emmons, in '79.

Derri approached the three men sitting on the bench.

"Hey Boss, can I get some popcorn out of the machine?" she asked Linton, but quickly looked over at Stark. She played with her flannel navel knot and slowly rocked back and forth while smiling at him. Kramer rolled his eyes, and then slowly leaned down in his seat and covered his face with his hat. Linton couldn't help but get a kick out of the whole situation.

"Sure Derri. How's your dad doing?" Linton asked.

Stark got up and filled a bag of popcorn for her.

"Well, I guess he's doing fine. He was wrapping his bowstrings when I left and we're gonna come up to the Elks club tonight for supper." Derri glanced back over at Stark and smiled her most innocent and seductive smile.

Linton also smiled, almost in a foolish way, and said, "Well I'm sure he's looking forward to seeing his little girl tonight." He punctuated his speech more in the direction of Stark than to Derri, but she couldn't help but giggle at that.

Linton and Kramer got up and walked to Kramer's cruiser. Both were uncomfortable around Derri's budding sexuality. Kramer opened the door and turned back to Linton.

"Do me a favor. Make sure that I don't have a complaint come across my desk from Jack Emmons tonight, would ya?"

Linton looked back at Derri and Stark. She was making obvious advances, but Stark was also trying his best to repel her with his hand motions, and he kept shaking his head no. Linton looked back at Kramer.

"I think he'll be just fine."

Kramer let out an exasperated laugh and got down into his car. He started it and put the car in reverse, but before he backed out he looked up at Stark, then at Linton and said, "That poor, tortured bastard. All those powers and nothing to use them on."

Jeff Stark had always had girls crawling all over him but he never seemed to bite. They were always too young, too tall, too old or too skinny. By now, Linton thought that poor bastard probably had testicles the size of tangelos, and any second he could just let loose and explode. But of course who was he to judge? He might have let them off the porch a time or two and Linton probably just didn't know about it. The truth was, Derri was only five years younger than Stark, and just a few more nudges might be all it would take to land him in the sack . . . and in the slammer without a job if Jack found out about it.

4

Chief Derr's office was very uncomfortable that morning with the heat wave rolling through and the smell of the 'Bend frying up mass quantities of ridiculously delicious breakfast food was just making it worse. Bret Holder had slept most of the night but could not quite make it past 8:30 a.m. He was not an early morning type of guy and most days his father's housekeeper woke him around one or two in the afternoon after a night of debauchery with his friends.

He rolled over on his cot and wiped the sleep from his eyes. The only thing he wanted right then was a cig, but Kramer took that away before he shipped him up to Fogstow. He also had to sleep in his bare feet without any socks because, well, fuck if he knows. The last thing he wanted to do was be stuck in this shit brick town on a Friday. It just occurred to him that his father still hadn't bailed him out. He wondered if his father even knew he was locked up in Fogstow.

Bret sat up and looked around, finding that he was the only one in the office and he was stuck behind the bars of this makeshift holding cell. *I guess if there's a fire, I will need to just suck it up. Pop will hear about this.*

One thing came to the surface as he sat on his cot rubbing his head – he was hungry! He could smell pancakes on the griddle sizzling in hot butter. That combined with frying sausage and the sound of the eggs popping had his stomach squealing in hunger.

And what is with this fucking heat? Isn't it October yet?

Sweat poured down Bret's face and the breeze from the open windows had done little to comfort him. His head was splitting and there was no one around to bring him a Percocet, or even an aspirin.

"Hello! Dumbfucks! Any dumbfucks around to give me a hand here?" he yelled toward the open windows. "Did you fuckwads even call my father and let him know you brought me here?"

He waited a moment then yelled again. "Hello!"

He could hear Chief Derr outside talking to someone and he could also hear a young girl innocently giggling. It made him smile as he closed his eyes and leaned against the wall. He had heard a lot of those innocent little schoolgirl giggles in his time and to him, they all looked the same. Small, slender, flowing hair and tight shirts that slid up and revealed their midriffs. They liked to twirl their hair around in their fingers while they talked to him because, well, he was just a highly desirable 22-year-old guy who can get them beer and make them feel good, or so he thought.

Bret slid his hand down his pants and caressed his groin. Just a few little harmless rubs to get the blood flowing. He listened to the sound of the teenage beauty and his vision of her pulling off those sweet little panties just before she climbed on top of him. The casual unclasping of her bra as she lowered it down and slid it off, throwing it behind her and straddling him at the same time, as if she couldn't wait to get right down to business. Oh yes, he remembered those things well.

Bret had rubbed himself until he was rock hard and the timing could not have been worse. The door flew open and *that little pis-sant Jeff Stark* walked in carrying his jacket over one shoulder and a to-go bag from the 'Bend in his other hand. He would have jumped out of his skin and covered himself with a blanket but he still had his pants on and was dry rubbing himself. Bret was embarrassed but he had to pass it off as no big deal, or else this *wet-behind-the-ears fool* would try to take his dignity away. This was, after-all, the same *little puke stain* that he and his friends used to pick on back in high school. He should be bowing down before him, not babysitting him and invading his privacy.

Stark looked directly at Bret when he walked in and saw the dry-rub going on inside the cell. He stopped, obviously perplexed by the situation, and then smiled and set down the take-out box on Linton's desk.

"Well, well, well! What do we have going on in here? A little early morning sunshine spray?" Jeff said.

"Go fuck yourself, puke stain! I have to piss and I was just trying to hold it in."

"Is that so?" Jeff took immediate notice of his little soldier saluting and quickly pointed to it. "I totally get what you're saying. I also get hard-ons when I have to piss," Jeff said and laughed in a condescending manner.

Bret stood up from the cot and walked to the edge of the cell. "Is that my breakfast?"

Stark pointed at the bag and smiled. "Yeah." He then sat down at Linton's desk and put his feet up. "I'll walk it over to you after I take my nap."

CHAPTER 2
A HARMLESS ADVENTURE

1

PLAYING BASKETBALL AT THE 'BEND was a tricky task, but there were no other goals around the Highland district to play at, and if no one would give you permission to play in their driveways, the 'Bend had to do. Noah Buchanon had been coming up there to play ball for as long as his 12-year-old mind could remember. Pete Brown had hammered the goal to the telephone pole years ago for kids like him, Joe Terrance and the Chapman brothers, Dean and Mark. That was where they had met about six years before when Noah, Joe and Dean were just starting kindergarten. They had been playing ball together ever since, along with Dean's little brother Mark. That gave them an evenly matched two-on-two game, and they could play for about two hours at a time on most days. During the summers they would have to stop and go swimming just to cool down, but they always came right back to the hoop.

Joe Terrance was a small, dark-skinned young boy with thick, flowing black hair. Both of his parents were Caucasians with German ancestry. A lot of the townspeople knew Joe's parents had a hard time conceiving and theorized that they had hired a Native American to help them. Even though there were plenty of Native Americans down the river in Illinois, the only one who visited Fogstow frequently was Shane Duncan Siders, and most people shuddered to think that he could be the father.

Noah and Dean both knew this. Siders was a tall and strong man with long black hair that he never combed. Most thought he was from Gallatin County in Illinois, but no one ever dared to ask. He spent a lot of time on the river in his makeshift houseboat and he frequented a lot of areas along the river in Ohio, Indiana, Kentucky and Illinois. When he came to Jamison County, he usually docked his houseboat near the sinkholes, closer to Derbie. He was a very private man, and when the boys came across him, he acted in an intimidating manner. He was always grumpy and intolerant, and sometimes, he was just downright mean. But for the most part, he kept to himself and wandered around the town. The boys had even seen him traveling up Pine Hill toward the Jeffries plateau and on other occasions, they saw him in the woods on the east side of the TC. They always dismissed him. Joe never made any connections to him and the other boys just thought that was for the best.

Playing ball at the 'Bend was always a challenge. The parking lot was gravel and playing basketball in gravel was no fun. But it was much better than playing on the Hastetter's goal in the side drive that led up to their barn. It had those large, meaty rocks that stuck out of the mud below it. Dribbling there was never ideal. Dribbling on the 'Bends gravel was much easier. It was small, white crushed stone, a lot like pea gravel, except white and more dusty than grimy.

They couldn't play at the Hastetter goal anymore, anyway, since that horrible Cindy Hastetter had run them off. They were playing on her goal one day when she was gone and they had thought she would be gone all day. She came home and caught them. You'd think they were breaking her windows or something by the way she came out of her car yelling at them. They all four ran and Joe turned around and flipped her off as they were leaving. That wasn't good for Joe, because she called his parents and poor Joe had to go out and pick his own twig. But Joe had learned early on that those small twigs hurt the worst when it came to getting a whipping, so he always came back with the large oak twigs that had a little moss and decay to them. When his dad swatted Joe with those, they usually broke off on his ass and his dad usually thought he had hit Joe too hard, so he'd pat him on the leg and tell him to run off and play.

It never really bothered the boys anyway. They played ball anywhere they could find a goal. Sometimes they got in trouble and had to run for it, but they never went without. If they were in the Highland district, they played at the 'Bend. If they were in Squaw

Creek, they played on any number of barn sides with the hard mud surfaces – same way with the Beach. But if they were in the TC, they had to watch out for those spoiled housewives who had nothing better to do than run them off and leave those damn basketball goals to just sit there and rot. Noah thought *it was just a damn crying shame and the biggest waste.* At least, that's how his pops would have put it.

Since that Friday was a special day and the county recognized it, it was built it in as a snow makeup day at school and they got it off if there were no snow days before it, which there never were in Indiana, at least not during September and October. The earliest they ever saw snow was late November and even that was rare.

Joe woke up at the crack of dawn that Friday and snuck in Noah's window to wake him up. Noah was always a hard case to wake up, especially if he had only gotten nine hours of sleep. But that Friday was the easiest Joe had ever woken Noah. Noah already had his clothes and shoes ready to go beside his bed. He slowly sat up and wiped the sleep from his eyes about the same time Kelly Doss was filling coffee pots and Lucy Doss was cracking eggs that morning at the 'Bend.

Noah and Joe crash-landed out the window, hopped on their BMXs and made a mad dash for the Highland. Dean and Mark were already at the 'Bend shooting a game of H-O-R-S-E when they showed up. They had actually been there for half an hour, just before the sunrise. Dean loved to torment Mark by challenging him to a game of slaps. He knew Mark was hell-bent on beating him, but every time, Dean would pound the hell out of Mark's hand and Mark would walk around half the day with his hands reddened and semi-bruised. Mark was tough as hell and Dean knew it, so he usually called it quits early on. He didn't want to bang his hands up too much, considering they both had taken their fair share of ass-whippins' from their stepfather.

Dean and Mark had lost their mother earlier in the year to breast cancer. Their mother was Mary Chapman, but she married Brad Oxley, so she was Mary Oxley at the time of her death. They had only been married for a year when they found out she had cancer, and she went downhill quickly after that. Their father had never been in the picture, and their grandparents were already in a nursing home. So that just left them with their stepfather.

Brad Oxley wasn't too bad of a guy. But after Mary died, the burden of losing his wife and raising her two boys became too much for him. He started drinking heavily and by March, he had lost his job because of it. He was raising the boys off their mother's social security benefits and he had stayed fairly close to only spending the money on the boys' needs, but he still had a habit to support, so he drew unemployment for awhile. When it ran out, he filed for state assistance. They were living in Mary's house, which she had inherited from her parents, so most of the bills were manageable. He did, however, force Dean and Mark to walk the roadsides and pick up cans so they could go down to the recycle lot in Derbie and sell them. It wasn't much money, but it was enough to keep a bottle in his hands most nights.

Although Brad had spent most of his time drinking or sleeping, he never actually laid a hand on the boys when he was drunk. It was never the drinking that the boys had to worry about with their stepfather though. He was a happy and peaceful drunk and did not get volatile. But the next morning, during the hangovers, he was always temperamental. He sometimes broke things, mostly Mark's stuff, when the boys were too loud or acting out.

By the time Noah and Joe showed up at the 'Bend, there wasn't much room left in the parking lot. They'd worked around it for a few years and they were about to today. Dean gave Joe a high five and passed Noah the ball. Since Dean was already warm, he gave them a chance to warm up with a few layups and defensive maneuvers.

"Hey man, what took you guys so long? We've been here for like an hour or so," Dean said as he grabbed a blank tape from his BMX rack and tossed it over to Mark.

"Don't look at me, man. Noah was the one still snoozing when I got there this morning," Joe said.

Mark started fidgeting with his jambox, which he always brought along because he liked to record rock songs off RBT-FM. Most of their collection consisted of recorded music from RBT because it was the only rock station in the area and it had the best reception.

"Hey guys! What do you want me to record today?" Mark said.

Joe and Noah were still warming up and Dean was fidgeting with the totes on the back of his BMX. He usually toted Mark around on it since he didn't have a bike of his own. Just after Noah powered in a layup, he looked over at Mark and said, "How 'bout some of that new music from Pearl Jam or Nirvana?"

Joe and Dean both agreed.

"Yeah that's awesome. But RBT doesn't always have them on, so they're hard to catch," Mark said.

Dean tightened his tote peg and looked up at Mark. "Just make sure you hit record this time instead of the mic-record. Last time you recorded the sounds of us playing ball over that KISS song. I don't want to play it back and hear us, just the music."

"I'll remember." Mark sat the radio on top of a blue '70s model Ford pickup and grabbed the ball from Noah. "Games are to ten today. No twos or threes and no stuffing me down low!"

Noah smiled as he followed Mark out to the check line and fidgeted with his hair. "Yeah, you wish!"

Mark tossed him the ball, "check," and Noah tossed it back. On the radio, RBT jock Wilson McGee blared loud on the warm, hazy morning while the sun was reflecting off the road behind them.

(94-9 RBT-FM kicking off a long block of Hoosier-Land rock on this beautiful Friday morning. We've got Alice-in-Chains, AC/DC and Springsteen coming up this hour, but first! Mellencamp! . . . on the thunder-city rocker!)

Joe heard that loud and clear. "Dude! Dude! Hit record man! That's JC! Hit record!"

Mark ran over and hit record. The boys always got excited and had a lot of fun when they played ball to Mellencamp. It just

seemed to flow right for them. Mark liked to make sure he recorded everything they could off the radio because tapes and CDs were
just so damn expensive and they always had to go all the way
down to Barrelton to get what they liked.

When Mark returned, he threw the ball back to Joe for a check
and their game got underway. When these boys played, it meant a
little more contact than the NCAA would allow, but they wouldn't
have any fun calling fouls on each other and shooting pointless
free-throws. The game was about action, not standing still with
their thumbs up their asses.

Mark dribbled and maneuvered around Joe, driving past him
only to meet Noah, so he threw the ball back out to Dean who sunk
a 12-footer from beside the pickup. Noah took the ball back and
drove in past Dean and missed a layup, which Joe quickly re-
bounded and put back in the basket.

(R.O.C.K in the U-S-A!)

The game lasted about an hour and the boys played hard all
through it, recording music and playing game after game until they
were just too worn out to stand. Mark was recording a Springsteen
song when they stopped to rest against the front of the 'Bend. Even
though Dean always told him to hit the "record only" button, he
forgot and pressed the mic-record, which recorded them as well.

(Born in the U.S.A.!)

Chief Derr walked out of the 'Bend and ruffled Joe's hair as he
passed by. They liked the Chief. He always seemed to be on their
side every time they got busted playing ball on someone's barn-

side. He just rounded them up and took them to the Co-op for pop-corn while he ate his peanuts and told them to stay out of trouble. He was always good to them, and he also watched out for Dean and Mark.

The Chief walked up to the Co-op and pulled the popcorn ma-chine out while Joe cooked up a plan for the day. He knew it was a long shot to convince Dean and Mark, but he wanted to go out to the sinkholes and explore the old caved-in areas west of the bluff park. The downside to that plan was that most of the teenagers around Fogstow, or even Jamison County for that matter, liked to hang out there and party. Most of them were pretty nice to the boys, but they sometimes got those occasional out-of-towners who liked to act like dicks and throw their bikes or their basketball over the high walls into the stripper pits. He knew they wouldn't be there this early in the morning but they always started showing up by noon, since school was out and the weather was nice.

Mark had a bad experience there in July when they came across a party while exploring the area on their bikes. The East Jamison teens were nice to them, and they even got along with most of the Barrelton High School teens. But Bret Holder was there and acting like a total dick. It was bad enough they had to deal with high school kids, but an older boy like Bret? That was just impossible. He first started shoving the boys around and would taunt them by spitting beer at them. He would laugh, but no one else would laugh with him. Most of the teens were actually scared of him. When Bret finally started to realize he looked like a fool, he backed up a little and told them to *get their asses home before he whips them.* The boys had hesitated for a moment and that was just a moment too long. He threw Mark off his bike and flung it over the high wall into the stripper pit. It hit every rock of the sidewall on the way down. The bike didn't sink immediately, and when they looked over the highwall, they saw that it had been destroyed, probably before it even hit the water. Mark started to climb down to get it, but Dean held him back. Everyone knew those stripper pits were deep and dangerous.

Mark was upset for weeks after that. He had just lost his mom that year, and now all he had were the boys. He thought they wouldn't let him come anywhere with them if he didn't have his own bike, and he really wanted to be with them. His stepfather wouldn't buy him a new bike. Brad Oxley said that *if he couldn't take care of the one he had, then he definitely wouldn't be able to take care of a new one.* Finally, Dean installed tote pegs on his BMX and he took him everywhere with them. Even though Dean sometimes teased Mark, he really cared about him and how he felt. In their minds, they only had each other to depend on.

"How about we hit the sinkholes and explore the old mine shafts before the dickheads come out?" Joe said.

Dean was up for it, but he didn't respond. He wanted to see how Mark would react. Even though Mark was nervous about the idea, he still wanted to do something like that.

"When do they start showing up?" Mark asked nervously.

"Probably around noon or so. But they may come later. That

gives us a couple of hours to get in and out before they get there," Noah said.

Mark was hesitant and even a little scared when he reached up to give Joe a weak high-five.

"Okay guys. I'm in."

"Okay, but we park our bikes in the bluff park on the river side of Floating Asshole where they can stay hidden. Then we hike there and back," Dean said.

Floating Asshole was a really steep hill that ran alongside the bluff trail. It was one of those dirt hills that had immense vertical grade going up and a quick overhang going down. If you got your BMX going really fast before you hit the hill, you could fly over it, and when you rounded the top to go down, it felt like your asshole was floating in anti-gravity.

Joe jumped up and high-fived Dean. "Deal!"

They all got up and went around the corner to fetch their jam-box and basketball. Mark's jambox was still sitting on the Ford truck, recording the Springsteen song when Brad Oxley stumbled up in shorts and a bathrobe He was holding his palm upside down against his upper eye bone. He swatted the jambox across the parking lot. It hit the broadside of the 'Bend wall and kept playing.

"I thought I told you two I wanted all those cans smashed and bagged before I got up this morning! Either one of you wanna tell why the hell they're not?" Brad said. He was obviously having a nasty hangover. Mark stood scared and frozen, and Dean just looked at him, expressionless.

"We didn't think you would be up until after noon, Brad! Jesus! Why the hell did you have to throw his jambox?" Dean said.

Brad walked over to the jambox and his it with his palm until it finally stopped. Dean jerked it out of his hand, put his arm around Mark and started toward home.

"Why the hell do you have to be such an asshole, man! It's not like we wouldn't have listened to you if you just came over and said your piece!" Dean said.

Brad didn't reply; he just held his hand up to his head. Linton had heard the commotion and walked around the corner to see what was happening.

"Everything okay over here, guys?" Linton asked.

Brad took a tired look at Linton and made his way back across the parking lot, waving the boys on with him.

"Get a move on!" Brad called.

They lived caddy-corner to the 'Bend, which was on the opposite side of Main Street, off the curve. Locust street terminated into their house as it came along the backside of the 'Bend.

Linton watched them go for a moment, and then turned to Joe and Noah, who were visibly stunned. They had trouble looking up at Linton at first.

"You boys wanna tell what just happened here?" Linton asked.

They both took a moment then Noah looked up at Linton with anger in his eyes.

"It just seems like Mark can't catch a break, you know, Boss. I mean, I can understand if he breaks a few things here and there, but it seems like every time he's mad at them, he breaks something of Mark's," Noah said. His anger turned to watered eyes and then he looked back down, just in case a tear rolled down his cheek. The last thing he wanted to do is look like a crybaby in front of Chief Derr.

Joe felt the same way, but he just kept quiet. He also knew Mark was getting it the worst. Even when Dean tried putting his old BMX trophy on the counter one morning when he knew Brad would wake up with a hangover and break something, he still found Mark's Sea Monkey aquarium hidden under the table and smashed it to pieces. Joe knew this. Noah knew this. But no one else did.

Poor Mark. Just because a kid didn't have bruises didn't mean he wasn't suffering. If only they could put it into words for Linton. If only they could make him understand. But none of the adults would ever understand. They would just pat their heads and say *chinup kid, things will get better*. But things didn't get better for their little friend. They just keep getting worse and at times, they'd just as soon Brad Oxley had taken a few swings at Mark, or even Dean. Just enough to put the bruises on them. At least then they would have a chance at a better life than the one their mother left behind.

Linton took a minute to think about what Noah had just told him and let them both stand there without questioning them any further. He knew that a broken jambox wasn't grounds for him to intervene, at least not yet. So he decided he would do the next best thing. But that would have to wait. He had to make his early morning commute out on the bluff trail and make sure everything was peachy there, which could sometimes be a burden.

Kelly Doss had seen and heard the commotion outside and let Linton handle the situation the best he could. When she saw it winding down, she came out to get the boys.

"Hey boys, you hungry? Lucy and Pete are making you both up some pancakes and bacon. Why don't ya come on in and get your hands washed? Sound good?" Kelly asked as she put her arm around their shoulders. Kelly looked back at Linton and gave him her half smile, only it was the kind that showed concern, not intellectual pity.

Linton turned back to the Chapman-Oxley house and gave it another once-over, then went back to the Co-op to dig out the three-wheeler and make his way up the bluff trail to the overlook park.

2

Linton had patrolled the bluff trail every morning for the past two years, even when he was off duty or sick. It was standard practice since the county provided the 3-wheeler ATV and alternative funds for it, even though it was outside of town jurisdiction. It certainly was a hassle, but one might have argued that the town should have been responsible for the area, given that it mostly served their townsfolk. So he made his morning trips up and down the trail, checking out the area to make sure it wasn't littered with booze cans or campfire debris from late night parties, which were banned by county ordinance.

Today was no different for him. He usually ended up finding the remains of the night spread sporadically across the trail and the overlook park. He kept a roll of trash bags on the 3-wheeler and scooped up about three dozen beer cans, a few liquor bottles and various smashed cigarette and roach butts. He kicked the butts in the river, threw the bottles in the park trashcans, then piled up the beer cans and put them in the bag. He figured when he came back to town, he could walk over to the Chapman-Oxley home with his bag of cans, and that would be a good way to get invited in to speak with Brad Oxley.

He knew of no other way to intervene on behalf of Dean and little Mark, so he was going to take advantage of the situation. What he was going to say to Brad had already raced through his head a few times. His first thought was he could take an aggressive stance and let Brad know he had his eyes on him and would know how he treated the boys. But that could be counterproductive, especially if Brad took an aggressive stance right back at him and kicked him out. His next thought was to just sit Brad down and try to get him to open up about his life and his troubles, and maybe just try to help him work through them the best he could. Lord knows he was no psychiatrist, but if Brad wanted to vent a little about his troubles, he could open up the platform. Maybe that might help ease his aggression toward the boys. But what if he didn't open up? What if he didn't want to talk to him and he just decided to accept

Linton's gifts and send him on his way? That would turn out to be a big waste of time, and Linton knew one thing for sure: Something had to be done. It couldn't keep going on this way. He was worried that eventually Brad would hurt those boys if he didn't try something.

3

The crowd at the 'Bend was starting to die down a little while Joe and Noah sat at the lunch counter and piled down pancakes and bacon. Joe had a tendency to eat way too fast, especially when he was hungry. He would stuff a lot of food in his mouth at once and spend more time chewing than actually enjoying it. His bulged cheeks about to give Kelly a panic attack; she was so afraid he would choke. Lucy sat right beside him on the red leather barstool and did the same thing with dry toast, mimicking Joe. That got Kelly even more worried, so she walked around the counter to intervene.

"Slow down you two. That food ain't going nowhere. Take smaller bites and chew your food good. Look at Noah; he's getting along just fine."

Joe slowed down and a smile filled his face - and exposed some of his chewed food. Lucy looked at Joe, then looked back at Kelly and did the same thing, which gave her a chuckle.

The door clanked open and in walked Cam Wright with a knapsack over his shoulder. He was wearing long underwear with a flannel t-shirt that had the sleeves cut out and a jacket vest on over it. He had his UMWA hat pulled down and he looked like he was about to go on a hunting trip. Kelly reached for her coffee pot and turned to the lunch counter to fill Cam a mug as he sat down and ruffled Noah's hair. Noah gave him a smile and opened his mouth so Cam could see his chewed food.

Cam had been around Fogstow all 29 years of his life and everyone really liked him. He always played ball with the boys at the 'Bend when he was in town, but most of the time he was gone on the barge. Cam worked *seven days on, four off* on the Bucky Cole barge, and that day he was coming in to catch the breakfast johnny back to the Bucky. He usually drove his truck out to the Cape Sandy dock and jumped aboard there, but his truck was sitting in his garage with the motor out, on a cherry picker. He had to tear it apart to figure out what was wrong with it and by the time he diagnosed the headers, he was going to be too late to get to work. He was supposed to be on the river working the Bucky for the next seven days straight, so his only option was to catch the next food johnny there in Fogstow.

"How ya doing Cam? You hungry?" Kelly asked.

Cam laid down his knapsack and put his thermos on the counter. "Well, a little bit I suppose. But I think I'm just gonna get a sack of those hot peanuts for now. The Bucky is keeping ribeyes on board now, so I'll eat those up this afternoon."

Kelly smiled and filled his thermos with hot coffee.

"Please tell me the Bucky called one in this morning. I need a taxi," Cam said.

Kelly smiled and put the coffee pot back. "Did your truck breakdown again?"

"Yeah, well it's at home with the motor torn apart. I didn't have enough time to get it back together in those four short days."

Kelly turned back to the lunch counter with a large brown sack full of the Bucky takeout orders. "Yeah, they called in four plates." She put a slip down on the table. "Go ahead and sign for them, will ya?"

"Yes ma'am." Cam signed the slip and tore the back copy off.

"They'll actually be here in a few minutes, so you may want to head on down. I'll radio Linton and let him know you're taking them."

Cam popped his hat on and off to straighten it and pulled his coat vest together. He hopped off the seat and grabbed the sack. "Well, then, it's off I go."

Kelly smiled and saluted him. She was confused about his coat vest, though. "Say, Cam. Why you got all those warm clothes on? Isn't it still hot out there?"

Just before he opened the door, he answered her. "Yeah, it's still warm. But that damn air pressure is dropping like a sum-bitch. That means it's about to get stormy, rainy, nasty and cold. I don't want to get stuck out on that god-awful river in my gym shorts, is all."

Cam shut the door and left. Kelly couldn't help but think that the schizophrenic weather here in southern Indiana would be talked about for quite some time.

Oh well. The thought left her mind just as quickly as it came. She got on the CB and radioed Linton on the trail.

"'Bend Deli to Chief Derr."

She waited a moment but got no response, so she tried again.

"'Bend Deli to Chief Derr. Linton? You out there?"

She waited a moment again before she got his response, which was slightly distorted with white noise.

"Go ahead Kelly," Linton said.

"Just wanted to let you know Cam Wright came in and took the Bucky order down to the dock. You can stay on task."

"Roger that. I'll be back late this afternoon sometime. You two get your bags packed for Carolyn's tonight after the Elk's dinner."

That made Kelly happy to hear. She had been to his mother's in Derbie a few times already, but she had never been invited to come and stay at the cabin. It made her and Lucy really feel like part of the family. And Carolyn was such a nice person and she was really good to Lucy. They really enjoyed going there.

Carolyn lived on a large "reservation," or so they called it. Actually, it was called the "Turtle Reservation," for no uncertain reason. It was basically a campground with 12 cabins around a beautiful lake behind the large house that Linton's mother had owned ever since he was little. It was all the legacy they had left of his father, Sammy, who went missing out on the Ohio River back in June of 1973. She knew his mother would keep that place until the day she died, hoping that somehow her Sammy would find his way home again.

"Roger that big daddy," Kelly said, quietly snickering before hanging up her mic and turning back to Lucy.

A couple of seconds passed before Linton responded, causing Kelly to spin around. "Over and out little momma."

That was enough to give Lucy a giggle, and even Pete in the back room had a laugh. Kelly was both tickled and embarrassed.

4

Allen and Russ Morgan pulled up to the Locust street entrance in their Co-op truck pulling a trailer full of hay and backed it in. The trailer was overstuffed with hay bales, just to make sure they didn't run out anytime soon. Burnley stood behind them and directed Russ backward until he reached the loading zone for the bales.

Allen got out as soon as Russ stopped the truck and saw that Burnley had stopped them about five feet away from the edge of the hay bale stack.

"Garsh-dangit Burnley. You got us walking five feet away from the stack for unloading."

Allen and Burnley always gave each other a hard time in their endeavors. It just made for good kinship in their eyes.

"Well hell Allen, you would have filled up the whole damn five feet with that first row of bales and then had to hop right back in your truck and pull it out further." Burnley pointed at his head a couple of times as he leaned toward Allen. "Some of us know how to think ahead, you mean old man."

Allen gave him a grinning smile while he pulled his work gloves on. Russ had already crawled on top of the hay bales and picked one up to start tossing over the edge to Allen and Burnley.

"Would you two stop pissing at each other and give me a hand?" Russ said.

Burnley and Allen both groped their balls, smiled and wiped their hands across their noses, an act they had done for years when someone called them out over their spats. Russ just smiled and shook his head while tossing down the first haybale. The old men started picking them up and stacking them along the storage wall.

Linton came rolling around the corner on his three-wheeler with a bag full of clanking aluminum cans and parked it behind the A&W stand, which is where he normally stored it, since he didn't have a utility shed to put it in. He needed it close everyday for his bluff trips.

He rolled off the 3-wheeler and was just about to go help them unload the hay bales when a grain truck came speeding around the corner and onto Locust Street. The grain trucks brought the grain in from most of the southeastern Indiana farms and hauled it out as well, when needed. Linton had seen them on several occasions taking those turns off the Main Street curve onto Locust Street at high speeds and had been meaning to hunt them down and talk with them about it. Every time they took the turn, he could see the load shift, and their driver's side front tire always lifted. If one of those trucks were to lose control and go over, they were liable to take out

the 'Bend and a few pedestrians. It also didn't help that Cliff Holder owned the trucking company and paid his workers straight haul
pay with no overtime, whether the job was done or not. It forced
them to work faster and harder for no extra pay.

Arn Simmons was driving the truck and he quickly pulled
around and backed it in front of the grain silos. Arn used to work
with Bob Stamps over at the Oarshire Mine, around the time they
brought the union in. Linton knew him well and they were halfway
decent friends, along with Bob and Russ. He was laid off like Bob
after the mine shut down and he had been struggling to make ends
meet, running the short-hauls for Cliff Holder and tending bar
down at the Stow.

Arn jumped down from the truck to swing the loading arm over
for unloading when Linton approached him, a little agitated.

"Arn?" Linton said.

Arn turned around while he was still working with the loading
arm. He had on an old work flannel and jeans that looked like they
had been worn in a rodeo during a hurricane. He might switch up
what he wore on a daily basis, but one thing that always stayed on
him was his UMWA hat. He was proud to had been part of the
United Mine Workers Association, even if the union was a short-
lived experience there in the region.

"Oh, hey Boss. How they treating ya?" Arn said as he kept
working the arm. He seemed anxious, as if stopping would cause
his heart to slow down and quit beating. He would carry the whole
conversation while working if Linton let him. He didn't mean any

disrespect by it; he just wanted to make sure his job got done quickly. That was his way.

"Arn, I'm gonna need you to leave that loading arm alone for a minute and talk to me about something. This is important."

Arn looked confused, but at the same time worried, as if Linton was about to tell him his mother just died. He quickly tensed up with worry and shoved the loading arm away, giving Linton his complete attention.

"What is it, Boss? What's wrong? Is everything okay? Carolyn? Bob?" Arn was genuinely worried. He thought the world of Linton and his Fogstow family. That was something Linton knew well, and after hearing that, he let all his agitation melt away and gave Arn a low-filtered smile before he responded.

"Yeah Arn, everyone's okay."

The tension dissolved on Arn's face and he took a deep, relieved breath as he looked one way and another and shook his head.

"Doggone it, Linton! Don't do that! You know things like that get me all worked up!"

"Okay. But there is still something important I need to talk to you about."

"Well, what is it?"

"It's about the way you're taking that corner over there off Main onto Locust. You're going way too fast for the turn, and every time I've seen you take that turn, I have also seen your load shift and pull your driver's side tire up about an inch and half off the ground."

Arn pulled his UMWA cap off and started to cower down a little, almost in shame.

"Gosh Boss, I had no idea. I'm just trying to meet Cliff's quota, you know. But I guess I didn't realize I was that bad with it."

Linton knew Cliff Holder would rather eat his own children than let his company take a net loss. Which would be just as well, because Bret Holder was still sitting on top of the Co-op in a cell, probably acting like a jackass to Deputy Stark right now.

One thing was for sure, Linton knew that Arn had a good heart and had always meant well to his family, his town and most other people in general. The last thing he would ever want to do was put someone's life in jeopardy. It occurred to Linton that his words may have depressed the hell out of Arn and made him feel a lot of undue guilt. So Linton put his hand on Arn's shoulder and tried to sympathize with him.

"Listen Arn, I know you mean well and I know you would never hurt anyone. Trust me. I know that. It's just, this Cliff Holder, well, he's got your nuts in a vice and he's forcing you to do things you wouldn't normally do. He's putting a blinder on you and taking advantage of you and that other guy's good nature."

"Brandon."

"What?"

"The other guy? You're talking about the other feller who makes these grain hauls with me, right?

"Yeah."

"His name's Brandon. Brandon Mackey."

Brandon ran the route along with Arn, but Brandon lived in Loudon, across the river from Barrelton in Kentucky.

"Brandon. Right! I knew that. I just couldn't think of it at the moment." Linton and Arn both shared a friendly chuckle then Linton continued. "But the point I'm trying to make is, Holder's got both of your nuts in a vice and he keeps twisting the crank. Squeezing just a little more out of you everyday and – I'm sure Russ, Burnley and Allen will agree with me – not paying you a lick extra for your time."

Russ, Burnley and Allen all stopped their hay bale work for a moment to confirm they agreed, then went right back to it.

"Well, I suppose that . . ."

Linton interrupted him. "Is he still paying you by the load with no overtime pay?"

Arn cleared his throat, sidled up to Linton and spoke low. "Well . . . yeah. But he still keeps us working."

"But does that mean the work you do every day is worth less and less? Why the hell should he get to keep all the profits for the extra work you dish out and give you nothing? Nothing extra, that is."

Arn thought about it for a moment and then cheered up, put his UMWA hat back on and re-secured the loading arm back to the silo.

"You know what – you're right! I'm gonna take this load back down to Barrelton and Holder can just haul it up here himself."

Arn started to take his work gloves off when Russ hollered over at him from the top of the hay bale trailer.

"Wait, Arn. Unload that grain into the silo first, then go shove that truck up his ass. I'm on your side, buddy, but we still need the grain," Russ said.

Arn quickly put his gloves back on and said, "Okey-dokey."

5

The noon hour was quite a bit slower than the early morning breakfast rush at the 'Bend. Kelly was able to get caught up over the hour and as 1 p.m. rolled around, Lucy was starting to get restless, so she let her play in the alley between the 'Bend and the Co-op. Lucy sat out there for awhile, drawing chalk lines on the asphalt that likened her mom and Linton as an old married couple with herself as a little rock star.

Elizabeth (Izzy) Brown opened the door to the 'Bend while Kelly was on a stool putting clean coffee cups back on the shelf. Kelly turned around just in time to see Izzy smile at her and she was quickly off her stool and around the counter, happy as hell to see her and gave her a hug.

"My God, you are just as beautiful as ever, young lady," Kelly told her.

Izzy was the young girl who went missing for three days over the summer of '92. Linton found her on July fourth, under the heavy light of the fireworks over the river, floating along in a johnny on the Ohio River, unconscious. She had traveled out on the boat with a boy she had met from Louisville three days before, but when she returned, he was gone and she could not remember where she'd been.

Linton immediately took her to the East Jamison Medical Center in central Squaw Creek and after finding her father, Pete Brown, they transferred her down to Jamison County Hospital for a complete evaluation. But the only thing they could find wrong with her was dehydration and a loss of memory.

Actually, Izzy remembered a lot of things, but she also knew that telling Linton or anyone else about them might have landed her in the state hospital down in Evansville, and she would be damned if she would spend any of her life there. So she just stuck with the amnesia angle. They had made her see a therapist, but all she wanted to do was put it behind her. Besides, it wasn't like she had been hurt or mentally scarred, or nothing bad had happened to that boy. It was just something had happened that she couldn't quite put into words, so she didn't.

Izzy pulled back from Kelly and said, "You're not looking so bad yourself, hot stuff! I hear you and the Boss have gotten together."

She stuck her pinky out for a mutual shake and Kelly obliged. Although Kelly was ten years older than Izzy, she had always identified with her. Izzy was a young musician who had chosen a darker element of rock music, namely goth rock, and she was always dressed in revealing skirts, her face painted white with black lipstick. But as anyone who ever interviewed her knew, she disliked being called a goth rock musician.

Izzy was interested in Wiccan culture and she liked to reflect that with her music in her band, "Izzy Lives." She tried to coin the term Wiccan Rock for her sound, but every magazine or newspaper that interviewed her always changed it over to goth rocker, so she just let it go. In southern Indiana, she had become quite an attraction. Her music had gotten some regional and midwestern notoriety, which translated to opening up for a few big names that came to the area around Louisville, Indianapolis, Evansville, Nashville and even St. Louis.

But Izzy preferred to play at smaller, more intimate venues around the area, which included a show in New Albany the next day. It was an outside show at the river park amphitheater and Type O Negative was supposed to be there. But in the past, many big names had made verbal commitments to show up and do an impromptu, only to later cancel. That happened more often than she cared for, but who was she to complain? She was an 18-year-old girl living the rock and roll dream, opening up for big acts, traveling and playing gigs with her own original music and a few covers, about to sign a recording contract. To put it simply, she was just going to keep going until they took the guitar out of her hands.

"Oh Jesus, Izzy. Whatever you do, don't call him Boss. He hates that."

Izzy smiled in confusion. "Why? I heard he set Bret Holder in his place last week. He deserves the title."

"You don't have to convince me of that, or anyone else, for that matter. But he told me he hated being called that."

They both laughed and gave each other another hug.

The kitchen door slammed open and Pete came charging out.

"Is that my baby rock star I hear gabbing in here?" Pete said as he reached in and lifted her off the ground in a bear hug.

Izzy was tickled pink to see him. Pete had told her several times he could go on the road with her and help her, which translated to protect her. But she always told him no, because she wanted to make things work out on her own.

"It sure is, Da-Da! I'm home for the night and I have a show in New Albany tomorrow night."

Pete let her down and gave her the look that said he had never been more proud of her.

"New Albany, 'eh? Hmm."

New Albany was only about a 45-minute drive from Fogstow. Izzy moved her face around with Pete's traveling stare so she could meet his eyes.

"Yeah, Dad —and of course you're coming with me!"

Pete's traveling gaze homed right on Izzy and he said, "Alrrriiiiiight," then picked her back up and swung her around.

Izzy just smiled and laughed with joy. As he swung her around, she tried her best to say what else she had to say, but it wasn't nearly as important. "I'm also playing tonight on the docks."

Kelly stood there and adored the two. It filled her heart to see such closeness between them after the near tragedy last summer. All they really had were each other, with the exception of herself and Lucy, of course. It was just such an important thing for her to see. Or maybe was more of an inspiring thing.

6

The day was starting to cool off and clouds were forming in the west. Linton guessed it to be around 67 degrees. If it got any colder, he was going to have to go get his jacket out of the Bronco.

After he finished off an A&W float, he picked up his bag of cans and made his way up Locust and across Main to the Chapman-Oxley house. As he walked up the front walk, Joe and Noah came racing through on their BMXs and said hi to Linton before they passed him and pedaled around to the garage.

Linton walked up the steps with his cans and knocked on the door. He had been putting this off for as long as he could. He wasn't quite sure what he was going to say to Brad, but he knew he was going to try to get invited in.

He knocked on the door and couldn't help but remember when he was a kid living on the reservation with his folks. They always seemed to have someone using the cabins all year round, and most of the time it was a woman and her kids. His dad used to tell him that when someone needed help, it was their responsibility as human beings to always lend a hand. It was their responsibility to make sure everyone was looked after, no matter who they were or where they came from.

Those words had driven Linton to join law enforcement, to maybe help in some way and let what was right, rather than what the law said, be a guiding factor. He always knew it was human nature for people to care for those around them, but it was also human nature to want more than they had, and sometimes, that could lead people to very dark places.

Linton had learned these lessons from both of his folks. Even after his dad vanished more than 20 years ago, his mother continued to teach him those values. His mom and dad were practically one and the same. That's probably why they fell in love, Linton surmised. They both wanted the same things out of life.

Only later, when he became a teenager, did Linton learn his mother kept those cabins ready at all times to house battered women and their children, who were on the run following a dirty court judgment. It was a safe place for them to come and hide until the next stop on their journey, the journey that would lead them to a better life, away from those who hurt them. Not once did Linton ever consider that the law might catch up with his family on this. Not once did Linton ever consider his mother or his father were criminals who aided and abetted women guilty of kidnapping. He trusted and supported them, both before and after his law enforcement career began. Even Sheriff Kramer knew the secret and went to great lengths to keep it hidden.

He wasn't just nervous to be standing at Brad Oxley's front door, about to pry into his life like no one probably ever had before. He was also nervous about tonight, when he would take Kelly and Lucy to Derbie for an overnight. Lucy had taken well to Carolyn, so he assumed that she had made up a room inside the big house for her to sleep in. It was just going to be him and Kelly out in that cabin together. Alone. And the thought of making love to her, well, he had never experienced a dull moment in bed with Kelly. But he was also going to let her in on a part of his life, his family's life, that could either make or break them, depending on how she took the news. He was going to tell her tonight what the reservation had really been used for.

He knocked again and after nearly a minute, Brad answered with a bottle of bourbon in his hand. He was dressed in blue jogging pants and a Kentucky Wildcats sweatshirt, and he looked like he hadn't had a shower in a few days. When he opened the door, he stumbled outward bit, and before Linton had a chance to try to get invited into the house, they were both on the porch and the door had closed behind him.

"Can I help you, Linton?" Brad said.

"Well," he began, and that was all Linton could get out before they heard all three BMX bikes rambling along out the side yard and directly over to the bluff trail.

Brad went to the side of the porch, leaned over it with his bourbon and yelled, "All those cans had better be smashed and in the back of my truck, or I will hunt you down and give you the belt!"

Brad turned around and stumbled over the bag of cans that Linton had brought for him. He regained his footing and walked down the front steps and around to the garage, where his rusty old '60s model step-side Chevy pickup truck was positioned so the boys could smash the cans in the garage and throw them in the back.

Linton had followed him with his own bag of cans, and by the time he reached him, Brad was leaning against the loaded truck. He seemed to be resting, or out of breath. The job was obviously done.

"What do you want, Linton? You here to bust my chops about me and my boys? What is it?"

Linton approached him slowly and held the bag of cans out to him.

"Well, first of all, I brought you this bag from the bluff trail. Found the leftovers of a party out there and I thought you guys could use them."

Brad tried to focus in on the bag and Linton for a moment, and then grabbed the bag and tossed it over the bed into the truck. "Thanks," he said, and started back into the house.

He had made it all the way up the steps to his back door when Linton tried to speak to him again.

"You know, Brad, I just wanted to check in with you, also. Just to see if everything was all right . . ."

Brad didn't even turn around before he went in the house and slammed the door shut. It was as if Linton wasn't even there.

Linton hesitated to leave for a second, but he also realized that if he had accomplished anything, he at least let Brad know he was on his radar. So he went ahead and left.

7

A wave of dust formed along the bluff trail as Joe, Noah and Dean thundered down the path on their BMXs, Mark on Dean's tote pegs. They were trying to gain as much speed as they could so when they approached the path to Floating Asshole, they could roar over the top of it like mountain kings and feel their assholes suck up into their stomachs.

The first one up the hill was Joe. With a thundering scream, he scaled the summit and cocked his bike sideways in the air. When he landed, he quickly pedaled off to the side because Noah was right on his tail and was sure to already be on his way down. Joe skidded to a stop, and not even half a second later, Noah skidded beside him. They could hear Dean in mid-air, with Mark on his tail pegs.

"Whooo-hoo!"

Dean landed on the bottom of the hill hard, and that was enough to send Mark flying into the dirt.

Dean dropped his bike and ran over to see if Mark was okay. Mark was lying on his belly. He slowly rolled over. Dean and Noah tried to help him sit up, but Mark didn't want to. He'd had the wind knocked out of him and he was trying to get it back.

"You okay, Bub?" Dean asked. "Can you breathe?"

Mark waved him off and Joe instantly knew what was wrong.

"You have to give him a minute. He got the air knocked out of him and he's just trying to catch a breath," Joe explained. He kneeled down and pulled the backpack off Mark's back and put his hand on his shoulder. "Just slow it down a little bit and let the air come back to you naturally, Mark. If you try to force it, you'll just make it worse. Just let it come naturally, buddy."

Even though Mark was visibly panicked, Joe's words calmed him, and after a few moments he got his wind back. They helped him stand up and they were all a little relieved. They all knew, but didn't say, that some terrible thing had yet again happened to Mark, as if he were a magnet for bad shit. That's why they all cared so much about him and always let him be there with them. They felt as though they had to protect him from some unknown force.

Fortunately, they were right where they wanted to be: on the south side of Floating Asshole. This was the best place to hide their bikes and make the walk out to the sinkholes.

Dean took the bungee cords off the jambox, which had been secured against his handlebars for the bike trip. He handed it over to Mark, who turned it on. The dial wheel must have been thrown off in the commotion, or when Brad Oxley pummeled it against the wall of the 'Bend, because Mark had to fine-tune it to get back to RBT-FM. One thing was certain: the recorder hadn't worked since Brad's tantrum that morning, and the cassette was stuck inside with the tape wrapped around the heads. That was something Dean had already promised Mark he would take apart and fix the next time he got a chance.

They all took off for the sinkholes and Mark started to lag behind while he tried to get the radio tuned. It wouldn't pick up a signal; it just kept going to static.

"Just wait until we get out of these trees. It won't pick up a signal until we get out into the wastelands," Dean said. The wastelands were the semi-barren lands that didn't have any tree growth, just junk brambles and brush.

Mark still fidgeted with it the whole way, until they reached the plateau just before the sinkholes. He got it tuned about the same time Radiohead started to play.

(Creep)

"So do you guys want to climb down this time? I hear that these sinkholes are happening because the mine company didn't fill in the tunnels and air shafts," Joe said.

"Yeah, you're right. My old man said they didn't want to spend any more money and just left them there," Noah said.

"That's right. Those fucking scumbags just left them to fall in and they could care less if it killed someone in the process," Joe said.

"Yeah, it's all about their greedy money. They came in and ravaged our land and left us with a shit-pile to clean up while they walk away with all the money," Dean said.

"Right, guys. I know. Fucking scumbags!" Mark said.

As they approached the highwall by the sinkhole, they saw a small group of teens messing around, trying to start a campfire. Their music was blaring from a Chevy truck with large mud tires and a suspension lift.

Mark started to lag behind, but Joe could see it was the Brownsman crew, and he knew they wouldn't mess with them. He turned to Mark and reassured him.

"Don't worry, man. That's Mike Brownsman and his crew. They're cool."

That was something Mark already knew, but he still felt a little skittish. He may not have had a bike for them to throw over, but he did have his backpack with all of their supplies in it, including a canteen, flashlights, gloves and peanuts in case they got hungry.

Dean and Noah were also sure they wouldn't catch any shit from the group, but they all started to pull together a bit with Mark in the middle, just to be sure.

As they approached, they could see it was just the main five from their crew, which included Mike Brownsman, Kurt Peters, Rush Amiano, Kate Liddel and Carrie LeBalte. The teens had seen them at the sinkholes many times and they had always been nice to the boys.

Even though they would have liked to, the boys couldn't just pass by without at least saying hello. So before they started down the sinkhole, they stopped in. Rush Amiano saw them coming and walked up to meet them.

"Hey, boys. It's good to see you four out here again. We don't ever see Bret Holder out here anymore," Rush said.

Joe walked up and gave Rush some skin. So did Noah and Dean. Mark stayed behind them and tried to stay hidden.

"It's good to see you too, Rush. What are you and Brownsman up to today?" Joe said.

Rush took a look back at Mike, who was trying to get the fire going, and then looked back at Joe with a smile.

"Just drinking some beer with the ladies and trying to do a little Boy Scouting."

That gave them all a laugh. Rush peeked around Dean's shoulder and saw Mark. He walked around him and ruffled Mark's Indiana Hoosier hat.

"How are ya, little dude? You didn't let that asshole Bret Holder scare you off from here, did ya?"

Mark shrugged his shoulders and drifted behind Dean. Rush faced Dean and gave him a sympathetic smile.

"Yeah, I wasn't there, but I heard what he did." He faced Mark and squatted a little to get to his eye level. "You know, that guy has been a dick to everyone that comes out here at least once. Hell, when I was your age he forced my candy-striped Cheaney number 40 jersey off my back and threw it over the wall. We've all had to deal with his shit at one point or another. Don't let him scare you away. We'll take up for you."

That made Mark smile.

"Besides, I heard he's locked up over the Co-op and he's about to get shipped off to do a stint in Terre Haute," Rush said as he fidgeted with Mark's hat again and smiled.

Mark smiled right back at him.

"Good! I hope he gets ass-raped!" Mark said to thunderous

laughs from the rest of the gang.

Carrie LeBalte walked up to join the conversation. Joe, Noah and Dean all stopped laughing when she approached. They all three had spent several nights standing over a bathroom toilet thinking about her.

"Okay, what's so funny over here?" Carrie said as she walked into Rush's arms and kissed him.

"Oh, you know. Just guy stuff," Rush said and winked at the boys. But Joe, Noah and Dean didn't see him because they were in awe of Carrie, standing there in front of them in her low-cut jean shorts, her luscious brown hair blowing in the wind. To them she seemed just like the women they saw in the Hustler magazines Brad Oxley kept hidden in the rafters of the garage (as if they weren't going to find those the second he moved in early last year).

One look at those three boys and Rush knew exactly what had hold of them. He snapped in front of the boys' faces and brought them back into the conversation.

"Guy stuff! Yeah! That's it," Noah said.

Carrie was flattered at the sentiment, but she was more curious what Mark had with him.

"Hey, whatcha got in there, little Chapman?" Carrie said, motioning toward his backpack.

"Nothing much, really, just some supplies for the tunnels," Mark said as Joe gave him a nasty *too much information was revealed* grin.

"What tunnels?" Carrie said.

"Ohh! You boys are here to explore the sinkhole! That's awesome, man! Something I totally would have done at your age!" Rush high-fived Mark.

"Did you ever go in?" Joe asked.

"Not from this end. We went in the other end that comes out in the TC. If you walk into the woods on the east side of it, you'll find a large air vent that's overgrown with brush and weeds. But we always thought of that end as the entrance. I guess we never even considered the sinkholes on this end were part of the old coal tunnels."

"How far did you go in?"

"Not very far. It was dark in there and we could also smell some sort of gas. Mike over there liked to smoke back then and we just knew he would end up lighting one and the whole thing would blow up on us, so we mostly left it alone."

"So are you boys really fixing to go in there?" Carrie asked.

"Yeah, but we have to climb down there and see if there's an opening. We're not 100 percent sure there even is one," Noah said.

Carrie started to fidget and bite her lip, but she kept quiet about the whole thing until she couldn't help herself. She turned and looked at Rush.

"You need to go down there with them. They could really get hurt down there and there won't be anyone around to help them," Carrie said.

Rush took a surprised step back.

"Babe, we'll be right up here. They can just holler for us if they need us," Rush said.

"But what if . . ."

Rush pulled her off to the side so he could talk to her alone. "Baby, I know this worries you, but if you send me down there with them, they're just gonna feel like I'm their babysitter. You have to let those boys be men. That's what their trip is all about."

"But they can get seriously hurt."

"I know, but they are also smart boys and can look out for themselves. And also, like I said, we'll be up here the rest of the day and into the night. They can just holler for us if they need us."

Carrie tilted her head in defeat.

"Okay, I guess. But we aren't leaving until they're back."

Rush gently put both his hands on her cheeks and kissed her.

"No problem, babe. We're here until they're back. Done."

He walked back to the boys and gave Joe and Dean another high-five, gave Mark some skin, and then turned back to leave.

"You boys be careful. My girl over there will kill me if anything happens to any of you."

The boys waved to him and all said okay. As Rush started to walk away Mark yelled for him.

"Wait a minute!" Mark said.

Rush turned around as Mark ran up to him and handed him his jambox.

"Can you hang onto this for me? It won't get no signal down there and I don't want it to get torn up," Mark said.

Carrie smiled at him and took the jukebox.

"It's in good hands," Rush said, and then turned with Carrie and left.

8

It took nearly half an hour for the boys to make their way to the bottom of the sinkhole. A pit of water had formed in the hole and it was covered by a thick top layer of golden soot. Joe theorized it was just pollution from the coal mine ruins and that the water probably had high levels of zinc or copper, or some chemical compound in it that made it look that way. They could see a few frogs hopping and mating along the top layer.

When they finally reached the bottom, or where the water had risen to, they found what appeared to be a runoff that wasn't letting the water rise any higher. The runoff had a small opening and there was a lot of loose rubble around it.

Joe and Mark starting clearing some of the debris and dead brush away, and they were finally able to confirm that their suspicions were right. There was an old mine shaft in there. It was musty and damp from the polluted water runoff, but they would be damned if they weren't going in. It held all their attention, and the only thing they wanted to do was explore it and see what was left behind.

Joe was the first one to squeeze through the opening, but Dean stopped anyone else from going through until they could get the entrance cleared away. He could see that even for Joe, who was rather small for his age, the opening was a tight squeeze. They had all the time they needed, so why not spend some more time clearing it away?

"Come on, already. It's pretty cool in here," Joe said as he shined his flashlight over the leftovers from what was once the main utility entrance for Oarshire's underground mining operations. Most of the equipment had been cleared away, but a lot useless stuff was left behind, including a metal utility cabinet, broken benches, some old pipe cutters and even a few hard hats with the brackets for flashlights on top of them still attached.

"I'm not letting anyone else in until we clear some of this shit away. There's no sense in letting the hole close up while we're in there. Especially if we get some rain and that nasty pit water starts pouring in," Dean said. But the real reason he wouldn't let anyone else in was because he was extremely claustrophobic and he wanted help making the entrance wider. All of them knew that about Dean, but they didn't rag him about it.

"All right, you guys clear it and I'm going to scope this place out a little. I can already see some badass shit down here!" Joe said as he picked up the hard hat. There was still an old flashlight in it, but it was well beyond its years. He started fidgeting with it and broke it loose of the brackets. When he tossed it aside, the metal broke apart on the hard, dusty ground.

It took him a minute to get the brackets to work right, but when he did, he was able to get his flashlight to fit inside them. Even with the brackets closed, it was still loose inside of them. When he walked with it on his head, the light wobbled and made looking in front of him harder. He decided to take it off and hold it. He put the hard hat back on and thought, *If it was good enough to protect them as they worked, then it's good enough to protect us while we explore.*

Just as Rush told them earlier, the mine let off the slight smell of some sort of gas. But it was a weak smell, so he assumed that it was probably safe. *Besides, what if it wasn't even a gas at all. I have no idea what natural gas smells like, or if it even has a smell. For all I know, there could be some dead shit down here,* Joe thought.

Dean and Noah were busy pulling away all the scattered loose rock and brush when they came across a branch that could have easily passed for a small tree. It seemed to be the key to all the other rock and dead brush around. It was sticking out of a muddy clay area, so all three boys lined up and pulled it at the same time. It budged a little, but they had to keep letting go and then pulling it again to try to rock it loose from the clay-like, muddy surface. It only took them seven tries, but once they got it to break loose, all the other debris came with it. When they pulled it far enough away, the opening gaped wide.

But with every great triumph comes unexpected dissatisfaction. Removing the tree broke the seal of the water line, and the pit water started draining directly down into the hole. Mark was closest, so he jumped across the streaming water so he could warn Joe.

"Joe! Joe! The water's flooding in! Joe! Can you hear me?" Mark said.

Joe received message loud and clear before he ever heard Mark. When the repulsive water poured in and covered his feet, he jumped onto a rock protruding from the wall.. The flow of the water was immense, and the only thing he could think was, *Great! Now that godawful water is going to flood our cave and there won't be no exploring today!*

"I heard you. I'm fine. Can you guys plug it?" Joe said.

Mark could barely see Joe, but he gave him a thumbs-up sign. "We're gonna try. Just hang on."

Joe looked down at the nasty flow of water and spoke in a low tone only audible to himself. "I don't think I have anywhere else to go."

Dean and Noah quickly started pulling the large branch back over with all the rock and brush attached to it, but the water kept getting in their way. They heaved it harder and harder, but every time they moved it further into the stream, the nasty pit water kept covering them. Mark got some in his eyes and it burned, but he just kept on tugging at the mess of debris.

Noah could taste it on his lip and even feel the slimy sensation on his arms and legs from where the water had doused him. They were finally able to get the mess of sticks and mud back into place, but not before the mine shaft filled with water.

The shaft itself pointed downward, so gravity naturally allowed most of the water to travel away from Joe. When they sealed the entrance, the opening that he came in was even smaller.

"You guys are just gonna have to leave it like that. Dean, I know you don't like tight spaces, but once you get inside there's plenty of room and nothing to worry about."

Dean wiped the slimy soot and water away from his face and he tried to spit the water off his lips. Even though he was deathly afraid of tight spaces, he really wanted to get in there and explore the area.

"Aw, shit! Just let me go first!" Dean said and cleared the path so he could crawl through the entrance. He stuck his feet in first, and when he could feel the opening closing in around his belly, he closed his eyes and hustled through.

Even once he got all the way through, his mind and body were still stricken with panic and it took him several minutes to calm down. Mark was the second one through and he immediately went to Dean, who was keeled over and breathing erratically.

"It's okay, Bub. We're through. No more tight spaces." Mark said, patting Dean's back.

Dean stood straight up and took a couple of deep breaths. "I'm okay."

Noah made his way through the opening feet first.

"Holy shit! This is awesome!" Noah said.

He went for the storage locker and tried to open it. It was locked, so they hunted for something to pry it open with. It didn't take long until they found a tool crib that was empty except for some rusty pipe wrenches, a broken drill and a corral of rusty re-bar. They all grabbed a rebar rod and started beating on the storage locker until Joe stopped them.

"Wait, guys. These aren't gonna get this thing open. We'll have to jimmy our sticks into it and pry it open," Joe said.

He stuck his rebar rod through a hole near the lock and they all started pushing down. After several attempts, they stopped to rest. Mark took the rebar rod out and put it through a hole near the top of the locker and pried it from there. He started with all of his might, but that was a mistake. The locker flew open and Mark flew into the wall. The lock was reinforced at that point, and it took very little force to remove this section, as long as you were prying it from the right spot.

When they got the storage locker open, they found it full of useless junk. Leftover personal protective equipment that probably wasn't even supplied before the union came in. Old hard hats with headgear for lights, safety goggles, ear plugs, ventilation masks with utility-grade dust and gas filters attached to them.

They didn't waste a second pulling them out and trying them all on. They could all smell the odd odor and they knew it could be a combustible or dangerous gas, given that all their families had at one time worked in the coal mines and had told them stories about the dangers of working underground.

Mark pulled the goggles out and put them on. The other boys were already outfitting their hard hats, and Noah got his flashlight to fit perfectly in the brackets over his head. They all pulled out the respirators and turned the filters clockwise to tighten them, and then put the masks over their faces. The nice thing about those was that they would usually last a lifetime if unused. When they pulled the masks over their faces, they could all breathe perfectly and could no longer smell the pungent odor of the mineshaft.

Joe pointed the flashlight at his eyes and did his best Darth Vader impression.

"It is pointless to resist, my son. The emperor is too strong!" Joe said, holding his arm up and making a fist.

The boys all laughed and realized that they could hear each other just fine with the masks on, except Mark, of course. Mark had already fitted his ears with earplugs.

Dean pulled his earplugs out and handed Mark a flashlight. "Here, keep this on you and keep those plugs out of your ears. The last thing you need is to end up at a Louisville hospital taxied by a helicopter."

"Huh?" Mark asked. Joe and Noah were also perplexed by the statement.

"Don't you remember what happened to those boys who swam in the channel? They went into the hospital with ear infections. They had to be flown by helicopter to a Louisville hospital. That's why I say we keep these out of our ears," Dean said.

(*the river will hide your bodies*)

Mark took a look at the earplugs in his hand and threw them away like he was holding a dead rat.

Joe shined his flashlight down the shaft the water had poured into, but they could only see so far due to the steep grade. The descending shaft was a much smaller space than the area where they stood. It was originally built only for the coal belt line and for utility workers to perform maintenance on them. The belt line was gone, but the tracks were still bolted into the rock floor.

"You guys ready to see what's down there?" Joe said.

They all put on their gas masks and rotated the filters so they could start breathing in them. They wore their hard hats, and Mark also had his goggles on.

"Your idea. You lead the way," Dean said to Joe.

Joe turned around and the boys started their descent.

9

The Brownsman crew was busy smoking pot on the bed of Mike's truck with the fire in front of them and Mark's radio blaring out new music from Pearl Jam when the sky started to turn gray.

(Evenflow)

Rush had gotten Mark's mixed tape out of the recorder and repaired the head bearings before he started toking on the joint. He had even recorded the Pearl Jam song for Mark and his friends to enjoy later on. He liked those boys and he felt sorry for Mark and Dean, for all they had gone through this year. He wanted to be that person who had done something nice for them, for a change.

Kurt Peters puffed on the joint and nudged Rush to take it from him. "So do you think those boys are discovering anything new in there?" Kurt said.

Rush puffed the joint and passed it over to Mike.

"Do you remember when we went in that shaft on the TC end?" Rush asked. They all laughed.

"Yeah, I remember you freaking out and saying you smelled gas," Mike said between drags on the joint. He passed it back to Kate Liddel, who was sitting behind Mike with her legs wrapped around him. Mike gave Kurt a playful smack on the head while Kate took a couple of hits off the joint.

Carrie was listening quietly and growing more and more worried about the boys. She knew Noah and Joe had parents who cared about them and would know to come looking for them. But Dean and Mark did not have that, and she felt responsible for making sure they were safe.

"Hey, you guys. I'm a little worried about the boys. I mean, if you guys smelled gas in there, couldn't that make them sick? Or maybe even cause them to pass out and possibly die from the exposure?" Carrie said.

Mike laughed, reached over and shook her shoulder playfully.

"Don't worry, Mom! That wasn't gas we were smelling in there. It was decomp," Mike said.

"What do you mean . . . decomp?"

Rush reached over and put his arm around Carrie, smiling like the joke was on her. "Decomp, baby. Dead things. The smell of them rotting away. There were bound to be all kinds of animals that went down there and died. The smell is just nature's way of confirming it has repossessed the body."

Carrie stayed quiet, but pulled her legs up to her chin and silently worried about them.

The sky was darkening and they could see lightning in the distance, but they couldn't hear any thunder. Everyone quieted down, and all they could hear was the radio.

The music played and the joint became a roach. There was no thunder and no rain, but they all knew it was just a matter of time.

The air started to thin out and the temperature was dropping. Carrie could smell the putrid stench of the river, the smell that only came when there was rain somewhere over its long stretch. It was the smell of fish, fish that had been out of the water for too long and were starting dry up and stink. That was the first odor that always went through the air there in southern Indiana after a rain. The odor told them that even though the rain wasn't falling on them, it was falling somewhere and the harder it rained somewhere, the more intense the smell.

Even though it was getting darker, they could still see along the horizon where the river lay. A tall man with long black hair was walking along it, dragging something that looked like a long roll of carpet, but he was too far away to tell for sure.

"Oh, shit! Someone's docked and walking up from the river!" Kurt said.

They all rushed to collect their stuff and quickly loaded it in the truck. Rush, Carrie and Kate all crammed in the front seat of Mike's truck. Kurt stomped the fire out, hopped in the bed of the truck and sat down on a spare tire.

Mike fired up his large muddy beast and made tracks, pulling out of the area back toward Highway 66 through the brush and mud trails.

10

The area sat silent for several minutes until Shane Duncan Siders walked up, dragging a gigantic knapsack that held a 32-year-old Louisville woman in it. Her life was cut short that morning before daybreak, when Shane strangled her to death and beat her lifeless body with a leather strap. When he got to the area beside the highwall, he saw the smoldering fire and reached down to feel its waning warmth. He stood up and looked in the direction the truck had gone. His face filled with anger and for a moment, he considered staying there and hiding just in case they came back.

Siders had been dumping bodies in the old mine shaft for several years now, trading them to the Jeffries who came down and collected them on the northeast end of town. The mine shafts were the perfect cover for getting dead bodies across Fogstow. He would drag them down there, at the southern entrance, which was mostly hidden under cover of the sinkhole.

His family originated in Gallatin County, Illinois, but Shane and his father spent their whole lives on the river, living in their houseboat. Shane's mother opposed this idea when Shane was young and insisted on him getting a formal education and establishing roots in the county.

Bill Siders was a tall and demanding man. He had taken in Moira Duncan after her parents had sold her off to him to settle debts, and after years of sexual abuse on the houseboat, she became pregnant with Shane at the age of nineteen. They moved into a river cottage for a little more than six years, until Shane was old enough to live on the river.

Moira cared for Shane in the cottage while her de Facto husband puttered up and down the river, making money any way he could and doing just about anything he wanted. When he came back for his family, taking Moira with him was not really at the top of his list. The last thing he needed was a *damn woman to interfere with his disposition to teach his son how to be a man and live off the river. She'd already given him two last names, and that was just outrageous!*

The last time he came home to their cottage, Moira stood in his way when he tried to collect young Shane and said she would never allow it. She would call the Sheriff if he tried. That enraged Bill and he picked her up by the throat with his massive hands and walked around the cottage with her suspended in the air. She clutched to his powerful wrists and struggled to breathe.

Did you really think I was just going to let you have your way with my boy? You're nothing but a river whore. A convenience for me at the time, and now, your purpose has been served!

Bill had slammed her against the wall three times. Shane counted each time, the breathless memory searing into his young brain. His mother's eyes filled with fluid and the redness quickly set in. Her face turned a pale purple and within a minute, Moira Duncan was dead.

Bill forced Shane to dig the hole that would eventually entomb his mother. Shane felt an emptiness, but he did not know the feeling of grief or loss. His father had always told him that weakness in this world would get him killed. *Only the strong survive, and if you are not the strongest, you're the deadest.*

That scared young Shane in the beginning, but before long, he wouldn't even feel fear anymore. The only thing he needed was a boat and a river. The rest would be easy pickings, just as his father showed him.

It wasn't until his sixteenth year that he finally decided to kill his father. The old man had wound down and could not keep up with him on their journey. He constantly had to nurse him back to health for some reason or another. They had never visited a doctor, and Bill Siders' liver was failing. They spent a lot of time docked on the north side of Derbie, in a quiet and secluded cove.

Shane had passed the time doing what he loved to do: swimming. He had swam in the Ohio River all his life, even when they were moving. He would just tie off on a rope, connect it to the exterior wall of the cabin and jump straight over the back into the river. He would let the boat drag him along most of the time and when they were stopped, he'd swim clear across the gigantic river and shore up in Kentucky. Sometimes he would hunt down squirrels or even steal a few pigs, but most of the time he just wanted to be away from his father and the miserable moans of a dying man.

One day when Shane re-boarded, he found his father sleeping

on the cot and decided that was the best time to end him. Just like his father had ended his mother so long ago. Shane remembered everything about that night, including burying his mother just before they left that cottage. The authorities never found her, though, and there was never an investigation into a woman who was never reported missing to start with. She may as well had already been a ghost years before she died.

Shane grabbed the paring knife they used to gut fish and approached his father's unconscious body. He looked pale and fragile lying there. Shane imagined that if his father were awake at that very moment, he would have looked into Shane's eyes and said, *Only the strong survive.* And that was all it took. Without a moment's regret nor any second thoughts, Shane rammed the paring knife into his father's throat, upward so it would penetrate his mouth as well. He did it once, twice, three times. His father barely came awake, but his body contorted and convulsed as Shane rammed the knife into his chest once, twice, three times. He stopped to gauge his father's reaction. The old man slowly stretched longways on the cot and it seemed almost like he was reaching for something. Maybe a ghostly figure stood in front of him and he thought he would be saved. This intrigued Shane, so he walked to the front of cot and stood directly in the path of what his father was reaching for. He smiled. He stuck the paring knife into his father's left eye once, twice, three times and pulled it out and stuck it into his right eye once, twice and three times.

That was the end of Bill Siders and the true birth of Shane Duncan Siders. He felt as though he had been searching his whole life for a more defining purpose, and now he had finally found it. This location was the most sacred to him. It was where he was born, where he became self-aware, and, most importantly, it was where he came home. It was where he would later dock and dispose of his trophies, and it was also where he met the young lady whom he chose to impregnate rather than kill.

Shane had killed so many people in his life traveling up and down the Ohio River that he couldn't keep count. He'd choke the life out of most. In the beginning he would dump them in the river, but then he started bringing them aboard his houseboat and dumping them in these old mine shafts. After he'd get them in the shaft, he would drag them down the tunnel until he reached the water and then float them across to the northeast end. The Jeffries would later pick them up and leave their loot behind as payment.

It was the perfect trade-off for him. He could snatch a body up from any number of towns along the river, in four different states. He typically avoided small towns because his victims were more likely to be missed and searched for. He preferred the larger areas around Louisville, Pittsburgh, Cincinnati and even Evansville and Paducah. He never killed anyone from Fogstow, or for that matter Jamison County (at least none that he could remember). That rule also spilled over the bridge into Loudon County in Kentucky.

He did sometimes stake out people in the little town of Santa Claus, Indiana, though, since the tourism there gave him better means to snatch an out-of-state traveler. It made him smile when he would close his eyes and think about it. Those summer days were some of his favorites. Young mothers taking their kids to a Midwestern dreamland full of Christmas spirit and summer fun. But he didn't spend much time there since it was so far away from the river.

It gave him great pleasure to choke the life out of people. He had never known much of anything in his life but rage and desire. He never carried a gun and only used his knife for simple tasks. He would never kill anyone with anything but his bare hands, unless, of course, the situation got out of control. He got no satisfaction from stabbing or shooting someone, with the lone exception of his father, the moment of his true birth. He felt his efforts would be wasted if he could not feel the life exiting their bodies.

He also took no pleasure in killing young children, teenagers or handicapped people. Although he did choke the life out of several men in his time, his favorite victim was young mothers. They gave him the most bang for his buck. All he had to do was make them believe he was going to hurt or kill their children. That was all it took to bring out the lioness in them. He loved it when they fought him, and he also liked to make them think they were winning. It was only when they believed they were winning that they truly fought until the bitter end. It was only when they had hope of survival that they would keep going until that very last breath. The last breath he allowed them to take before he took them.

After years of hunting up and down the Ohio, he came across Ceril Jeffries and his merry band of inbreds. He had disposed of an old farmer about five miles north of Fogstow in a gully deep inside the Hoosier National Forest two days before. He had liked that spot and decided he was going to take the farmer's wife there after he went back and beat her to death. When he returned to his new dumping zone, he found Ceril Jeffries there, overseeing two other men who were dragging the dead farmer, his dead farmer, through the woods. He laid the wife down and covered her with loose brush and leaves, and then followed the Jeffries. For all he knew, they were pulling him back to the highway, on their way to call the police. He knew before they could get there, he was going to have to deal with them. But they didn't go anywhere near the highway. Instead, they tracked through the woods toward Fogstow. But they didn't make it to Fogstow. They went directly to their plateau, where he knew the family had been squatting for generations and had laid claim to. And this was the moment he knew that the stories were true. The Jeffries were cannibals.

When they pulled the farmer into a makeshift barn, Ceril came outside and lit a cigarette. With the stealth instincts endowed to him by his nature, Shane managed to sneak up on Ceril Jeffries and apply a choke hold that rendered him unconscious. He carried his body into the cellar of a nearby house (a makeshift house built over the abandoned remnants of a military bunker) and found some duct tape, which he used to bind his hands, legs and mouth.

When Ceril woke up, he was scared to death. That puzzled Shane to no end. Why would a murderous cannibal like him be scared? Sure, no one wants to die. But this man was supposed to be like him. Not once in his new life had Shane experienced fear. Not once had he had an emotional breakdown, or so he thought. So why would this guy respond in such a strange way? Did he not have the necessary instincts? Did he not possess the necessary drive to carry out these tasks?

But then it started to become clear to Shane. This man served his people. His people were not killers. They were scavengers. They were those wretched birds who flew in circles over the carcasses of the dead and waited for their opportunity to swoop in for a meal. They were poor folk who did not leave their home to labor or socialize. They did not even leave their homes to mate. They hunted down their animals in the woods and picked up the roadside meals. They didn't let anything go to waste, including human meat.

A smile appeared on Shane's face. He couldn't help but wonder what happened if they ran out of food. Did they dig up bodies at a cemetery and dine on them? It made him laugh out loud while Ceril Jeffries sat there, engulfed in fear and crying with snot covering the duct-tape on his mouth. He struggled to breathe through his congested nose.

He squatted down beside him and laughed into his face. "Tell me something. Has anyone from your family ever died from poisoning? Maybe from something like, oh, say, . . . formaldehyde?" Shane asked.

He stood up, already knowing the answer. Ceril calmed himself down and realized that Shane already knew. Shane pulled the duct tape partially off his mouth so he could breathe and speak.

"So why is it that I see you pulling a body out of the forest and you don't take it to the police, but instead, you take it . . . here?" Shane said, spreading his arms to indicate the room.

Ceril bowed his head in shame, and then looked up at him with the most despondent answer he could find. "So why is it that you find us pulling a body out of the woods, see us bring him home and you snatch me up and bring me . . . here?"

Shane just snickered and turned to look around the cellar. In all the excitement, he had not even realized what was in the cellar with them. Various pieces of camping gear, boat motors, grills, small propane tanks, coolers, fishing gear, jamboxes, outdoors clothing and even empty purses.

The Jeffries were indeed vultures. Those who stole from campers and hikers in the national forest. Those who stole from cars broken down on the sides of the highway and the interstate. Those who made do with whatever they could, by any means they could find. And most importantly, those who ate whatever they could find to survive on.

Shane and Ceril made a lasting arrangement that day. The Jeffries would dispose of his bodies, and Shane would dispose of their loot. It was an even trade between two very different devils. A win-win pact that made no waves. An understanding.

11

Joe Terrance and his gang were making progress, slowly descending the dark mine shaft. They knew that at some point they were going to hit that filthy water that had poured in earlier, but they wanted to see how far it went and whether or not it really made it all the way out to the other side of the Turkey Crossing.

The walls of the shaft were starting to crumble, little by little. There were supports still in place in most sections, but in others they had given way, and if more were to give way, well, the shaft could end up collapsing and the town would have another sinkhole to worry about. If too much of it collapsed, then the entire TC could end up buried beneath the surface, and that was some dangerous business for the community. That could kill a lot of people.

"Guys, I think we need to report what we found here as soon as we're done. This entire shaft could cave in and all those people over in the TC would be goners," Mark said.

They were all thinking the same thing and they all agreed at the same time. It just made good sense to let the Boss know if his town's in any danger. Of course they had all assumed the worst when it came to the reclaim land from the old mines. Most of the townsfolk were all pretty hip to theory as well. But it was these boys that were going to come back with the confirmations. If they could just make it all the way through to the TC and come out the other end, before they had to give it all up. That's all they wanted to do. Complete the adventure. Have something to tell their grandchildren about someday, which would include how they saved a lot of lives by discovering the mineshaft and letting the Boss know about it so he could evacuate the area and make sure no ended up dead.

In their minds, that was how it was going to play out.

They had approached a portion of the shaft where the rocks and junk stone had broken loose from the walls on both sides. The rock must have rolled all the way down to the bottom of the shaft, because it was nowhere in sight. And by the looks of the holes in the wall, those rocks must have been house-sized boulders, because they could have easily hidden a car.

"Jesus Christ! Look at these! They could be new tunnels and lead to more places down here!" Mark said.

Mark and Joe went into the one on the right and Dean and Noah went into the one on the left.

"Just explore and come right back, we don't want to get separated for long. Got it?" Joe said to Dean and Noah.

They both confirmed and both parties went their separate ways.

Joe stood at the entrance to his side while Mark was already deep inside exploring the cleared cave-in.

Joe could hear something from behind them, from the direction they had come in. He stood there for a moment praying the water barrier had not broken loose, and then he saw light. It wasn't sunlight because it was bouncing around. It was a flashlight. It was coming from their entrance. At first, he thought it might have been

Rush and his gang, but then he heard a man grunting and something dragging along behind them. He quickly shut his light off.

Dean walked back to his own side entrance with his light on and Joe motioned to him to turn it off. When the strange man got closer, Joe waved for Dean to go back into the wall and hide. Dean gave him a scared nod and retreated back into the wall. Joe also found Mark and turned his light off. He whispered into Mark's ear what was going on and Mark went quiet, obviously scared out of his mind.

Outside their walled hideouts, the man made it to where they were at in the shaft. Joe peered around the corner and could see by the wavering shine of the man's flashlight that it was Shane Duncan Siders.

What in the world could that lunatic be doing here? And what in the hell is he dragging along behind him? Joe thought.

Then he could see clear as day. That gigantic knapsack was actually a feed mill bag that was commonly used when people came into the Co-op and picked up their grain. Some used those extra heavy sized sacks to cram more into their loads. But there was no way that bag was packed with grain. That's when he saw it, the hand that was hanging out of the sack. And he knew right away it was a woman's hand because there was a ring on the finger, which looked like it might have been an promise ring. Kind of like the one that Jaci Pinker wanted Noah to buy her when they went on the Louisville field trip to the museum and they saw it in the gift shop.

It all became clear to Joe in a single moment that Shane Duncan Siders was dragging a body deep into the ruins of this old mine shaft, and it probably wasn't the first one. They had always known that there was something off about that lunatic but they never could know for sure. All the times they encountered him, he was always grimacing, as if he was in pain at the mere sight of them. When he saw them, he looked as though he had just stubbed his toe on the edge of a table and all the pain was in his face. He didn't talk to anybody when he came to town and always disappeared for days, weeks, even months at a time. It didn't surprise Joe one bit that Siders turned out to be a murderer. Seeing with his own eyes was enough for him to believe.

Joe looked back at Mark to see if he saw the hand, too. Mark was standing against the wall with his hands over his goggles, covering his eyes. That was something Joe used to do when he was in his room all alone and scared something was going to get him. He used to think all he had to do was cover his eyes and that would somehow cloak him from any monster, or keep anything scary away from him, as if it would just move on to the next person and leave him alone. He wanted Mark to see what he saw, just so the others wouldn't think he was crazy, but he could not make any noise, so he just let it go and turned back to the main shaft.

Luckily, he could see Noah peeking around the corner too, his face white as a ghost, and he knew right away that Noah had seen the same hand and the same bag. Siders might have groaned a few times as he dragged her, but if it were Joe and his buddies, they couldn't have even moved her a few inches.

Shane heaved the knapsack by the boys, and just before he passed their hideouts, he picked the sack up completely and gave it toss down the shaft. The body thudded and tumbled the rest of the way down for several seconds, and then they could hear a splash. Shane smiled when he heard it hit the water, and then picked a cigarette out of his pocket and pulled a match out of his trousers. But just before he lit it, he sniffed a couple of times and looked around. He sniffed again, then continued to look around as if he was trying to locate the source of a smell.

Joe and Noah on both sides started to get very frightened and Joe said to himself, *Okay. This is it. He can smell us now and he's going to find us. If he does, I'll punch him in the dick and we'll all jump out and push him down the shaft, then we make a break for it.* He just hoped that Noah was thinking the same thing. God, he hoped so! The last thing he wanted to happen was for him to get Siders off track and for no one to come to help. They could miss their opportunity to get out of this alive, and then they would be the next ones in a grain sack being tossed down a mineshaft into that god-awful water below.

Shane sniffed around a few more times and looked at the match he was about to light and smiled.

"Oh no. Better not this time, old chucky," Shane said to no one in particular as he put his match back into his pants. He put the cigarette in his left front shirt pocket and took off down the mineshaft.

Joe peered around the corner to make sure he was gone and then walked back out to the main shaft. He motioned for everyone to come out and shooed them with his index finger. He pointed to all of them and pointed back up the shaft to the exit. They all just nodded their heads in agreement and quickly, but quietly, hustled up the shaft and out of the mine.

* * *

It took them less than five minutes to run all the way back to Floating Asshole, where their bikes were stashed. They still wore their protective gear, and when they got there, they started pulling it off and hiding it all in the brush.

"What the fuck was that?!" Noah yelled at Joe.

Joe was out of breath and still in a state of panic. He hunched over to catch his air and he could not answer right away. Dean, although he knew that the situation was tense, had no idea what Joe and Noah had seen. He checked Mark over to make sure he was okay. Mark was vulnerable to situations like these and he sometimes would withdraw.

"You okay, bub?" Dean asked Mark.

Mark just stood there, still wearing his goggles, and didn't say anything. He just whimpered. Dean grabbed his shoulders, gave him a little shake and pulled his goggles off.

This upset Mark, and he quickly pulled the goggles out of Dean's hand and put them back on.

"Mark! Talk to me, bub! Are you okay?" Dean said. He looked around and saw they were in a completely hidden area. No one was around and the danger was all gone. "Look, Mark. Look around. There's no more danger. Nothing to be scared of anymore."

Joe and Noah took a moment to observe them. They were more interested in making sure that Mark was okay than discussing the hand of the dead lady they saw in the grain sack. They also didn't want to upset Mark anymore.

"Mark, we're safe, buddy. No one can get to us here. And Siders didn't even see us, so he has no reason to come after us," Joe said.

Mark felt safe with his goggles on. As if they were the only things that protected him while they were in the cave. They were what gave him his invisibility and they would keep him out of the sight. No one bad could hurt him when he had those goggles on. He knew those boys thought that he was just a young kid and could not understand what Shane Duncan Siders was pulling along in that grain sack, into an abandoned mineshaft. He knew all too well that man was a criminal, just one who hadn't been caught, and he scared the hell out of Mark. There was no doubt that Siders was dragging a human body along behind him. That is why he covered his eyes. If Siders saw him, he might just pass him up and decide that Mark wouldn't know anything and did not need to be killed. He also covered his eyes at home when he did not want Brad Oxley to break his stuff. It never worked and Brad just kept on breaking everything that Mark cared about and he knew covering his eyes wasn't working anymore. But this time, he had his goggles on and Siders didn't catch them. This time, he was truly invisible to bad things. His goggles saved their lives.

"I, I just . . . I need to keep these goggles with me. That's all," Mark said.

Dean looked relieved, and he took his hands off Mark's shoulders. "It's okay, bub. You can keep them. Just always remember to talk to me when something's wrong. That's all."

Darkness was starting to fall. The skies had covered in what seemed like an approaching thunderstorm from the west, but they could not see nor hear any rain. Noah checked his watch; it was rounding 5.

"Let's just get back before we get poured on. It looks like a wicked storm is rolling in and we don't wanna get caught in the middle of it," Noah said.

They all agreed and slowly wheeled their bikes up over Floating Asshole and glided down the other side, straight onto the Bluff Trail.

Joe and Noah didn't stop at the Chapmans' house. They rolled straight through to Joe's, which was deep in the heart of Squaw Creek. Noah lived right beside Joe.

CHAPTER 3
THE DUSK BEFORE THE DAWN

1

THE A-FRAME CABIN Bob Stamps had rented just a mile away from Patoka Lake smelled a lot like no one had been inside it for a couple of years. Although everything seemed clean when Bob and his children hurried inside to get out of the pouring rain, it still had a stale, musty smell, like it had been sitting empty for a long time. Bob certainly didn't mind, nor was he surprised. That's what he expected out of this trip: a smelly log cabin, no TV, fishing on the Patoka in a rented pontoon boat, a table and a kitchen supplied with cooking utensils and a small refrigerator to keep their food and root beers cold.

As Bob and his children, Sebastian (Bob called him Sebby) and Ellen, stepped into the cabin, he took a deep whiff, breathing in the dusty smell, and then remembered that Ellen had severe allergies and the dust might bother her. The kids smelled the odor right away also and Ellen was less than happy about it.

"Oh my God, Dad! Could you have gotten us a crappier place to stay?" Ellen said as she laid down her suitcase and covered her nose.

Bob turned around to face her and smiled.

"Oh, come, now. This isn't so bad. It's just what a cabin smells like. It's good to be one with nature. That's what this is all about," Bob said.

Sebby set the tackle box and fishing poles down beside the door after he closed it, and then walked through the cabin. He traced through the first level, climbed the ladder to the exposed loft and only found a bed.

"Seriously? No TV? What in the heck are we supposed to do all weekend?" Sebby asked.

Bob just smiled at that as he pulled his coat off and started putting kindling in the makeshift fireplace.

"How about we make supper, and then play a card game?" Bob said as he ruffled Sebby's hair. "I'll teach you how to play poker."

Sebby shrugged his shoulders, but he looked interested in the notion. Although he really wanted to watch TV, he had also always wanted to play poker, especially with his Dad. But he didn't want his Dad to know he was no longer disappointed, so he just shrugged his shoulders and wandered away.

They had gone directly to the lake when they got to Patoka and hadn't even checked out their cabin first. Sebastian was excited about fishing on such a big lake after all the stories Bob had told him. Bob had said they would not only be fishing on the pontoon boat, but they would also be seeing a lot of flamingos (which were actually heron, but he didn't tell Sebby that), bald eagles and maybe, if they were lucky, they might even be able to spot a bobcat drinking from the lake. This last part scared Ellen, but Bob had reassured her that they would be in the boat the whole time and that bobcats couldn't swim out to hurt them. He had also pulled her aside and said that bobcats were more afraid of people than people were of them, so it was more likely they would not even see one while they up there. He didn't want his little Sebby to hear that, though, since it took a lot of convincing to get him to come up there in the first place. Bob really loved taking his kids places and seeing them happy. But they were also being heavily influenced by their mother (and grandmother) to believe that Bob was a bad person, and the kids had expressed a lot of negative sentiment toward him lately. He just wanted to do whatever it took to make them like him again.

Things weren't going so well that weekend. First of all, when they got there, they didn't catch any fish. They didn't see any herons or bald eagles, and when they saw the wild turkeys, they were somewhat small and unimpressive. After about an hour on the boat, the kids started to get restless and bored. Ellen complained several times that she just wanted to go home and Sebby sat back and stayed quiet. He even looked disappointed, but only when he could see Bob looking at him. When the rain started to pour down, they had made their back to the dock and packed up all their stuff and run back to Bob's Jeep Wagon.

For Bob, it seemed like it got cold way too quickly and even though they were having an unseasonably warm day, he didn't like the sudden shift in temperature. He didn't think too much of it, though. He had stopped at a small store on the way to the cabin and picked up hamburger meat and Grippos barbecue chips. They already had the root beers in the back of the wagon, so now all they had to do was make supper. He was sure that at some point that night he could get them in better spirits and maybe make them a little less disappointed in him.

They ended up playing cards that night, but Ellen did not want to learn how to play poker. She only wanted to play Go Fish, so that's what they played. Sebby's disappointment ended in him going to bed around 7:30, not long after they ate supper. Ellen read her teen magazine until she fell asleep around 8:30. That just left Bob, awake and concerned that he was losing his kids. They had kept telling him they wanted to go home.

For Bob, home just meant going back to the same old thing. They would sleep in their rooms at his two-bedroom apartment in the Beach and he would sleep on the couch all weekend so they could each have their own bed. But it might have also have meant going back to the home they shared with their mother. Bob's old home that he still paid a monthly mortgage on. The home where he had built zip lines between the trees for the kids to glide across the yard. The same home that he bought before he met Sandra, in hopes that he would one day raise his family there.

I don't want them to be unhappy. Maybe I shouldn't have brought them out here. Maybe we should just pack it up tomorrow and head back to the channel and salvage what's left of the weekend with something that will make them happy.

Bob went over all the options in his head that would make them happy. Just a year ago, it was a lot easier. He would take them one weekend to Holiday World down in Santa Claus, another weekend they would drive down to Opryland and other times they would visit the zoos in Louisville, Cincinnati and even Indianapolis. They had such a great time and they were always smiling and so happy to be with him. Now, they seemed to loathe being around him.

Bob fell asleep around 2 a.m. and they all left Patoka the next morning at 8. That would be the last trip Bob would ever take them on.

2

The day was darkening from an impending thunderstorm looming somewhere west of Fogstow over the Ohio River. Kelly was busy wiping off the lunch counter and getting ready to shut the 'Bend down at quarter to five that evening due to the town coming together for the Elk's Club brain sandwich dinner that night.

Izzy Lives was going to be playing down at the Stow Tavern later in the night as well, and Kelly and Pete always shut it down for the Friday night events. Pete wouldn't have stayed anyway. He would never miss one of his daughter's live shows, even if they were playing that goth-rock music that Izzy wrote so passionately.

Kelly had turned the pretzel warmer off and pulled the last pretzel out and put it on a plate. She would have shared it with Lucy, but Allen and Burnley came over and took the girl to the hay bales so she could jump around and play on them. They always did that in the early evening hours. They loved Lucy, just like most of the town.

The bell chimed as soon as the door opened. Dr. Amy Strange walked in. Kelly was sitting behind the lunch counter picking apart the giant pretzel when Amy approached and casually sat at the counter across from her.

There had always been an unspoken tension between Kelly and Amy. Linton had dated Dr. Strange for a couple of years and had even stayed with her when he needed to stay in Fogstow for one reason or another. That was before he made accommodations above the Co-op in his office.

Amy Strange was a few years older than Linton, and they had had a passionate relationship. A little more than a year before, they talked about children, and that was where the relationship started to fade. Amy did not want to have kids at that point in her life. Linton, although he wasn't unsympathetic to her feelings, drifted away from Amy and eventually broke it off. A month later, he had started seeing Kelly and things had blossomed quickly.

Although Kelly had seen Amy around town on occasions, she had never really spoken with her after she got involved with Linton. Every time she might have had a chance to, it always felt like this giant elephant was in the room, and she cowered from the task. She supposed Amy knew this and might have come here at that moment with just that in mind. Although there was no animosity between them, it just seemed like the right thing to do: To allow the awkwardness to pass and live together in a small town. They both had equal standing in the town, and being on the same page meant being comfortable and happy around each other. They at least owed it to the town, so that the townsfolk never felt like they would have to pick a side.

Amy did not look at Kelly as she sat down, and Kelly plucked away at the pretzel. She was fairly confident that Amy wasn't there to a put an order in, so she just stayed there and waited for Amy to speak.

When Amy finally looked up, Kelly joined her. Amy smiled at her in a sympathetic and caring way, but Kelly could not return the gesture. She was taken off guard, as if she had been backed into a corner. She didn't feel threatened by the situation, just unprepared. Kelly quickly looked back down at her pretzel and tore the already-torn pieces into smaller pieces.

"I know this has been awkward for you," Amy said as she fidgeted with a straw on the counter. "It's been awkward for me, too."

This calmed Kelly's anxiety. She picked apart a piece of her pretzel, looked up at Amy and finally gave her a smile. Not a manufactured smile or one of her patented half-smiles, but a smile that said she cared.

Kelly pushed her pretzel plate halfway between them both and picked a piece for herself and nibbled on it. "It doesn't have to be."

That relieved Amy, too, and the two shared bites of the pretzel for the next ten minutes in a comfortable silence.

When Amy picked up her purse and jacket to leave, she gently touched Kelly's four fingers sitting on the counter. Kelly did not look at her, but smiled and accepted the gesture.

3

Linton was wrapping up his rounds in Fogstow. He parked his Bronco in front of the Co-op just as he saw Kelly walking out of the 'Bend and locking the front door. It was already past five and he wanted to check in on Stark and Holder before he left for Derbie that night. He and Kelly had to make sure to stop at the Elks Club and drop by the Stow for one of Izzy's songs, so they were both hustling so they wouldn't get caught in the weather that was guaranteed to drown them.

"You got your things packed? Where's Lucy?" Linton asked her.

Kelly walked up and kissed Linton and they both walked into the alley toward their separate stairwells. "Will you run over and grab Lucy from Burnley? I think he has her, since Allen's running the grill over at the Elks."

Linton abruptly turned around and went for the front of the Co-op.

"Linton?" He turned back to Kelly. She slowed down and

smiled at him as she went up her stairwell. "I'm glad we're going to Carolyn's tonight."

Linton just smiled and shook his head at her as he made his way to the co-op.

* * *

Burnley had Lucy in the back lot, letting her jump from hay bale to hay bale and then into his arms. When Linton walked in he could hear her laughing and jumping. Burnley might have been an old man, but he was never too old to play with the youngsters.

"She keeping you young, old-timer?" Linton said to Burnley.

Burnley caught Lucy in mid-air and turned around, an abundance of joy on his face. Lucy was still laughing when she called out for him.

"Win-ton, Win-ton!" Lucy said as Burnley let her down and she ran into Linton's arms. Linton pulled her up and she immediately kissed his cheek.

"You ready to go, little gal?"

"Yep! Momma got our luggage packed last night and we're alllll ready!" Lucy joyously punctuated that with her arms spread wide open.

Burnley picked up Lucy's drink and handed it to Linton. Lucy carried around a large plastic Indiana Hoosiers cup that said *1987 National Champions* on it. She always had to have orange juice or lemonade with her. She thought that she could die from dehydration if she didn't. Kelly washed it every night for her and filled it up then put it in the refrigerator so her drink would be good and cold the next day.

Lucy had been fighting a fall cold and she'd been prescribed amoxicillin, which came in a pink liquid. Burnley had run down to the store and picked it up for her and had given the first dose just about an hour ago. Kelly had asked Lucy if she wanted her to mix it into her drink, but Lucy liked the taste of the pink stuff by itself.

"Hang on just a second, Linton. I have her medicine in the fridge," Burnley said. He went and got it. "Also, Marvin Kramer called and said you don't need to be back at 10 a.m. tomorrow. He said Cliff Holder tugged a few purse strings and got a judge to set bail. Stark let him go about an hour ago."

Linton let Lucy down and handed the medicine to her. "Run this up to your momma, sweetheart. She needs to put it in her travel bag."

"Okay," Lucy said. She took off like a lightning bolt out the front door.

They both watched her go and shook their heads.

"I think she's really excited about going to Derbie tonight," Burnley said.

"Yeah. Last time we were down there, Mom made homemade donuts and glaze with her, and she told Lucy they would make fudge when she came back."

"Sounds like she's taken to Carolyn."

"Mom really enjoys her. They usually send me and Kelly off somewhere else so they can do things by themselves. Well, I should say Lucy sends us off. Last time, we went to a movie down in Barrelton."

"What'dya guys see?"

"'A League of Their Own.'"

"Oh yeah? Didya know they filmed that down in Evansville?"

"Well, they filmed some of it there. I think at an old stadium named Bosse Field."

"Yeah, that sounds right. Old Walt took little Renny down to sit in the stands while they were filming it. They did a drawing there for all the spectators in the stands and little Renny won five hundred bucks. Ain't that the darndest thing. That five-year-old boy had more money than his own grandpa."

About that time Alice Konicke was pulling her car in front of the Co-op. She liked to creep her car forward and tap whatever was in front of her. Fortunately, the parking spaces in front of the 'Bend, the Co-op and the Elks club were angled in, so she just tapped the telephone pole. Several people in town had tiny dings in their vehicles, though, from Alice's car. Allen had pleaded with her to get her eyes checked, but she was too stubborn to do it. No one really minded. Alice was just a sweet old far-sighted lady who always eased her way into places.

They both had a good laugh at that. Linton patted Burnley on the shoulder before he left and thanked him for watching Lucy.

He waved to Alice as he walked by, and when she got out of the car, she asked him if he would be at the dinner. He told her he would, but only for a few moments because he had to get down to Derbie to eat at his mother's house.

* * *

That night was going to be a great one for Linton and Kelly. But first, they had to stop in at the Elks Club dinner and then drop by the Stow for Izzy's performance. Linton had told Kelly they wouldn't be staying long so they could get on the road and be at Carolyn's before it got too late.

They both wanted a brain sandwich at the Elks club, but only had time to chat with other townsfolk. Lucy did not like the brains and she wanted to save her appetite for when she got to Carolyn's. The truth was, she likely would not be eating much supper in Derbie, either, because she was craving the homemade fudge.

Most of the people who frequented the Elks club dinners were older folks. They always brought their grandchildren, and there was a table set up just for the grands, who liked to carry on with juvenile stunts and conversations. The boys would do silly things like make fart noises with their hands in their armpits. The young girls, even though their grandparents dressed them up nicely for the event, would crowd around the boys and take part in the crude behavior. One thing about southern Indiana girls: They might be pretty and nice, but they were also women of the world and did not subscribe to the posh etiquette of civilized society.

Linton made his way around to each table for a visit and a handshake. He had shaken many hands, including those of Herb and Milly Rogier, Barry and Tracy Denton, Patty McCallister (whose husband was elsewhere shaking hands) and Alby and Maggie Peters.

Alby, Roman, Herb and Alice Konicke were all on the town council along with Allen Morgan.

Alby and Maggie, who were sitting at a table beside the serving booths, were tickled pink to see Linton. They had always thought Fogstow was going to hell in a hand basket with the modern state of youth and their general disrespect for elders. But Linton had been quick to turn that trend around. And given what had just happened with Bret Holder the week before, they were more certain than ever that Linton was the best man for the job.

"Well, hello there, Alby," Linton said as he reached out to shake his hand. The room was noisy, with everyone talking about the upcoming basketball season and their chances of a sectional victory over Smirna, who were East Jamison's main rival in the area for Class 1A. Barrelton was obviously closer, but they were Class 3A, which meant they would never meet in the post-season.

Alby couldn't hear Linton, so he stood up to converse closer. He grabbed Linton's hand firmly and shook it. Like most of the older generation in Indiana, he believed a firm handshake between men was a sign of respect. "Hello, Linton. How's your day been?" he asked.

Kelly approached behind Linton with Lucy in tow. They were squeezing between tables, and most of the older women were admiring little Lucy by touching her hair and telling her things like, "Don't you just look precious tonight, darling." Lucy smiled and giggled at the first couple of ladies, but she quickly retreated inward and became shy. She had her right index finger in her mouth and kept her head down while Kelly guided her by the left hand through the dining traffic.

When Kelly approached, Maggie Peters stood up and hugged her. "Hello, dear. You both look gorgeous tonight," Maggie said.

Kelly blushed at the compliment. "So do you, Mrs. Peters."

Lucy lost her shyness and gently waved at Maggie. She was starting to come around.

"Say, Linton. Have you gotten any news on the state rankings yet? I hear Smirna's at number 5 in class 1A," Alby said close to Linton's ear.

Linton fielded questions like this often, so he turned around to find Roman McCallister. Roman always kept him up to date on topics like this, especially if they were talking about Hoosiers college ball. But he was the most knowledgeable about all things basketball on the local and regional level. He found him standing beside a table talking to Burnley and Alice Konicke.

"No, Alby, not yet. But I'm getting ready to go talk to Roman and I will send him over with the info after I'm done."

Alby gave him a thumbs up, because talking in the Elks club had become impossible due to the noise. When he sat back down, Maggie joined him, and as Linton and his crew were leaving, Lucy turned back to Maggie and gave her an ambush hug. Maggie loved that.

Linton made his way over to Burnley, Roman and Alice, who had saved them a seat. He shook Roman's hand as he pulled a chair out for Kelly, and then picked Lucy up and put her in a chair beside Burnley and Alice.

"You better get over there to Alby. He's interrogating everyone about the Class 1A rankings," Linton told Roman.

Roman was hunched over the table next to Burnley when he shot up in comedic fashion, which always made Lucy laugh. "Well, I better get over there and give him his medicine," Roman said as he patted Burnley's back and walked away.

Alice was straightening Lucy's dress while Kelly struggled to fix her ponytail. "How are you, little Gidget?" Alice asked Lucy.

That always confused Lucy. Alice Konicke was the only one in town who called her Gidget. She called all the little girls her age Gidget. By now, they were all used to it.

"I'm okay," Lucy said, but it was more of a packed sentence with the words pushed together. *Imokay.*

This gave the whole table a chuckle.

Derri Emmons walked up to the table with a waitress apron. Even though she was not dressed in such revealing clothes as she was earlier in the day, she still oozed of that budding sexuality, and she gave Linton one of her newly manufactured smiles that said, *Look at me and you will have good dreams tonight.*

"Hey, Boss. Allen sent me over to see if you want a couple of quick brainers. You heading up to Derbie tonight, Boss?" Derri said.

Linton looked over at Kelly and wanted to know if she wanted to eat, but he only gave her the look so he didn't have to say anything in front of the crowd.

"It's up to you, Boss. Your Momma's cooking and she will want us to be at least a little hungry when we get there," Kelly said, snickering at her own use of the word *Boss*. Even Alice chuckled because she knew that Linton disliked being called that.

Linton looked back at Derri. "Just bring us one and we'll share it." He hated passing up a brain sandwich because they so rarely got served here in Fogstow. Mostly at special dinners and festivals.

"Ew! You're gonna eat a brain?" Lucy exclaimed.

Linton smiled at her, pulled out a dinner bib and tucked it below his collar. "Yep," he answered.

"Hey, Gidget. Will you do me a favor?" Alice asked.

"Yep!" Lucy replied while pulling a dinner bib out and tucking it into her own collar, mimicking Linton.

"Will you make sure you don't ever go into that river? Don't even touch it. Can you do that for me?"

Kelly was always uncomfortable with other people telling Lucy what she could and could not do, but she knew Alice Konicke well enough to just leave it alone. Alice was always worried about kids getting into the Ohio, at least ever since her son Randy left town for Seattle to be a roadie for the emerging rock scene there. Randy hadn't been home to visit Alice in nearly a year, and Kelly knew she was lonely and just wanted to be part of people's lives.

"How come?" (*howcome*) Lucy asked while fidgeting with the triangle peg game that was laid out on every table for the younger kids.

"Because, sweetie, that river is polluted with vile chemicals and that can make you really sick."

Lucy looked up and stared at Alice for a moment. "But what if I want to go swimming or splashing?"

Alice was little taken aback. "Oh, Gidget. Please, sweetie. Only swim and splash down at your Grammy's lake in Derbie."

Lucy was still a little confused. "Gammy?"

That was Kelly's cue, since it implied that she and Linton were married and Carolyn was now her grandmother.

"She means Carolyn's, sweetie. Down at the Turtle Reservation. Remember her lake out in the back, with all the cabins around it?"

"Yeah, Momma," Lucy said, and then went back to playing her triangle peg game.

Allen walked up from the kitchen with a styrofoam to-go tray. He had a cook's bib on that said East Jamison Brainers, which was both the school logo and the Elks Club's flagship dinner entrée.

He handed the tray to Linton. "Here ya go, Boss. I put an extra one in there for Carolyn. You guys better get going. It looks like a storm's rolling in."

Linton stood and took the tray, putting his coat back on. "Yeah, I guess you're right."

Kelly and Lucy both got up and put their coats on as well. Allen tickled Lucy on the stomach and said, "Say, little gal. You making sure Burnley's behaving out here around my girl!"

No one was really sure if he was referring to Lucy or Alice. But they all enjoyed Allen and Burnley's exchanges in regards to their romance with Alice. They knew it meant a lot to Alice to be treated with such pleasantries.

"Yep! Burny's been good!" Lucy said.

"Well, all right then!" Allen said and went back to the kitchen to fry up some more brains for the rest of the party.

"We'll see you guys tomorrow," Linton said to Alice and Burnley. They made their way out.

* * *

It was already dark out when they left. Even though there was no rain, lightning illuminated the distant clouds. They could hear far-off rumbles of thunder. The three made their way quickly down the steps to the dock and went into the Stow Tavern, where Izzy and her band, Izzy Lives, were playing covers for the older crowd. Izzy would later play her original goth music, but for now, she went with old Alice Cooper, Iggy Pop and Credence Clearwater covers for the sake of the older generation, who were all having a blast.

When Linton walked in, Pete was working behind the bar serving beers to patrons, such as Harry Keethers, who was the county coroner down in Barrelton. Pete always worked behind the bar when Izzy was in town because the crowds came from all around the region. She was becoming a big name these days and locally, she was a celebrity.

Linton approached the bar and sat Lucy down next to him. Kelly sat beside them and dipped her hand in the popcorn bowl and gave some to Lucy.

"Say, little gal. You got your ID on ya?" Pete said to Lucy as she munched on her popcorn. When she smiled back at Pete, she showed the chewed popcorn and kernels in her teeth and Pete could only laugh.

"We just wanted to come down and hear Izzy play a couple of songs before we left for Derbie," Kelly said.

"She's only playing covers right now," Pete said as Izzy rolled out a Mellencamp song. The crowd was on its feet, dancing and having a fantastic time.

"We can't stay but a few minutes," Linton said. Pete filled a couple of cups with strawberry soda and served them up to Lucy and Kelly. He handed Linton a beer, which he only took a few sips of before they left.

Kelly waved at Izzy and Izzy waved back. She pointed at Lucy. Lucy was intrigued and started to dance up and down on the bar stool.

They sat through a couple more songs and when 7:30 rolled around, they figured it was time to leave. As they were beginning to walk out, Izzy finished up a song and announced that the covers were over and the magic was about to happen, which meant her loyal fans were about to hear some of her original music that would soon be produced, likely in Nashville. The crowd cheered.

Kelly turned back to her, sad to be leaving when her music was about to start. Izzy flashed her a peace sign and waved goodbye.

They were heading out the door when Izzy said over the PA, "Welcome to the jungle, people. This is your captain speaking . . ."

This grabbed Linton's attention. He knew he'd heard that before, sometime when he was really young. But for the life of him, he couldn't figure out when or where. Eventually, he just gave up trying to remember and walked out.

The rain had already started pouring down, so Linton picked Lucy up and held her under his jacket as they raced up the steep steps to the Highland district and to the Bronco.

4

Noah and Joe sat inside Noah's room. They had already talked about what they had both seen, and they were trying to figure out a way to get the news to Chief Derr without him knowing where it came from. The last thing Joe wanted was for Siders to figure out they had seen him and to come looking for them. They just wanted Linton to know about Siders hauling a body down into the mine shafts and to put him in jail. They were both scared to death and didn't know what they were going to do.

"We could always sneak back down there and drag the body back out where it would be found," Noah said.

"Yeah, but then our fingerprints would be on the body and they might think we killed the girl."

"How do you know it was a girl?"

"Didn't you see the ring?"

Actually, Noah had seen the ring and he knew it was a girl. He was just a little delirious and clung to denial for the moment. All he knew was that he was scared.

"Well, we could still drag her out and leave her where people would find her. We can use gloves to do it and no one would be any the wiser. No fingerprints on her except . . ."

"Yes! She would still have Siders' fingerprints on her! That's the perfect idea! We can drag her out. She would be found. Siders would get busted by fingerprints and our names would stay out of it."

"Yeah, but what if he comes back while we're doing it? What if he never left? Maybe he's down there right now, just camping out."

"I don't think so. Remember that smell. I know we smelled that putrid death smell. But there was another smell in there. Like a gas or something. Maybe methane. I think even Siders smelled it when he decided not to light that cigarette."

"First of all, I don't think you can smell methane. But why does that mean he's not down there camping out?"

"Because he wouldn't want to be down there breathing it in. And he can't make a campfire or smoke down there because it could blow the entire shaft up. So he probably left."

"Yeah, I guess you're right. But even still, what if he's close?"

"Siders only shows up on that stupid looking houseboat he sails up and down the Ohio. We've seen him dock it down by the clearing just off the channel. That's probably how he got the body up to the mine shafts to start with, without anyone seeing him. We can just go down and check to see if his rig is docked and if not, he's nowhere around. Simple as that."

"Well, yeah. But even still, this is some serious shit we're about to get ourselves into. I mean, I'm scared shitless right now just thinking about doing it."

Noah's mother called them in for supper. She always made them homemade pizzas when Joe spends the night, and then they would sit in his room all night and watch the Sammy Terry late night fright flicks, beamed down through cable television from Indianapolis. Noah's little 13-inch television was rigged to display through the front of his bottom bunk and they both crowded in with the covers up over their heads.

But that night, they wouldn't be watching any Sammy Terry fright flicks. They would both lie in their beds all night, unable to sleep. Because the next day, they were going to go and do something frightful and scary enough that no blankets would be able to keep them safe if they got caught.

They had decided they were going to tell Dean about it and see if he wanted to come along. They didn't want Mark there because they were afraid it would be too much for him to handle.

Linton, Kelly and Lucy got to Carolyn's in Derbie at just before eight that evening.

5

The Bucky Cole had just arrived at the Cape Sandy quarry after a tumultuous journey from the Cannelton Locks and Dam. The river had turned into a screaming child's tantrum since the storm started on the south side of the locks, and everyone was watching for rotation in the clouds. But it was dark out and hard to see. They were relying on the readouts from their on-board units to give them warnings.

Cam Wright had learned earlier in the day that the barometric pressure was dropping and the storm that night had the potential for disastrous fallout. He was taught to read a barometer as soon as he started working on the barges.. The trick to it was not just being able to read it, but to interpret it, as well. The last thing they should have been doing was lugging empty barges up the Ohio River for loading at the Cape Sandy quarry.

But there they were, docked and processing all the stone the mines could push out. The quarry kept operating no matter the weather. Most of the work took place below ground, but if the weather started to turn deadly, they pulled their surface people below for safety until the threat passed. The barge crew did not always have that opportunity, though, especially if they were in the middle of their tour. Cam had heard that tornadoes had been known to hop across rivers, and if they were in the belly of the beast, the only place for them to go would be up.

It wasn't usually the tornadoes that had him and the crew shaken. It was the lightning. Although the Bucky Cole had preventative measures in place, extreme injuries could still happen. On the journey from Cannelton to Cape Sandy, the crew was remanded inside the cabin. The fierce storm they were trudging through could have been more disastrous if they had been working the barge lines. The

Bucky kept them safe through the trip and they had made it another day on the deadly Ohio River.

Deadly in more ways than one.

As the barges were being loaded, Cam stayed on the Bucky and cooked up steaks for himself and the rest of the crew. The belts were loading the stone, and they only needed two people working the tugger and barge lines.

It was his normal six-hour "off" shift, but he couldn't usually sleep when the weather was bad. His "on" shift would be starting in about 40 minutes, so he decided it would be best to stay awake and work his six hours, and then try to get some sleep later, in the early morning hours.

Cam had grilled eight steaks for the crew by the time they got the barges loaded. The captain decided everyone would sit down and eat while the rain was still going. But the rain stopped abruptly, so he got them en route shortly after, around 11:30 p.m.

By the time they had made their way onto the river, Cam had already gone on shift. There was very little to do while you were on shift at night except sit on the deck and watch the stars. When situations arose, he had to deal with them, but other than that, he would just sit there and roll down the river with the tide.

The sky was overcast that night, even though the rain had already stopped. The air had cooled, so he bundled his jacket around himself and took the occasional drink of coffee from his thermos. He was glad he had worn his long underwear. He could still see cloud-to-cloud lightning and even hear the occasional rumble. The cover wasn't enough to keep the bright shine of moonlight out, though. And the sound of the restless river was loud enough to keep him alert.

The river had undergone a sudden conversion when the rain fell. The warm river water had mixed with cold falling rain and the currents were at odds with each other.

They were within a half a mile of the river bend that fed into the Fogstow Channel. The river became more restless, and he could see fish, likely carp, jumping at an alarming rate. Something was changing below the surface and the fish were reacting to it. A few even landed on the deck of the Bucky, and he tossed them back in the river. But there was something frantic and desperate about them. They were fighting him with violent spasms, as if they wanted him to let them stay aboard. He would lose his grip and drop them. He'd try again, but they fluttered violently on the deck and flopped away from him. More and more were jumping aboard and he did not know what to do with them.

Then he noticed something he had never seen in all his life. A fog was lifting from the river. Not across the entire river, just in a section that stretched its width. He had seen fogs lift on the river before, but this fog seemed to be coming in straight, from the Indiana line to the Kentucky line, just as the Bucky was passing over it. Hundreds of fish were jumping out of the river and the fog kept coming. More and more of it kept rising, and after the Bucky passed over the line of lifting fog, Cam could see that it was forming into a cloud over the river behind them, growing bigger and bigger.

It wasn't just a fog on top of the river now. It was a full-mass cloud . . . and it was mobile. It was now moving toward the Bucky, as if it were chasing them, and it was quickly catching up. Cam's heart started to pound and for the life of him, he could not figure out why he was so scared of this fog catching up to them. Like it rose out of this polluted river, from the pits of hell and now it was after them. It was going to devour them and all Cam could do was watch as it approached. He looked ahead and saw the river bend approaching and he knew that once they got around that bend, the fog would keep rolling straight ahead and stop chasing them. It would get swallowed up by the warmth of the land ahead and dissipate.

The river curved left and as they approached it, the Bucky navigated around the bend and sure enough, the cloud of fog did not follow them. It did the exact opposite: it veered to the right of the bend and entered the channel.

Holy shit! This fog just changed directions and it's now heading into the Fogstow channel. Cam knew he couldn't let this fog touch him, for reasons unknown. Even the fish were trying to escape it from under the water!

The Bucky Cole was out of the way of the cloud, but Fogstow was directly in its path. Cam could not imagine what might happen when it covered the town, but he knew it wasn't good.

6

The Stow Tavern was filled inside and out with patrons from around the county who had come to see Izzy play. As Pete and Arn served drinks behind the bar, Izzy and her band rolled out song after song. Pete liked to help Arn out when his daughter came to town to play at the Stow. Her shows had a tendency to draw too many people with not enough help.

Izzy wailed out the lyrics to her song "Black Annie" as scores of people drank and danced. Most of the teens had congregated on the outside patio with the doors open so they could hear her play. Some snuck inside and got their hands on some booze, but others stayed outside and smoked their joints in the cool night air.

Harry Keethers sat at a table with his friend Perry Dupont and Perry's girlfriend Erin Mills. He motioned for a beer from Pete. Izzy announced that was the last song of the night, so Pete grabbed a few beers and sat down beside them. Harry and Pete had known each other for a long time and frequently came out and supported each other at things like this, although Harry was known to drink a lot and would have probably been there with or without Izzy playing.

When Pete got to the table, he handed all three of them a beer and sat down.

"Izzy really is quite talented. I'm very impressed that all of that music is her own," Erin said.

Pete took a drink of his beer. "She gets it from her father."

Harry lifted his can and said, "Cheers to that."

They clinked their beer cans together and took a drink.

Izzy approached them and sat down beside Pete.

"Did you bring me one also?" Izzy asked her Dad.

"Sure I did. You'll just have to wait two years before you can drink it," Pete said.

Izzy cocked her head and stuck her parched tongue out, thirsty. Pete laughed and gave her a quick drink of his beer.

"You know, young lady, that's some impressive music you've got going up there," Harry said.

"Well, thank you, Harry," Izzy said with a smile as she leaned back in her chair, exhausted.

"Long night?" Erin asked her.

"Yeah. All I want to do now is go home and sleep in my own bed for a change. I feel like I haven't had a good night's sleep in months," Izzy said.

"Are you ready to go on home?" Pete asked her.

"I have to help Mickey and Jason pack the equipment up and then we're off."

"We'll help you," Harry said, nudging Perry.

"Yep," Perry said.

Izzy leaned toward Harry. There was something she had been meaning to ask him for awhile now, but she had never gotten around to it.

"Say, Harry. Why'd you leave that awesome job up in Indy to come back here and run for county office?" Izzy asked. She knew

Harry liked to make up funny stories about things. He'd been doing it ever since she was little.

"Well, my dear, it's kind of a weird and funny story. Do you want the long version or the short version?" Harry said.

"Um, how about the extended short version?" Izzy said.

This made Pete laugh. Harry's extended short version is what most people call the distorted truth.

"Well the truth is, the M.E. job in Marion County was great. It paid well, had great benefits and I liked my work. But that was all I really had up there. You see, my real friends were down here in Fogstow and Barrelton," Harry said as he patted both Perry and Pete on the back. "So I decided to take a bribe and came down here to run for county coroner. The end."

They all laughed at that.

"Don't you know you can't start taking bribes until after the elections?" Pete said.

"Po-ta-to, Po-tah-to," Harry said.

Izzy smiled and rolled her eyes. She had known Harry would just feed her a line of bullshit, but it didn't matter.

They all got up and Izzy started breaking down her equipment with Jason and Mickey. They had been in her band since last winter, and they were enthusiastic about getting into the recording studio with her. Jason played lead guitar and Mickey was her drummer. Izzy both sang and played bass.

Pete pulled Izzy aside.

"Where are those boys sleeping tonight?" Pete asked.

"Don't worry, Dad. They sleep in the van every night."

"Well, okay."

When Izzy walked away, Pete started to think about where Izzy herself slept when they were on the road. Did she sleep in the van with them, or was she using the money he had sent her for hotel rooms? That thought made him quiver for a moment. But just like any father with half a brain, he immediately asked himself, *or do those boys come in and sleep inside the hotel room with Izzy?*

He knew he'd better stop thinking about it at all if he didn't want to fight the ulcer that had been tracing around in his stomach now for years. Izzy was 19 years old and able to make her own decisions. *She needed to live without his constant interference*, or so he imagined her saying.

He finished helping Izzy and her band load up their equipment, and then took her to their home in the Highland district, which was about twenty yards away from the 'Bend off Locust Street.

7

When they arrived in Derbie, Carolyn had a tenderloin and biscuit and gravy dinner ready for Linton, Kelly and Lucy. Linton had put the brainers in the refrigerator for lunch the next day and they all sat down and ate a fantastic dinner.

Even though Kelly worked around tasty food all day, she always loved eating at Carolyn's. She felt like they were around family.

"Oh, my God, Carolyn. That was so good," Kelly said as she wiped her face and leaned back in her chair.

Carolyn smiled at her and said, "I'm glad you liked it. I was really excited about seeing all three of you tonight and I wanted to give you my best."

"Well, I'm stuffed," Kelly said as she patted her belly.

"Me too," Lucy added, and patted her belly, as well. It was funny because Lucy had not eaten but maybe two bites, and they were both from the buttered biscuit. Kelly had insisted early on that she eat some of the green beans, but she let go of it pretty quickly because she knew that Lucy was too excited about making the fudge after dinner.

"I got the cabin all made up for you two. There are fresh sheets on and towels in the bathroom," Carolyn said, winking at Lucy.

Lucy was getting more and more anxious. She wanted to start making the fudge right then, but she knew she had to wait until her momma and Linton were out of the house.

"I also got a room all made up for Lucy upstairs, right next to my room," Carolyn said.

"Oh! Oh! Can I go see?" She turned to Kelly. "Can I, Momma? Can I? Can I?"

Kelly was taken off guard. "Well, I suppose. As long as it's okay with Carolyn."

"Of course it is, sweetie," Carolyn said as she took Lucy's hand and walked her upstairs.

Carolyn's house was gigantic and made of logs sealed from the inside out. The home could have easily doubled as a secluded get-away for summer folks. When they reached the top of the stairs, Lucy saw that not only did Carolyn have a room ready for her, but the bed had Strawberry Shortcake sheets and the walls were painted like the ocean, with sea turtles and dolphins. Carolyn had attached a night light to the back of the bed frame and had left several pages of stickers lying on top of the dresser so Lucy could put them wherever she wanted.

Lucy turned to Carolyn and asked,, "Is this my ACTUAL room?"

Carolyn smiled down at her and answered, "Of course it is, sweetheart. I made it all up just for you. So now every time you come here you have your own room."

"What about Momma and Win-ton?"

"Oh Lucy, sweetheart, they're grown-ups. They need more space, so they sleep in the cabin out back."

"But what if I get scared in here all alone?"

"Just come right next door." Carolyn led her to the bedroom next to hers. "I will be right beside you. You will never have to be scared. Ever. I will *always* be right beside you."

Lucy smiled at that. "Okay."

Lucy went back into her room and looked around, joyously. She reached for a hug, so Carolyn picked her up and held her.

Lucy whispered in her ear, "Are you my Gammy?"

Carolyn pulled her away so she could look her in the eyes. She would certainly accept the title if Kelly would allow it. If Linton and Kelly got married, she would be by default, but could she be so bold as to take the title before they ever made such plans? She knew if she did, she would be backing Linton into a corner and forcing undue pressure on him, which she didn't want to do. But she also knew that Lucy had likely spent her entire four years wishing to have a grandmother, especially one that cared for her and did things like build a room just for her. Carolyn had already done that, and she was probably overstepping her bounds a little bit, but she did not care. She wanted to be Lucy's grandmother.

Carolyn spoke in a soft, low tone when she answered Lucy. "I'm whatever you want me to be, sugar. If you want me to be your Grammy, you just say it and poof! that's what I am."

"Is that because you love me, Gammy?"

Carolyn smiled. "That's right, sugar. I love you very much."

"Do you love Momma too?"

Carolyn tickled her nose. "Can you keep a secret?"

Lucy shook her head yes, firmly looking into Carolyn's eyes.

"I love your momma too. And from what I can see, Linton does also."

Lucy reached her arms back around Carolyn's neck and held her tight. She gently pat Carolyn's back with her four small fingers and a tear rolled down her little face. She was happy. She wanted it to stay this way forever. She had a Grammy now and she didn't ever want to let go of her.

As she started to regain her voice, she said, "We love you too, Gammy."

* * *

Linton and Kelly walked outside to make their way to the cabin. The rain was still coming down hard and it was a good 50-foot hike to the front porch of the cabin, where Carolyn had left the front porch light on for them. They both pulled their raincoats over their heads before they left the porch of the main house.

"You ready?" Linton said

"Ready, Freddy," Kelly replied. They made a mad dash out into the stormy night and across the gravel parking area onto the path that led to the cabins. As soon as they reached it, they stopped and shivered, laughing.

"Oh my God, that rain was cold! I felt raindrops hit my back and roll down my spine -- and it almost gave me a seizure," Kelly said.

Linton shook off his raincoat before he opened the door.

"I know. What a drastic change in the weather we've had today. This morning, I thought I was going to have to change into short sleeves. Now I could use that long underwear packed away at the office."

Kelly took off her raincoat and gave it a shake, then cuddled up to Linton, trying to warm up.

"Say, handsome, what do you want to do now?" Kelly asked as she gently ran her hand down Linton's chest. She smiled up at him like an innocent schoolgirl. Linton smiled back and pulled her close as he kissed her gently, running his hands firmly up her arms.

"Well, I guess the first thing I need to do is warm my girl up."

Kelly smiled at him in a way that confirmed she was okay with being seduced.

"Then you better get me out of these wet clothes."

Linton shut the door and rapidly turned Kelly around, embraced her and started kissing her. He ran his hand down her back and groped her bottom. She reached her arms around him and rubbed his neck as they both panted with desire.

She lifted his shirt and he raised his hands. The wet shirt pulled against his skin as it resisted removal, but Kelly yanked it quickly like she was pulling a Band-Aid off a wound.

Linton undid the belt to her jeans and they slid off her with ease. She removed her shirt and Linton removed his pants. As he held her, he moved closer to the bedside table and turned the lamp off. They both removed their underwear and as soon as they were naked, Linton firmly lifted her with both hands from her bottom. She wrapped her legs around Linton and he slowly climbed onto the bed by his knees, holding her suspended in front of him, still in the air.

She reached down and grabbed his manhood, then quickly realized there was no need to stroke something that was already primed and ready for delivery. She kissed him one last time before they looked each other in the eyes, for only a moment. Kelly, still holding his unit, angled it up. Linton held her effortlessly in the air in front of him. Her legs were still wrapped around him, feet firmly locked together behind his back.

They both knew it was about to be the greatest experience of their lives. They'd had sex before, but never quite so passionately. Their desire for each other had grown since then and it was still growing. They had not even reached their summit, and they both knew that staying together meant years of happiness.

Linton slowly lowered her down. She let go of his unit as it made its way inside of her. One inch, two inches, then a full invasion. Linton was still on his knees as they passionately made love. Not one part of Kelly's body had touched the bed. Kelly buried her mouth in Linton's neck in an attempt to stifle her strained sounds. Linton muffled his own mouth on her shoulders.

But they had gained too much momentum and they could not hold their voices at bay any longer. Strained excitement and joy released into the night, only masked by the hard-pouring rain and thunder outside.

* * *

The rain was starting to let up about the same time Cam Wright was sailing down the Ohio on the Bucky Cole and Izzy Brown was packing up her equipment at the Stow.

Linton and Kelly lay side by side in the bed. Kelly pressed her back against Linton under the covers, and Linton wrapped his arm under her neck, hand resting on her naked chest. They had turned the bedside light back on and were lying there, devoid of energy but still too involved with the each other to fall asleep.

Linton had been making small strides to confide in Kelly the parts of his life that he hadn't told anyone about. He was now at the point where he felt like he could trust her with anything.

She held his hand on her chest and gently caressed his thumb. He had made her feel the joy of sex that no other man had given her. Although she had been with three other men in her life, that was the first time she experienced the wonderful release of an orgasm. She knew it was not just lust. She trusted him and she allowed him to open her up. He had done so with such ease. As if he were destined to set her free.

Kelly rolled over to face Linton. She rubbed his shoulder and kissed his arm. He slowly ran his hand through her hair as they both relished in the revelations the night had brought them.

Linton knew that if he wanted her to be a part of his life, her and Lucy both, then he had to open up to her about who he was and, more importantly, about who his family was and what they did. It was something that being a lawman puts him at odds with, but a necessary struggle to help people who need it.

"Do you ever wonder why Mom has so many cabins around the lake, but not very many tenants?" Linton said.

Kelly was a little taken off guard, but delighted to discuss the topic. "Well, I supposed that Carolyn has had enough financial security in her life that she can pick and choose who enjoys the reservation with her." Kelly sat up beside him. "Don't the boy and girl scout troops in the area camp here in the summers?"

"Well, yeah, but that's only one week at a time. Two weeks total for both troops combined."

"So what does she do with the other fifty weeks of the years?" Kelly asked, amused at the topic.

"That's just it. She has a purpose for the reservation, but no one except me and the Sheriff know about it. Well, actually, a few others know about it, but I can't mention who they are."

This piqued Kelly's curiosity. "Okay, so does that means she runs moonshine in the back cabin?" she asked with a foolish half smile.

Linton stood up from the bed, still naked, and looked out the front window of the cabin. Kelly sat up a little higher and pulled the sheet over her breasts.

"Linton, I was just kidding," she said.

Linton sheepishly looked back at her and smiled, then sat back down beside her.

"I trust you, Kelly. I have reached a point with you that I've never reached with anyone else. I want you to know everything about me, including where I came from and what my family does."

Kelly looked concerned and reached up and caressed his face. "It's okay, baby. I feel the same way about you. What most people don't realize is that trust and love, they are two of the same things wrapped in different boxes, one with a bow tie and another with a hemp string."

Linton stared into her eyes and knew that her knowledge of things, her ability to adapt to the greater good, were ever-present. He knew he could trust her completely.

"Well, for starters, we're not a family of moonshiners," Linton said jokingly. "And we've never robbed any banks, at least not that I know of."

Kelly was both amused and attentive to his words.

"Go ahead."

"Well, you see, Mom, her and Dad, they got together back in the '60s, when this area, just like so many others in the country, was particularly tolerant to male dominance over women," Linton said. He took a breath to search for his words. "Dad wasn't a wealthy man by any means, but Mom, she came from a family of entrepreneurs, some of whom owned the docks up in Fogstow."

Kelly nodded. She knew that was the old Weyerbacher Coal Docks, and she knew Carolyn was a Weyerbacher.

"But Mom, she came together with Dad . . ."

"Sammy, right?" Kelly said, cutting Linton off.

Linton smiled. He was amused that she knew his Dad's name.

"Yeah, that's right," Linton replied. "Mom and Dad, they came together because Dad was helping a woman and her two children escape an abusive man, whom she lived with across the river in Loudon. Mom helped Dad get the woman in contact with a network of volunteers that help women run away from abusive husbands and establish new identities."

Kelly was rubbing his hand, awestruck by his story. She seemed to be holding Carolyn in high regard.

Linton continued, "This reservation here, this is something that Mom and Dad built together after they were married. My grandmother gave them the financial support to do it, as a wedding gift, sort of. I've often thought that she knew what it was for and she may have been supportive of it, but she never revealed that to me.

My grandfather died before I was born, so she was less than naïve about counter-culture and even a little . . . partial to it. But like I said, she never let it be known to me.

"Over the past thirty years, or I guess I should say my entire life, we've been a part of that network, housing women and children, from out of state of course, until the network could set up their permanent homes and new lives."

Kelly was speechless. She stared at him in awe. It worried Linton because he was not quite sure how she was taking the news.

"Please, Kelly, say something."

Kelly shook her head as if she was still registering the news.

"I promise you, honey, these women, they would have been badly hurt or even killed by their husbands had we not intervened in their lives. Their children, too. Please tell me you . . ."

Kelly reached out and held his face, gently. She had a look of both concern and kindness, a fragile kind of stare.

"As if I ever needed a reason to love or trust your mother. But now, she has given me even more pride in being part of something that is bigger than just you and I. She's making the world a better place and I humbly accept the secret. The man I love and his mother I adore. You can always trust me with this."

Her response slowly soaked within him. His tension evaporated and slowly, a tear rolled down his cheek. He had finally been able to define love. The moment hadn't passed him by. He had grabbed onto her and now he was never letting go. He pulled her into him and they embraced each other for the first time as transcendent lovers.

Holding Kelly was just the right time to reflect on what was important to him. When his father disappeared back in '73, he was only 10 years old. He remembered that day with vivid clarity. His mother had cooked him a fried bologna sandwich on a grilled cheese. She made him wait in the house while his dad geared up their johnny across the street on the boat ramp. He'd had a baseball game that day and he still wore his jersey with the team sponsor's name on it, Rudd Insurance. His mom took the sandwich off the stove, opened it up and squirted some mustard on it for him.

He'd raced out of the house while chomping on his grilled bologna and cheese. The mustard had spilled on his shirt, leaving a stain. He had always gone with his dad out on the boat, so he assumed that he was doing the same thing that day.

Linton had pounded across the dock and was just about to board the johnny when Sammy Derr stepped in front of him.

"Not today, son," Sammy said. "Your momma has some things she wants you to take care of in the cabins and I have a few runs to make in Fogstow. You go back and take care of your momma's chores and I'll come back to get you tonight. We'll do some night fishing."

"But I want to go with you. I can take care of the chores tonight," Linton had told his father.

"Sorry, buddy. Rules are rules," Sammy said as he fired up the johnny motor. "Make sure you wipe that mustard off your shirt. You know your momma don't like those stains."

Linton looked down at his shirt and saw the mustard stain, and then looked back up at his dad with a smile. Sammy was just pulling his leg. Carolyn never minded getting stains out of little Linton's clothes.

Sammy buttoned his flannel shirt, which was red and white with black stripes down the front. He wore an unbuttoned vest coat, but he took it off because the day was getting so hot. He revved up the johnny motor and pulled away from the dock.

"Remember, do what your momma says, buddy."

That was the last time he ever saw his dad.

8

The rain had stopped pouring down and people were leaving the Stow Tavern for the night. Deputy Jeff Stark was making rounds in the parking lot, shining flashlights in people's cars, making sure they weren't too drunk to drive. A lot of people had come from counties in the surrounding areas and were making a longer drive home than the patrons from Fogstow.

A group of teenagers had congregated on the north side of the Stow, smoking cigarettes. Some smoked joints or discreetly drank beer.

Embedded within the group of smokers was Bob Stamps' ex-wife, Sandra, and her mother, Candy Odair. Rush Amiano stood beside Mike Brownsman, who was drinking a beer and talking with Carrie while Kurt Peters passed a joint back and forth with

Kate Liddel.

Sandra made her way over to the Brownsman circle and started puffing the joint with Kurt and Kate. Candy had followed and moved uncomfortably close to Kurt.

Kate saw this and felt a little grossed out by the two older ladies invading their space. Sandra puffed the joint and turned to speak with Rush.

"Say, handsome, where you staying at tonight?" Sandra said.

Rush was taken off guard, and Carrie noticed it from the corner of her eye even as she talked with Mike. It was okay, though. She trusted Rush and had no worries about him giving into a nasty older tramp like Sandra Stamps.

"Um, well . . . I think we're all gonna camp out tonight by the sinkholes," Rush answered.

Sandra gave him a seductive smile and closed in on him, pushing her breasts against his chest. She put her hand on his shoulder and said, "Who does 'we' include?"

"Well, that would be me, Mike, Carrie and a few others. You know — high-schoolers," Rush said, hoping she would get the point.

Sandra looked over at Carrie and Kate and let out a small, condescending laugh. She pushed herself against Rush and firmly grabbed his penis.

"Why would you want a little girl when you could have an experienced woman who knows how to please a man?" Sandra said, squeezing his penis more tightly.

Rush raised his hands and jerked backward, stunned. Carrie threw down her beer and pushed Sandra away from Rush.

"Why don't you go somewhere else and try to rape a child, you smelly old whore!"

Sandra had been smiling at the intervention, but when Carrie said "smelly" and "old," that set her off. She started to come at Carrie with clenched fists, but Candy put herself between them.

"I think that we will just let this one go, sweetheart," Candy said. Their agenda for the night did not include going to jail, and there was a county deputy in the same parking lot.

Candy and Sandra knew that several of these teens lived in the TC with their rich parents, and when they could get one of them to sleep with Sandra, all they had to do was pretend that Sandra was pregnant and blackmail their fathers. Candy would tell them *a little cash would keep them quiet and pay for an abortion.*

Sandra had actually been barren ever since she gave birth to Ellen, whose real father was unknown. They pinned it on Bob, though, given that Sandra and he were married at the time. He would have never suspected otherwise — that do-good, worthless, working-class nothing of a man. Even if he did suspect, he wouldn't have done anything about it. *What a sucker!*

"Let's just all calm down and go our own way," Candy said to the small group and pointed Sandra the opposite direction. They both started to walk away, but before they left Candy whispered in Kurt's ear.

"Sandra really wanted you, but she was too shy. If you want her too, meet her behind the Marine supply shop in ten minutes," Candy told Kurt before she walked off.

Kurt did not know how to take that. It was creepy that this nasty old lady was pimping out her own daughter, but at the same time, he was the only single guy in their group and he was horny as hell. Although the idea repulsed him, he was so turned on by it that he had to at least try. He waited for them to drive off and then told everyone else to go on without him. He said he would catch a ride to the sinkholes later.

Rush and Carrie knew exactly what he was doing, but they didn't try to stop him. Poor Kurt had all kinds of trouble with the ladies and Rush knew he had to get it somewhere. Might as well let it be.

As Kurt walked away, Rush caught up with him.

"Just make sure you wrap it up, bub. She's been with everyone within a hundred miles of here," Rush said.

"What?" Kurt said, trying to look like he didn't know what he was talking about.

Rush pulled a condom out of his jean pocket and handed it to him.

"Just use this," Rush said. He walked away before Kurt had a chance to say anything.

* * *

Stark made his way over to the crowd of teens and everyone started stomping out their cigarettes and joints. Rush and Mike put up the tail gate to hide the cooler of beer.

"I don't want to spend all my time ruining you kids' night, so go ahead and clear out of here and I'll pretend I didn't smell that reefer from clear across the parking lot — or see that cooler in the back of your truck," Stark told Rush and the crowd.

"No problem, Jeff," Rush said. He turned around and whistled for everyone to clear out.

They didn't mind because they would just end up going back out to the sinkholes and continuing the party there. Stark knew this, because that was him just a few years back.

Before they packed up in Brownsman's truck, Carrie approached Stark.

"Hey, Jeff. I know Derri Emmons approached you earlier today and she was probably flirting with you. But I just wanted to let you know she was out here tonight with us and now I can't find her. She was supposed to go with us, but she's nowhere around. Can you keep your eyes open for her?" Carrie asked.

"Could she have left with someone else?" Stark said.

"I don't know, maybe. It's just — she was supposed to stay at my house tonight and now I can't find her. Oh, well, I guess she'll turn up. She's been getting a little wild lately and she might've snuck off with a boy or something."

Stark smiled. "I'm sure she's fine, but I'll keep an eye out for her."

Carrie loaded into the truck and they all took off, hooting and hollering as they left.

That gave Stark a laugh. He remembered those days like they

were yesterday. He didn't miss them, though. He was never really much into getting laid or partying, at least not all the time. He just remembered what it was like not to have all this responsibility and to be, well, carefree. It was only three or four years ago. He wondered if people like Linton or Sheriff Kramer could remember things like that, considering how old they were.

Most everyone had already cleared out except for the Izzy Lives band van, which bore a picture of Izzy with pale skin and black lipstick to go along with her black hair. He knew those two boys were camping out in it, since Pete wasn't going to let them stay at his house with his daughter, so he walked over and tapped on the door. Mickey Crowley opened it. He only had a pair of boxers on, and Jason Gumpner was lying down behind him under a sheet, apparently naked.

"You boys all set for the night?" Stark asked.

"Yeah, we're dog-tired so we're about to crash out. It's been a long month and I'm kind of looking forward to getting back to Bloomington after our New Albany set tomorrow," Mickey said.

Stark looked around inside their van and he could see no other cot on the floor. He wondered if they were sharing the same sheet or if Mickey just slept without a cover.

"You boys know it's going to be cold tonight?"

"Oh yeah. We're good. We have blankets and pillows."

Stark double-tapped their door. "All right, then. G'night boys."

Mickey pulled the van door shut and Stark could hear them rustling inside. The van windows had a tint to them so no one could see in, but he could hear them as he walked away. They were laughing about something and rustling around, making the van shake.

Stark had a pretty good idea they were gay. He never knew why, but he had always been able to peg someone for gay. He had been a little unsure about his own sexuality for years now, given that he had women always crawling around him, but he'd never been drawn to them.

He got his flashlight and started to walk along the brush off the side of the docks that led up to the bridge connecting the town to Alcatraz Beach. He crossed over the bridge and shined his flashlight along the wooded area. The night was bright enough from moonlight shining behind the overcast clouds that he didn't really need the flashlight unless he was in the shade of the trees.

He could hear some rustling in the woods up ahead, but he was not quite sure what it was. He had to walk about forty feet up Squaw Creek past the bridge before he could figure out was hearing. When it became more audible, he could clearly make out the words *please* and *no*. That was it! Someone was saying *please, no*, and then he heard *not again*.

He held his weapons belt as he jumped across the ditch and scurried further into the woods. He heard a commotion and someone saying *just shut up, bitch!*

Stark hurried in the direction of the voices and commotion. When he got there, he could see that Bret Holder had Derri Emmons on the ground. He was holding her hands behind her back as he rammed his naked body into her from behind.

Stark could see no real option. The pale moonlight turned a more defining red and his vision became distorted, as if the world around him was changing colors. He could feel the rage tearing at his guts, and when his vision was restored, he could hear and see perfectly, as if he had night vision. The redness gave everything a more defined presence.

Holder pounded himself into Derri's tiny little frame over and over with such force that her tight bottom rippled. Blood leaked down her legs. Massive bruising would soon settle in and she would likely need surgery for the pelvic injuries Holder was inflicting.

Stark's approach was subtle. He didn't run, he simply walked and did not stop. He would accomplish his mission in a calm and orderly fashion. There would be no arrest. His rage had only reasoned with him enough to suggest that the punishment should not be played out later, in a long, drawn out due-process. Justice was going to be served at the moment the damage had occurred.

Bret had just reached his orgasm with a roar before he heard someone approaching. He barely had time to turn and look before Stark hit him with a metal flashlight. The impact knocked Bret to the ground, unconscious.

Derri was crying as she looked up at Stark. Stark was not looking at her. He was only looking at Bret on the ground. He pulled a pair of gloves out of his back pocket, put them on, and squatted beside Holder's unconscious body. He had time to consider how he was going to carry out justice on Bret.

Derri tried to stand up but had a hard time with it. She kept expecting Stark to come and help her, but he hadn't even looked at her. She thought maybe he was disgusted with her and didn't want to see her. She wanted so badly to tell him the truth, that Tim Jacobs had lured her out there to smoke a joint and make out, but when she got here, Bret Holder was waiting and Tim Jacobs was sent packing.

She wanted to tell him that she tried to stop Bret but he was too powerful, just as he had been when he raped another girl at his party a week ago. She wanted Stark to be the first man she truly made love to, not Bret. But that choice had been taken away from her by that horrible man. And all she wanted was for Jeff Stark to love her and protect her and tell her everything would be okay.

But none of that was happening because Stark wouldn't look at her. It was as if he didn't even know she was there. More to the point, Stark looked more like someone else. Someone she'd never met. His eyes studied Bret Holder and the area around them. He was making a plan. He seemed to be operating on a different plane.

She used all her energy to force herself up and pull the pants over her beaten legs and pelvis. The pain shrieked through her. She could barely walk, but she managed to limp over to Stark.

He was still scanning the area when Derri put her arm on his shoulder. He jumped violently backward and started swinging his fist with his eyes shut, as if he'd been awakened from a sleepwalk. Derri also jumped backward and gasped with her hands across her face.

"Derri?" Stark said.

"Jeff. Jeff, you helped me. You stopped . . . stopped him from hurting me more. Please, Jeff. Please help me," Derri said as she started to collapse.

Stark shot over and caught her.

"Derri, it's okay. I'm sorry, I don't know what came over me. I couldn't focus on anything except — except hurting Bret."

"I'm okay, just lean me against a tree," Derri said. "Just don't let me sit down."

Stark leaned her against a tree and stepped away.

"I know about you, Jeff. I know why you didn't have any interest in me. And I also know that doesn't stop you from caring about me."

"Derri, I . . ."

"It's okay. I also know what you were going to do to Bret."

"Let's just get you home, Derri. I will deal with him when I. . ."

"Do it! Do it now, Jeff. I have to see it happen. He's just going to keep on and we both know I can't send him to jail, considering who his father is."

Jeff looked back at Bret, who was starting to regain consciousness. He knew the law could be of no comfort to her, either. But he couldn't do what he was going to do in front of her. It would scar her for life.

"What is it that you think you know about me, Derri?"

"I know you like men. And I know you were about to give him

a taste of his own medicine. I want to be here when you do it. I want him to see my face while it's happening to him. Do it. Don't even think about it, just do it. No one will ever find out about it," Derri said.

In a way, he was glad she knew. Even he had been lying to himself all this time. He just thought he did not like women. He never even considered that he liked men, or that men could arouse him in the same way others get aroused. He'd been turned on by men before, but he dismissed it, thinking it was something that happens to every man at some point or another and that it just went away. He had always considered himself normal because he knew no other way to be. But it was true, he was aroused by men and he knew what he could do to Bret Holder that would scar him for life. He knew he could serve justice on him right now and no one would ever find out, because he certainly would never tell anyone a man had raped him. He also knew that it would give Derri some sort of peace, to know that raping her had consequences, and she could sleep easier knowing that Bret knew this.

"Just stay there and turn away if gets to be too much."

Derri just nodded her head and stood lightly on one of her legs, taking the pressure of her right side, which hurt her the most.

Stark slung Bret over on his back and lifted him with his shirt just high enough to beat him over the head a few times. Bret was conscious now and he rolled over, spitting out blood. Stark took his handcuffs out of his back holster, wrapped Bret's arms around a downed tree and handcuffed him.

As Bret became more lucid, he exclaimed, "What the fuck!" His pants were still down below his knees and now, he was to be the receiver.

Stark unstrapped his belt and lowered his pants. He was hard as steel, with an overdue lava load lying in wait.

Bret started wrangling with the handcuffs, and then violently jumping around on his knees trying to free himself. Stark easily beat him a few times with his gloved fists and Bret became immobile.

"Fuck you, man! Fuck you, you faggot-assed queer! You touch me with that thing and I'll fucking kill you!" Bret said.

Stark beat him a few more times, until he was barely on the verge of consciousness. Before he could go out, Derri walked in front of him, smiled, and then spat in his face.

"It's your turn, you bastard!"

Stark lowered down and violently raped Bret Holder. It lasted less than a minute, but it was long enough for the frothy mix of blood and semen to leak slowly down his badly discolored legs and pelvis.

"Every time I see you, this is gonna happen again," Stark said when he was done. He then beat him unconscious again and removed the cuffs.

Bret just lay there, his breath making cloudy puffs in the cold night air. Stark took Bret's shoes and socks off and threw them in the creek. Frogs chirped in the water under the bright moonlight. A breeze blew a cold chill on them and leaves blew around the small gully, hidden from the view of Squaw Creek.

Stark and Derri left him there. Stark dropped her off at home and told her to call him if she needed him again. As Derri watched him walk off, she smiled and knew that her romance with him was one in a million, if at all. He was her hero. She was lucky to have him in her life, even if he was gay. She had no doubt she would never have to worry about Bret Holder again. She would keep Stark's secret for the rest of her life, and he knew it.

9

It was getting close to midnight and Arn was wiping down the last of the tables inside the Stow. Harry, Perry and Erin stayed behind to help him. They sat down at a table beside the stage and drank a few beers before they locked up for the night.

"My God! I am pooped!" Arn said as he tipped his can of beer back and rubbed his calf muscles.

"I hear that," Erin said as she drank the last of her beer and stood up. "You ready to go, old man?"

Perry drained his beer and stood, too. "Yes, ma'am."

Harry also rose and Arn threw the cans in the trash as they made their way to the exit. The wind was blowing outside. Normally, dust would be swirling everywhere from the gravel parking lot, but the rain had weighed it down.

"Jesus, what is wrong with this weather today?" Harry said.

Erin was just about to answer him when the wind suddenly

stopped. It surprised her.

They were standing on the east side of the building on the out-side patio when they saw it. The wall of fog was rolling in from the channel. It was traveling fast, and they all felt that same sense of dreadful, unknown terror that Cam Wright had felt when he saw it emerge from the river and chase the Bucky Cole downstream. The fog danced on the sides of the bluff walls and billowed as it drew near, as if it was expanding to swallow them.

They all headed to the north side of the building toward their cars, trying not to let on that they were bothered by it, but walking fast nonetheless. The cloud enveloped the building and as it moved past, they could no longer see the Stow, but they saw the fog quickly closing in on them.

Erin took two more steps and was trying to fish the keys out of her purse when the cloud swallowed her and Perry whole. At first, for only a moment, it was inconsequential.

Their anxiety shot through the roof when it first reached them. A second passed, and then it hit them. It was pain, pure pain. They felt the sensation of hot fire boiling through the pores of their skin, as if they had been submerged in liquid nitrogen and reheated with steam. Parts of their body felt the burn, other parts felt like needles. It poured through them like their skin was ripping apart.

They all screamed in agony as the fog swallowed them whole and continued to move north toward Squaw Creek. The cloud was a quarter mile long and kept coming and coming, merciless. They felt stuck in a flow of lava, running against gravity. It hurt so badly they could not even continue screaming and they all fell to the rocky surface in agony. The cloud just kept moving through them, digesting their bodies with its agonizing torment.

Mickey and Jason opened their van to see what was happening. The fog quickly rolled in and engulfed them as well. They felt the same agonizing torment as Erin, Harry, Arn and Perry. It just kept coming and coming.

* * *

Sandra Stamps and Kurt Peters were both naked in the back of Sandra's Chevy Caprice, which she'd gotten as part of the divorce settlement with Bob. Sandra was on top of Kurt, straddling him like a rodeo diva. Kurt's head was rolled back as he enjoyed the sex, trying to forget the fact that Candy Odair was in the front seat watching them, occasionally reaching down to tickle his balls as if she were trying to make him ejaculate quicker.

"A little harder, honey. You want to make sure that he unloads like a dump truck," Candy said, which made Kurt quiver a little.

Kurt would've been doing just fine if Candy had not insisted on being there with them. He'd agreed to leave the condom off because Sandra said she liked sex better without it. He even let her rub her nasty snatch, which smelled and tasted like a lasagna that had been left in the smoldering sun for a week, across his lips.

Kurt could see Candy in the front seat playing with herself, masturbating while she watched them fuck. *My God! That is one fucked up bitch!* Kurt wanted to get the hell out of the car but he could not find a reason to, and Sandra had already gotten him so hard that he would have a month-long case of blue balls if he quit now.

"Call me Mommy," Sandra said to Kurt.

"What?" Kurt said as he fought back the urge to blow his load. She was humping him so hard that it was getting harder and harder to hold it back.

Sandra reared back and smacked his face.

"I said to call me Mommy, you little bastard! You ungrateful little shit!"

Kurt was hesitant. The slap stung and he had unexpectedly gotten harder each time she had said it.

"I, uh . . ." Kurt said, and Sandra started to reach her hand back again for a slap. "Mommy! Mommy! I love you, Mommy!"

Sandra pulled her hand back down and kept riding him, her sloopy breasts waving back and forth, the nipples barely catching his nose with each thrust.

"That's it, baby. Do you like what Mommy gives you? Do you like it when Mommy puts your winky inside of her?" Sandra said, pulling her feet forward and sitting them on the bench seat beside him to straddle him with more force.

"Uh-huh." Kurt wasn't sure what else to say. Candy was again reaching down and tickling his balls with the same fingers she had inside her vagina. He could smell the stench coming from those fingers.

Sandra was now starting to moan louder, and she was reaching a screaming point.

"Oh baby! Mommy's about to come. Can you come for Mommy, too!"

"Uh-Huh!" Kurt said, and quickly released. It came out in a splintering stream. Sandra could feel it, so she slowed and then stopped.

She kissed his forehead as she put on her bra and condescendingly said, "Good boy."

Candy smiled in an evil way and turned around to face the front dash. Sandra opened the back door and stepped out behind the Marine supply store, beside the Stow. The fog cloud quickly surrounded her and filled the car, afflicting everyone inside with the same fate as it had everyone in the Stow parking lot.

* * *

Bret Holder awoke next to the log where he'd been raped. His thighs ached and his anus was leaking blood down his legs. He was freezing and his shoes and socks were gone. The cold air bit at his skin and the woods offered very little cover. He could not make out which way would take him back to town, and he could barely see.

He felt like every part of his body had been violated to the point of no redemption. He could never look anyone in the face again. If his father found out what happened to him, he'd be kicked to the curb and left with nothing. He found himself wishing he had left with his mother ten years ago, when she moved to Illinois and started a new life. She was the one who really cared for him, but he had wanted to stay with his dad. His dad was a strong man who didn't take shit from anyone. Everywhere he went, he was the boss, and people listened to everything he said.

Right now, though, he wanted his mother. He wanted her because she cared about him and she would tell him everything would be all right. The last thing on his mind was making it with young girls or getting stoned . . . or drunk. He just wanted to be safe.

He had finally made his way out of the woods into a residential area of Squaw Creek when the fog clouded came barraging over the district. He could hear screams. The cloud surrounded him and danced around every corner of his body. The pain he had felt before was no comparison to what this felt like.

* * *

The fog passed through for another forty-five seconds before the end finally reached the Stow and rolled on past. Everyone in the original Fogstow district of Squaw Creek got the same surprise as it rolled in and squeezed through windows, doorjambs and chimneys. Some with weatherproofed homes were spared, but not many.

Everyone left at the Stow could hear the screams, including Arn and Harry, who stood up despite the residual pains they were feeling. It had mostly calmed down on their skin but now they could sit in their guts. Stomach tensions, colon pain, bladder pain.

It seemed so preposterous that they could have been painfully swept by something so powerful, yet so simple as a cloud. But it had come from the Ohio River, and that thought occupied the back of their minds.

Harry knew that they couldn't go through something like that and not feel the aftereffects. His time at the Indiana University Medical Center and as a medical examiner for the Marion County police department had given him enough experience to know that those kinds of symptoms came with a price.

That's when it happened. Their bodies started releasing their wastes. It first came out as uncontrollable urine, then defecation and vomit. Harry thought it would lead to relief so he pulled his pants halfway down to let it come out unrestricted. But it wasn't just a little; it was everything. It just all kept coming and coming until every last drop, every last ounce of toxicity and waste had been eliminated. When it was over, all they could do was lie there under the bright lamppost. The cloud cover had cleared out and a few stars accompanied the bright moonlight. They all looked up at the stars and then fell unconscious.

A strong breeze blew cold droplets of water from puddles across the parking lot. There were no more chirping crickets or croaking frogs. Residents of the Squaw Creek district were reeling from the cloud, and just as had happened to everyone on the old Weyerbacher docks, their bodies purged themselves. Agonizing moans could be heard echoing throughout the area for several more minutes, then silence.

Everyone affected by the cloud had lost consciousness just like the Stow crew and all was quiet, except for the breeze. The wild brush that grew alongside the bluff rasped with the wind, but even the wind eventually died down and silence creeped over the town, awaiting the new Hoosier dawn.

CHAPTER 4
THE NEW HOOSIER DAWN

1

THE MOON HAD BEGUN TO DIM as dawn crept on the horizon in Fogstow. The wind was still blowing and most of the area had dried out, with a few puddles left standing in the parking lot at the docks.

The sky had returned to a grey overcast and the sun barely breached the tree line, still low at the base of the rolling hills and forest, on the morning of October 2, 1993.

A possum sniffed around the tires outside the Chevy Caprice behind the Marine supply shop, where Sandra lay naked on top of Kurt, both asleep in the back seat, with Candy in the front, her dark stained underwear pulled down to her knees. Their mouths were crusted with vomit and their bowels had broken loose inside the car.

Kurt laid immersed in Sandra's waste and the smell of piss lingered heavily in the car as Sandra's eyes slowly opened, wincing at the small amount of light that was breaching the surface. She lifted herself off Kurt. Her whole body hurt. It felt like she'd taken on an orgy with 20 men the night before, but she was quickly realizing that Kurt was her only score. She remembered that she and Candy were due to blackmail his father soon, and the first thing that crawled through her mind, besides the intense hunger she felt, was the idea that she needed to get him out of the car and get home.

She tried to pull him out of the car by his legs with what little strength she had, but it hurt too much. Candy started to come awake as well, feeling the same pains and waking in the same pile of waste. She was hungry as hell and severely weakened. She opened the front door and saw Sandra struggling with Kurt. She immediately saw what they had to do and she started to help Sandra, but soon stopped, exhausted.

They both sat on the ground; they could hardly move. Sandra was still naked except for her bra. She reached over Kurt's shit-stained body and pulled her clothes out to get dressed.

Kurt woke up at the same moment and jerked in surprise. Sandra pulled back out of the car and started dressing as Kurt looked at his naked body, covered in Sandra's piss and shit. He was thoroughly disgusted, and he noticed that he himself had let out the loads underneath him. He rose slowly (and painfully) as he became more aware of where he was and started to recall what happened the night before. He felt disgusted with himself and tried to get dressed as quickly as possible, despite the pain that was rolling over his body. He didn't even care that he was putting his shirt on top of the mess glued to his chest and legs.

He crawled out of the car and looked around, disturbed. He didn't say a word as he walked away as fast as he could, although his weakened body, wracked with hunger, would not allow him to move too fast.

He could smell something appealing wafting off the docks from the river channel. It reminded him of smelling his neighbors' grill when they cooked steaks or hamburgers, mixed with the simmer of Worcestershire sauce.

But this smell was different. It wasn't a steak, but it was appealing like a steak on a grill. He wanted to make his way over to the docks, but he hesitated as he looked back at Sandra and Candy sitting beside their car and decided to get the hell out of there.

He walked across the bridge to Alcatraz Beach and was out of sight by the time Candy realized it.

"I thought you said he lived in the TC," Candy said as Sandra got dressed.

"How the fuck should I know? What's the fucking difference anyway?" Sandra replied.

Candy walked up to Sandra and viciously pulled her hair back and grabbed her throat, although it physically hurt her to do so.

"The difference is he's from a poor working-class family and we will have little to no leverage to get his daddy's money, you stupid little bitch!" Candy said and then let go of her hair.

"Whatever, mother! We'll just find another horny little fucker!

They're crawling all over this place."

Candy crossed her arms and looked doubtfully at Sandra. "Also, what the fuck was with that 'call me mommy' shit last night? Did you get off on that or something?"

Sandra pulled her pants up and closed the back door, then got in the driver's side. "Let's just get the fuck out of here, can we, please?" she begged.

Candy got in the passenger seat and dismissed the idea outright. She was more interested in finding the source of the smell. It had her stomach rumbling with hunger. The memory of the fog weighed heavily on her. Candy had been through a lot of shit in her 56 years, but nothing like that. She'd been pulling these scams with her daughter for a long time now and never had they encountered anything that matched the strangeness of that fog.

Maybe it was a bad idea, after all, when they decided to scam that dimwit Bob Stamps eight years ago. Although they had really cashed in on him, and it had given them a base of operations. *But this town is a real shithole, and look what happened to us last night. It's been ravaged by coal mines and pollution and there's no telling what was in that fog that made them piss and shit themselves.* On the other hand, they didn't live out of motels or random apartments anymore.

They once lived in the house of a man whom they'd accidentally killed during a routine scam in the backwoods outside Louisville. It had played out pretty much like the night before with Kurt, except things went wrong and the man chased Sandra naked around the outside of the car. Candy had no other choice but to put the car in gear, and it rolled over him killing him. They put him back into his cheap tuxedo, which looked like one of those old tuxes that men wore to weddings and proms back in the '70s. Then they dumped him in the river, and they saw him sinking as the current caught him.

It was supposed to have been simple, but Sandra couldn't get his penis hard and she finally ended up calling him a faggot. Candy knew that it was probably because he was drunk, considering they met him at a bar and heard his life story over shot glasses.

They stayed at his house because they knew he had no family and no one checking in on him. He had lived in a secluded area, so they just holed up for a bit, biding their time. That is, until they ran into that dipshit Bob Stamps and Linton Derr at a nightclub one night.

"Can you smell that?" Candy said.

Sandra sat there with her hands on the steering wheel. She smelled the same thing.

"Yeah. I'm fucking starving, Mom! Let's get home and eat."

"Let's go. We're gonna need our strength tonight because we're heading west to the riverboat casino. No more wasting time with these small town hacks. It's time to cash in."

Candy noticed Sandra's eyes after she said it. The whites were changing. Not getting darker, but lighter. There was a clearer presence in the white and she could even see what appeared to be tiny vessels. They were in a 3D like image, suspended in a hazy liquid, attached to other parts of her eye. But she could care less about it. All she wanted was to get to that casino tonight and possibly retire.

Sandra put the car in drive and wheeled away. They both looked back at the docks as they were leaving, trying to figure out where that delicious, foreign smell was coming from.

* * *

Arn and Harry both awoke to the sound of a car crossing the parking lot. They saw the Chevy Caprice pulling through and exiting the docks. They were both hungry as hell and Harry felt around his body, giving himself a physical.

Erin and Perry both awoke and found themselves covered in their own vomit and waste. Arn held his arms around himself and shivered. The temperature was 55 degrees and his body felt pre-hypothermic.

They looked around and could see a few people coming out of their houses in Squaw Creek, bundled up in winter coats and appearing severely jetlagged. Harry people were probably going to be crowding into Amy Strange's office at the East Jamison Medical Center. The least he could do was to get the four of them feeling better, somehow.

Harry stood up and said, "Let's all get back inside the Stow. We need to get ourselves warm and cleaned up before we get any sicker."

They all got up and followed him. Just as Sandra and Candy had, they quickly picked up on the strangely attractive smell coming from the river and realized how hungry they were. Arn came out in front of them and used his keys to unlock the door and let everyone in. He went to the thermostat and turned the heat on.

"Arn, do you have anything to eat in the kitchen?" Harry asked.

Perry was holding Erin by her waist and one hand, trying to help her the best he could to get her to a table to sit down. Arn gave Harry a thumbs up.

"Yeah, I think we have some hamburger meat. It's raw, though, so we'll have to cook them," Arn replied.

"Let's do it," Harry said, and patted Perry's back. "We'll be back in the kitchen if you need us. We need to get some food in our stomachs."

Perry waved him on and paid strict attention to Erin, who seemed to be faring worse than the rest of them. Her eyes were turning strangely clear in the white and her body wasn't retaining any heat. She should be shivering right about now, but her body was too weak. Her mind seemed to be a little scrambled. She had not spoken anything, just replied with nods and simple headshakes.

This worried Perry. She was a small woman with a tiny frame. He needed to warm her up and get some food in her. He himself was hungrier than he'd ever been, but he needed to feed Erin first.

"Can we get some hot food out here?!" Perry yelled into the kitchen.

Harry walked out of the kitchen with a frozen burrito in his hand.

"Is she getting worse? I can always throw this in the micro-wave. I'm not sure how old it is, though, and it might taste horrible. Not to mention the fact that burritos are a horrible food to eat when you're ailing."

Perry looked at Erin and she shook her head no. "No, just get those burgers on the burner as quick as possible."

"Is the 'Bend open?" Harry said.

"No, they're closed because of opening day," Arn said from the kitchen.

Harry walked back into the kitchen and started helping Arn.

Erin suddenly stood, and Perry stood with her. He put his jacket around her. She started smelling around the room and walked to the side door that led out to the dock. Perry followed her, smelling the same thing. Erin walked outside onto the dock. She kneeled and reached down and felt the cold water. She quickly pulled her hand back in pain. The cold shot through her with a jolt. She reached her hand up to her mouth and tried to exhale warm breaths on it, but then the smell intensified. Perry kneeled behind her and wrapped his hands around her shoulders. She stopped breathing on her hand and considered something she had never considered in her life.

Perry turned her to face him, her river-wet hand was still near her mouth. He looked deep into her eyes. He knew what she wanted. He wanted it, too. All logic had told them their entire lives to never ingest anything from the Ohio River, but there was something about it that had sweetened to their tastes. The smell led to a pure desire, unnatural to the common folks who resided along the Ohio River. Neither one of them wanted to do it, but there was nothing else they craved more than to taste it, right at that moment. A tear rolled from the changing white in Erin's. She could see the same thing in Perry's eyes, but their minds had yet to reconcile with the truth of their desire. It was like betraying everything they were, everything they had come to know.

Erin slowly put one finger in her mouth. The beads of water disengaged from her finger and rolled down her esophagus, bonding to the surface of her throat tissue.

She pulled the finger out of her mouth and Perry saw it happen. The white in her eyes changed like a dissipating storm cloud. Tiny blood vessels emerged through the clearness, appearing out of nowhere. He could see tiny cells running through them, carrying blood to the eye. Feeding it, and then taking away the waste.

Perry had never witnessed such beauty, such a metamorphosis. Her eyes had retained the central iris color, but they were now immersed in a translucent mass that left the center more exposed.

He reached both hands into the water and cupped them, bringing a larger sample back up. He wanted so badly to drink it himself, but instead he offered it to her. She lowered her head into his hands and drank all of it, and then flipped her head backwards as if she had just snorted a line of cocaine.

Perry reached down and did it again, this time drinking the water himself. It was invigorating, satiating. He ran his hands through the water.

That's when it came to the surface and gave Perry the shock of his lifetime.

2

Jeff Stark had not slept well the night before. The thought that he had raped a man hadn't sat well with him. But he also thought about what Bret Holder had done to Derri Emmons, and it seemed to weigh out equally in his mind. It was a burden he would have to carry for the rest of his life, but it was worth it to have seen Derri peaceful the night before. She might have been banged up a little, but she wasn't going to spend her life in terror of that man.

Maybe I should go look for him. Make sure that he isn't stewing for revenge. If so, he could take it out on Derri and the whole thing would have been for nothing. It angered him to think about it, but it still weighed on him.

He was still awake at 6:45 a.m. when Cliff Holder came barging into Derr's office like a maniac on a power trip. Stark rose to his feet, his weapon drawn.

"What the fuck do you people think you're doing up here in Fuckstow!" Holder yelled, completely ignoring the gun Stark was pointing at him. For all Stark knew, Bret had gone home and told Daddy what happened to him last night, and Cliff Holder was there to shoot him.

"You care to elaborate on that, slick?" Stark said, still aiming his gun at Cliff.

Cliff shook his head and approached Stark, shoving the gun away from his face.

"Was it you or that good-for-nothing lefty piece of shit Derr?"

"You had better get to the point before I bullet in you, old man," Stark warned as pointed the gun back at Cliff.

That didn't sit well with Cliff Holder, and his voice took on a more threatening tone as he spoke.

"Come downstairs and I'll show you, tough guy!" Cliff said. He walked down the stairs and around to the grain silo, where a man was unloading grain from a short-haul truck. Stark followed, firmly holding his service revolver. A pungent, repulsive smell filled the air; he immediately attributed the stench to the river. Awful smells came off the river three or four times a week, but this one was enough to make him a little nauseated.

"This man right here has been working double and triple hauls because of you self-righteous cocksuckers. I want to know which one of you fucking pissants spoke your left-winged gospel to my driver yesterday. That motherfucker brought my truck back and said he was done until he got paid more for the hauls. He also told me that he was convinced by the Fogstow cops. Now, you tell me if it is was you or Derr," Cliff said.

Stark put his gun back in his holster, relieved.

"This isn't our problem, old-timer. Go somewhere else and take care of your business," Stark said as he turned to head back.

Cliff grabbed Stark's shoulder and whipped him around.

"Don't you turn your back on me, you little worm!"

Stark grabbed Cliff's hand and twisted it easily, forcing Cliff to double sideways in pain.

Cliff started to reach behind his back for a concealed gun when a voice emerged.

"It was Derr," said Bret Holder in a soft, weak and shy voice. He was covered in dank soot and blood stained the legs of his jeans. He was still barefoot, just as Stark had left him the night before, and his body was so pale and weak-looking that he appeared on the verge of death. Stark released Cliff, who was looking at his son with shock.

"It was Derr, Dad. I heard him through the cell window yesterday, just before I got out," Bret said.

"What the fuck? What the fucking fuck! What in the hell happened to you, boy!" Cliff exclaimed.

"Well, no one showed to pick me up last night, so I had to stay here," Bret said as he cast a glance at Stark. He quickly looked away, scared.

Cliff walked up and put his hand gently behind Bret's neck. He could not quite figure out what to say to him for a moment, so he just went with what was obvious.

"Let's just get you to a hospital, boy."

Bret slowly shook his head yes. He kept his eyes down as he walked around to his dad's extended cab truck and got in the passenger's seat.

Stark watched them drive away, and then he went inside and gave Linton a warning call from the office. He had to use a handkerchief to mask the nasty smell rolling over the town.

3

Bob Stamps had set out early from Patoka that morning with the kids. As much as he would have loved to stay with them, he just didn't see the point in forcing them to do something they obviously didn't want to do.

He had stopped off the highway and taken Sebby out for a couple of casts in the Ohio River, but nothing was biting, so they just packed up and continued back toward Fogstow. Ellen stayed in the back seat and slept as they rolled down Highway 66, en route to home.

"Hey, Dad," Sebby said.

"Yeah, buddy?" Bob answered.

"Let's just try to go back when the weather gets warm, next spring or something. We can probably catch some fish then."

Bob rubbed his head and smiled.

"That sounds good, Sebby."

Ellen was waking up in the back seat. They had passed through Derbie. Next stop: Fogstow.

"Can we go eat at the 'Bend, Dad?" Ellen asked, hungry and tired.

"I think they're closed, sweetheart. But I can cook you up some bacon and toast at home. I also have some syrup — you can dip your bacon in it," Bob said as he looked in the rearview mirror at Ellen, hopeful.

"No. I'll just go back to Mom's. I want some of the leftover lasagna she gets from the store."

"How about I go and get you some lasagna from the store and make it up for you? It's real easy and it comes in a frozen box, so it won't take nothing."

Ellen thought about it for a moment while she stared out the window at the sun, which was perching over the horizon.

"No. I want to go back to Mom's."

Bob let it go. He didn't want to upset her while she was tired.

He faced back toward the road and saw a black extended cab truck heading directly at them. It was in the wrong lane and he had nowhere to go but the shoulder of the road, which dipped off at an incline. He quickly swerved the wheel of his Wagoneer to the right, and they bounced off the shoulder and down an embankment. The Jeep safely made it into the gully, but had not lost enough speed to avoid the dead-fallen tree that was pointing straight at them. The Jeep plowed into it and a long, hard branch speared directly through the windshield and into Bob's neck.

* * *

Cliff Holder was making his way west down Highway 66 when he looked over at his son with disgust. *That little pussy let someone beat the piss out of him last night. There's no doubt about it. He is such a disgraceful piece of shit, always drunk or stoned, or on whatever the fuck they're into these days.* He looked back at the road for a minute and then cracked his window and pushed the cigarette lighter in on the ashtray. He pulled a cigarette out of his pack and leaned down with it in his mouth lighting it with the truck utility lighter.

When he sat up, he found he was in the wrong lane and heading straight for Bob Stamps' Jeep Wagoneer. He tried to swerve back into his lane, but the Jeep had already swerved off the road and down the ditch.

Cliff turned around to look and then turned back to the road.

"What happened to them?" Bret asked.

"Nothing, boy. They're fine. Let's just get you to a hospital and checked out."

Bret tried turning around to see for himself, but the Jeep was too far off the road for him to make anything out. He turned back and huddled against the door. He tried to sleep, but he was in too much pain and he was also ravenously hungry.

* * *

The Jeep had come to a stop with the tree limb firmly embedded through the windshield and Bob's neck. Ellen was frantically crying in the backseat and Sebby sat in the front seat, in shock.

"Da-Da! Are you okay? Dad?" Ellen said.

Bob was only partially conscious. He couldn't move, and although he couldn't see or feel it, he was fairly sure there was a lot of blood.

"Da-Da! Please answer me!" Ellen cried from the backseat.

Bob came around a little more and Sebby saw his Dad's eyelids moving.

"Dad! Dad, can you heard me?" Sebby asked.

Bob couldn't move and could barely talk. The tree limb was

firmly lodged in his neck. He spoke with a raspy, labored voice.

"Okay kids. It's going to be okay. Dad needs your help right now. Can you both do something for me?"

Sebby nodded yes and Ellen climbed forward from the back seat and whispered yes in Bob's ear.

"Okay, sweetie. Here is what I need you to do. Dad can't move from this spot right now because of the tree branch. It could also hurt me to move, so I need you two to walk into Fogstow. It's only a few hundred feet up ahead. Dad needs you both to walk and get Chief Derr for me. Tell him what has happened and he will come and help me," Bob said.

"Yeah, Dad. We will. No problem. You just stay right here and we will go get him," Sebby said in a worried voice. "Just stay here and we will be back in jiffy."

Bob knew that his situation was dire. He could not feel anything below his neck and he saw Sebby looking down with fright, likely seeing the blood that just kept flowing.

He realized he probably wouldn't make it out of this and he didn't want the kids to watch him die. Despite their mother's coldness, those two kids had very kind hearts. He just wanted them to grow up with the least amount of pain as possible.

"No, buddy, I don't want you to come back with him. Just call your mom to come and pick you up and let Chief Derr come and help me by himself."

Ellen leaned forward, tears rolling down her face. She leaned her head on Bob's right ear.

"I don't want to leave you, Dad. I won't leave you," Ellen whispered.

"I know you don't want, to sweetheart, and Dad loves you very much, too. But I need you to go with bubby. I need you to both go so you're both safe on the road. You can both look out for each other on the roadside on your way in. Please, honey, go with your bubby."

Ellen sat there, cuddled against her Dad's only good side. Sebby didn't want to leave him either, but he knew he had to get him help. He also knew his Dad wanted him to take charge and get El-len to come with him.

"Come on, Ellen. We need to go now before he gets worse," Sebby urged, yanking on her sleeve.

Ellen wouldn't budge. Sebby hated to do it, but he pulled her out of the car and she screamed as he walked away with her. She kept screaming back at her Dad.

"Dad! Da-Dad! I love you, Dad!"

4

Linton and Kelly lay peacefully sleeping when the faint sunlight began filtering through the shades on the window. A knock at the door awoke Linton. It was Carolyn.

"Yeah, Mom," Linton said from inside the closed cabin.

"Deputy Stark is on the phone and he said he needs to talk to you. Don't worry, I won't come in. Just come to the door and grab the portable," Carolyn said.

Linton slid his pants on, cracked the door open and took the phone. Kelly slid up in bed and leaned against the back frame with the sheets pulled over her breasts. She felt a little embarrassed, but Carolyn did not look inside. But she knew Carolyn knew there was a good reason not to look inside, which made Kelly self-conscious.

"Thanks, Mom," Linton said. He closed the door.

"We've got homemade donuts in the house with fresh glaze," Carolyn called as she stepped off the porch.

Kelly shivered in the bed at the rush of cold air that had come in when the door was cracked. It had gotten considerably colder out, and she was definitely underdressed.

Linton walked into the bathroom and took the call from Stark. She could hear him in there, talking to on the phone while the urine splashed against the toilet water. She rolled her eyes and thought, *Men! They are so primitive when they're together.* That gave her a chuckle. She got up and dressed herself. She knew Linton probably had to go deal with something in town,, so they would likely be leaving soon.

Linton walked out of the bathroom with the phone in one hand and his other hand adjusting his manhood. Kelly laughed.

"Golly gee, Romeo. Did you get them to settle right?" she asked.

Linton smiled at her, sat down and took his pants off again.

"I don't think now's the time to be doing that," Kelly said.

Linton slipped his underwear on.

"I just need to get these underwear on or else the stones get in a bind," Linton said.

Kelly chuckled and pulled on her sweater and jacket.

"Do we have to leave?" she asked.

"Well, I have to. Got an issue to deal with. Cliff Holder's up in Fogstow throwing his weight around. Why don't you and Lucy stay here with Carolyn and enjoy the donuts? You'll love her homemade icing."

Kelly was famished.

"Now that sounds good," she said. She kissed him just before they walked through the door and headed for the main house.

Lucy opened the door, still in her pajamas and with a major case of bedhead, right before they got to it.

"Come on in, you two yahoos," Lucy said in a sleepy little voice.

It was apparent she had already dug into the donuts because she had icing stuck to her cheeks. Kelly walked in and kissed Lucy's forehead. Linton did the same, then he grabbed a donut and went back toward the door.

"I'll be back this afternoon to pick you two up," Linton said.

Carolyn walked over and kissed his cheek as he was leaving.

"Don't rush, son. Let the girls have some time together this morning," Carolyn said.

Kelly put her arms around Linton's neck and planted a warm and loving kiss on him.

"See you later today, soldier," Kelly said.

Linton nodded, and just before he left, he said, "I love you."

* * *

Linton pulled his Bronco out of the reservation and onto Highway 66, where a black, extended-cab truck sped past him. He thought it was Cliff Holder, but he was not sure. He could have always chased him down for speeding, but he decided not to. *Not my jurisdiction*, he thought.

The drive back to Fogstow was a quick one, and as soon as he rounded the curve into town, he saw Bob's Jeep in the ditch.

Linton pulled off to the shoulder and turned his emergency lights on. He figured no one was in the Jeep, but he had to go down and make sure.

He carefully made his way down the incline and as he approached the Jeep, he could see Bob inside, with a tree limb stuck in his neck.

Linton jerked the door open and blood spilled off Bob's pant leg and spattered on the ground.

"Oh, no! No, no, no, no! Bob! Can you hear me, buddy?"

Bob's eyes were closed.

"Bob! Wake up, buddy!" Linton said, gently shaking Bob's arm.

Bob's eyes fluttered open, but he was weak. Talking was out of the question.

Linton looked around the Jeep for the kids, but he didn't see them. There was no blood anywhere else, which was a good sign. Either they were fine and had gone for help, or they hadn't been in the car with him. That awful Sandra could have come and taken them with her, but that was unlikely.

Linton had started to get on his radio unit to call for help, but he saw Jeff pull up on the three-wheeler.

"Stark! Call and get an ambulance here right now!" he ordered.

"I already did it, Boss. His kids came and got me at the office. I got an ambulance and a fire engine coming with an emergency saw from Barrelton."

"Where are his kids?"

"They're back at the Co-op. I left them with Burnley. He called their mother to come and get them."

"How far out is the ambulance?" Linton yelled. He was becoming hysterical. There was no way to compress the wound. Blood flowed steadily down Bob's body.

Linton reached down and grabbed Bob's hand. Bob had no family but the kids.

"Bob, you hang in there with me, bub! We've got help coming. You're gonna be just fine!" Linton said.

Blood welled in Bob's eyes. He could barely see Linton, but he was glad he was there with him. If he'd had a brother in this world, he would have wanted it to be Linton.

Linton gripped Bob's hand and tried to find some way of holding the blood in. He reached around his neck, but it was coming out everywhere. He frantically grabbed in every possible place around the tree limb on his neck to stop the blood loss, but it just kept gushing, covering Bob and Linton both.

Bob's eyelids were getting heavy. He struggled just to keep them open. He wanted to say something, but it was too hard to get any words through his throat. He muttered something indistinguishable to Linton. Blood sprayed out of his mouth with each attempt.

"What, bub? I can't understand you," Linton said. He held his ear close to Bob's mouth.

Stark stood back and watched, his own eyes starting to water. He knew Bob wasn't going to make it.

Bob muttered something again, spraying blood on Linton's ear. Linton did not move, but he could not make out what Bob was saying. He thought he heard him say *Tell them,* but he wasn't sure. He didn't want to worry Bob, so he pretended he had heard him.

"Okay, bub, I'll tell them," Linton said.

Bob smiled. He weakly ran his finger across the blood-stained side of the door. He wrote the word "SORY" on it.

Linton grasped Bob's hand again. Bob squeezed Linton's hand for a moment longer, and then his grip weakened.

Bob Stamps died with his eyes open, staring at his best friend, his brother.

5

Arn took a couple of hamburgers off the stove and laid them on a plate. The whole time he'd been cooking them, they smelled wrong, as if they had spoiled or something. He hadn't noticed anything wrong with them when they were raw, but now that they were cooked, they just didn't smell right.

He decided he'd better try one before he sent them out to Perry and Erin. Even Harry was standing off to the side, smelling them and eyeing Arn with suspicion.

"What's wrong with them?" Harry asked.

"I'm not sure. They seemed just fine before I grilled them. We just got this batch in yesterday, so they ought to be fresh enough," Arn said.

Harry opened the cooler door and noticed that it seemed to be working fine. None of the other meat seemed to be spoiled. He closed it, and then looked back at Arn.

"Let's just give them a bite and see if they're okay to eat."

"Okay," Arn said. He took a bite of the burger then wrinkled his nose in disgust and spat it out immediately.

"I take it that one was no good," Harry said.

Harry picked up another one and took a bite; he had the same reaction. It tasted like wet paper, as if it were not meant for human consumption. But it did not taste like it was rotten.

Harry glanced back toward the dining entrance and wondered what to do. The most logical thing was to load everyone in the car and take them elsewhere to get some food. He had soup at his house, and that was probably the best thing for them. His own hunger had risen to an agonizing level.

Arn was looking at Harry in a kind of daze. He didn't seem sick, just confused. Harry himself felt a little dazed as he looked back at Arn. He looked at Arn's body and a sick thought went through his mind. The sight of Arn's body, the veins that bulged from his skinny hands and the cords of his neck, made him hungry.

Harry knew that fog had done a real number on them, and even though he was aware of his craving, he could not seem to bring himself away from it. Harry knew Arn was looking at him the same way, with those horrible thoughts going through his brain. The only other thing he could think of was the increasing weakness in his body. His eyes felt dry and all his teeth were beginning to ache, as if he'd bitten down on hard candy and the sugar-crusted coating had lodged there, eating away at the enamel.

They stared at each other for half a minute before a scream from outside on the dock broke their gaze. They ran out of the kitchen to find Perry and Erin gone. They went to the dock and found Erin holding her hand over her mouth while Perry kneeled beside the dock with his hands pulled back as if something had come out of the water and bite him. He hadn't stepped away from whatever it was.

Harry approached Perry and found him looking at a dead body that had surfaced next to the dock. It was the body of a woman dressed in a brown overcoat. One of her shoes was missing and her pantyhose had been torn in many places. By the looks of her body, Harry guessed she'd been in the water for weeks. Her skin was grey and bloated, with patches of discoloration.

Harry knew if someone were to try to pull her out, her body would likely tear apart. The combination of skin pigment and bloating indicated the muscle had already dislodged from her bones and that only her overstrained skin was holding it all in..

Harry also realized why Perry hadn't pulled back yet. It was the same reason he himself continued to get closer to the body floating before them in the river channel. It was the smell emanating from her corpse. It was horribly attractive.

Harry sat down in cross-legged beside Perry. They both stared at the body. Neither questioned the other, and they were eventually joined by Erin and Arn. They all sat there, unconcerned about see-ing a dead body or reporting it to the police. The only thing on their mind was their hunger. They were changing, and they craved something new. Something that scared them all, but nevertheless had attracted them to the dock in the first place. They could have gone home and eaten something from their own cupboards, but the smell had led them back inside the Stow. And now, they sat in front of the rotting corpse of a lady none of them knew. The only thing they could understand was what they felt, not what they saw. Because the only thing they saw . . . was food.

* * *

A few other people had made their way up to the docks from Squaw Creek. They were all confused, pale and weak, guided only by the smells. Darvin Brown and his wife Connie were among them. Darvin sat down beside Harry, looking at the floating body. He hesitated at first, but then he put his hand in the water beside the body. He touched the corpse and the skin broke, releasing a liquefied cloud into the water.

They all reached down and cupped their hands in the cloudy water and pulled it back up to their mouths like they were drinking soup. The thought of their actions horrified them, but they couldn't stop. The water was comforting them, making them feel better. The cloud dissipated and Harry poked the corpse again and more came out.

No one was bold enough to do much more than poke the body until Arn lowered himself into the cold river water. He held himself afloat by the side of the dock and they all watched him intently, hoping he could do what they had not been able to bring themselves to do. Arn pulled the lady's corpse to his face, and without hesitation, bit into her abdomen. Her liquefied organs ran over his face in a silky black gush.

The group pulled the corpse partially out of the water and everyone starting biting her to pieces. Piece by piece, the dead woman's body was being consumed. More people approached in horror, but they eventually participated, too.

Gasps were heard behind them as the people of Squaw Creek had come out of their homes and to the dock. They were terrified of what they saw, yet still drawn to the event. The smell, coupled with their agonizing pains, had led them there. By the time the greater Squaw Creek populace arrived, the body had been devoured and the bones sank into the channel.

Harry leaned against a post in shame. Despite all his training in the medical field, he had absolutely no answer for what had caused him to do this. It was beyond anything he had ever known or experienced. It was incomprehensible. But one thing was certain — he was starting to feel better.

Several people were ladling handfuls of water from the channel and into their mouths. Harry realized the community had already taken to its new biology, no matter how horrifying it was to them. The pain within them demanded it. The river water would partially satiate their hunger, but it would not be enough. Harry alone had had to fill his stomach with the rotten meat of the corpse before he felt whole again.

Even still, he felt the weakness and pain that he'd imagined dying people felt just before they passed on. His best guess was that they were indeed dying. Their bodies were changing, and consuming human flesh only delayed the process — the process of decomposition. His joints ached, his head hurt, his muscles were sore and weak and his back felt contorted. It hurt to see, hear, taste and feel. The only thing that gave him comfort was his sense of smell. His teeth ached, and he felt as if some of them were loosening.

The real question was, *how long before he needed more? How long before all of these people needed more?* He knew the fall of Fogstow was likely imminent. He had felt the hunger, and he knew how powerful it was. It hadn't taken him long to consume the dead woman, and when the pain returned, how bold would they all be when it came to relieving it?

Harry wiped his face off. His nails scratched him, and when he pulled his hands back to look, he noticed the nails had grown thicker — much thicker. His body still felt weak, but his fingernails were very hard. They had grown about a quarter inch past his finger, and he guessed they were about an eighth of an inch thick. They were also itchy — excessively itchy. He tried running them along the dock planks to scratch them, but once he pulled his hand back, the itch would return.

The terrible annoyance, of this coupled with his new biology, was overwhelming. His brethren were gathered around him, scooping out river water polluted by the remains of a rotten corpse. He watched Perry and Erin sitting side-by-side across the dock, scratching their nails across the wooden planks obsessively. Arn scratched his against the outer wall of the Stow, and Darvin was using small rocks on his nails, like he was sharpening a blade.

This was bad. Very bad.

6

Joe rolled out of the top bunk of Noah's bed and woke him as soon as the sun was up. He had changed his mind about pulling that body out of the mine tunnel. It just seemed like a better bet to tell Chief Derr about it and let the police handle it.

"Hey, man. I'm not going back to those mine shafts without the Boss," Joe said.

Noah sat up in his bed and didn't even have to wipe the sleep from his eyes. He had lain awake nearly all night long thinking about what they were going to do today.

"I don't want to, either. I agree; let's just tell the Boss and let them handle it."

Joe was glad that Noah was onboard with the new plan.. *They're the police, that's what they get paid to do.*

Noah wondered if Joe was catching on to the possibility that Siders could be his father. He certainly wasn't going to say anything to him, but he knew Joe was a smart kid, and he also knew that his dad wasn't of any Native American descent, so what else explained his complexion?

"Do you want to go and tell him now, or what?" Noah asked.

Joe just sat there and needled the idea around in his head for a few moments. He, too, thought Siders might very well be his real father. But the worst part of that was, *what if he figures it out, too? What if he comes back to get me, to take me away? If he finds out it was me who ratted him out, he'll kill me too, just like that lady in the grain sack.*

"Let's just get some breakfast first," Joe said.

They both went downstairs and found Noah's parents looking out the living room windows, drinking coffee in their robes. Noah's dad had weatherproofed the house two years ago and the fog hadn't made it in the night before. They had slept like babies last night while the rest of Squaw Creek was submerged in the cloud.

"What's going on, Dad?" Noah asked.

Norman Buchanon would have spent that Saturday morning reading the newspaper, but this Saturday he was more interested in the unrest happening outside his home. On a normal day, he would have answered Noah's question with *That's nice* or *Have fun out there*. But this morning was different, and he barely noticed Noah or Joe. He felt like he needed to keep on top of what was going on, especially considering how everyone he'd seen looked as if they were fighting the plague. And for some reason they were all bundled up in winter clothes. He knew it was cold out, but not quite cold enough for a winter coat, long underwear and snow boots. They were also moving in the direction of the docks, as opposed to heading toward East Jamison Medical Center, where they obviously needed to be seen.

Margie Buchanon usually fielded Noah's questions. When he came in, she let the drapes fall back into place and she walked up and hugged Noah, careful not to spill any of her coffee on him.

"Come on, boys. I've got some bacon on the stove and scrambled eggs," Margie said.

"But what's going on outside, Mom?" Noah asked.

She gently led them away from the darkened living room..

"Well, it's nothing the county can't handle. It looks like there may be a nasty virus going around, because everyone seems sickly. Let's just get you boys fed and we'll pull some board games out of the closet and make a day out of it."

The boys were perplexed, and they knew that if Noah's mom wasn't letting them go outside, then they wouldn't be able to tell Chief Derr what they had seen the day before. And they couldn't tell Noah's mom, because if she found out they had been exploring the old mines near the sinkholes, they would both get their asses whipped.

Norman walked into the kitchen, looking worried.

"Margie, did you lock up the back door and the garage door?" Norman asked.

"I'm not sure. Why?"

"They're walking through the yard now."

Margie and Norman both dashed out of the kitchen for the garage and back door. Noah and Joe seized the opportunity and went to the window to see what was going on. Outside they saw people hobbling with limps in both legs, holding blankets across their backs and wrapped around their bellies. Their faces were pale; some seemed to even be turning blue. They shuffled slowly, like they were zombies, or as if they were in pain. There must have been a hundred people migrating down Adams Street. They saw the boys in the window but just looked away, intent on their destination. The docks, maybe? All the boys knew was that it looked like a scene straight from *Dawn of the Dead*.

When the herd started thinning out, their fear deepened. Shane Duncan Siders stood across the street, looking directly at them. His face showed no emotion; he just stared at them as if he was casing out the house. He made no attempt to look away when they saw him. He just kept on staring.

The boys stood there, frozen, for nearly a minute. Margie and Norman came back into the room and told them to get away from the window. But the boys were so scared, they couldn't move. Finally, Siders departed and walked north up Adams Street, in the opposite direction of the herd. He stared at them as he walked away.

Joe dropped the shade and looked at Noah. Neither one could say anything, but they knew they were thinking the same thing.

How could Siders know we were there yesterday? If he knew, he would have killed us right away instead of letting us go. He wouldn't have given us the chance to tell anyone.

But one way or another, he had to have known. Why else would he be outside their window, staring them down? They had never seen him do that before. Noah though that maybe he was just casing out Joe. Maybe he was looking for his moment to kidnap him. But why hadn't he done it before? Why now?

Noah wondered if Joe had the same thought.

7

Burnley sat on top of a hay bale behind the Co-op and held Ellen Stamps while she cried. Sebby sat beside them both, his elbows on his knees. He did not accept the notion that his Dad was going to die.

Burnley had already called Sandra Stamps, but there was no answer. He had left a message on the answering machine. He also called Carolyn's in Derbie to try to reach Linton, but found out he was already on his way in. Normally, he wouldn't tell Carolyn something like this over the phone, but he knew Linton was likely going to find Bob out on Highway 66 and he thought Carolyn should know what Linton was about to go through.

Stark rode up on the three-wheeler with Linton following him in the Bronco. Linton pulled around the other side of the 'Bend so the kids could not see his bloodstained clothes. He was covered in it. Pants, shirt, face, ears.

Stark pulled into the back of the Co-op and made sure everyone stayed there to give Linton enough time to head up the stairs in the alley and get cleaned up. Seeing Linton with all of that blood all over him would be too much for the kids. It was not his place to tell them what happened. He only needed to tell Sandra, who would be responsible for breaking the news to the kids. And she would be a total monster about it, he thought. But parents had the right to decide on matters such as this.

He wondered if Sandra would try to milk Bob's life insurance dry before they could even pay for his burial. There was no one else to take care of those details for Bob, so it would likely fall on Linton to make his funeral arrangements.

"Sebastian, can you take you sister into the Co-op and get her some popcorn? You both need to eat. Dad's orders," Stark said.

"Dad's okay!" Sebby replied enthusiastically.

Ellen rose from Burnley's lap and smiled.

"Dad's okay! HE'S OKAY!" Ellen yelled at him.

Stark knew that he'd fucked up. He couldn't tell them that their dad had died, but he also couldn't lie to them and say he was going to be fine. He removed his jacket and held it in his hands, staring at the ground, trying to think of the right thing to say— something that wouldn't break their hearts, but also wouldn't give them false hope.

It was Burnley who read him loud and clear, and quickly released the hopeful smile on his face.

"WHERE'S MY DAD?!" Sebby yelled, and pushed Stark. He pushed him again. "WHERE IS HE?!" He kept backing Stark up with his surprisingly powerful pushes.

Jeff Stark did not know what to do, so he carefully and gently scooped Sebby in his arms.

Sebby fought him at first, but then gave up and cried into Stark's chest for a few seconds before he ran out the back lot and into the front of the Co-op. Burnley followed Sebby with Ellen in his arms. He gave Stark a look as he walked away, thinking to himself, *Nice job, screwup.*

A moment later, Carolyn pulled into the back of the Co-op in her white '70s model Ford F-150 pickup truck. Kelly and Lucy were riding with her. Kelly jumped out and approached Stark.

"How's Bob? Is he okay?" Kelly asked.

Stark was still holding his jacket. He had about as much luck telling Kelly about Bob as he had trying to hide it from the kids.

Kelly stepped away from Stark and held her hands to her mouth in shock and sadness. She turned around to avoid facing him, and only Carolyn and Lucy saw her grief. Carolyn knew right away what had happened from the look on Kelly's face, but Lucy still had not been told anything. She looked up to her for an explanation.

"What's wrong with Momma? Is Win-ton okay?" Lucy asked Carolyn.

Carolyn picked her up.

"Linton is fine, sweetheart. Your Momma is sad about something else. She will tell us later, sugar," Carolyn said. She gestured for Kelly to go up and be with Linton. She would take care of Lucy.

* * *

Linton let the shower run over his head in the small makeshift bathroom above the Co-op. The whole day seemed like it hadn't happened. He still believed he was going to see Bob on Monday when he got back from Patoka with his kids. It still seemed likely that Bob was going to pull up to the Co-op with a whole mess of fish on a stringer, and that they were going to clean them and freeze them until next Friday, when they would have a fish fry out back with his kids. Kelly would be there with Lucy. Russ would be there, and so would Allen, Burnley and Alice.

They would put the fish fryer on Locust Street and close the street down, detouring traffic to Main. They would put hay bales on the street and let the kids jump from bale to bale. They would break out the soda fountain and Lilibaum's would provide enough potato salad for half the town. They would get a cooler of beer and assign Stark to it, to make sure the teens didn't swipe any and run off to the sinkholes.

The kids would run wild playing tag on the street, and later in the night they would play Marco Polo with blindfolds on. The adults would play lawn darts across the road in front of the old Co-op warehouse, which now housed Allen's tractor that mowed the Bluff Trail. Marv Kramer would stop by with his deputies and hand out bronze-colored toy badges to all the kids, and they would run around shooting pretend zombies in the woods behind the warehouse.

The parents would then round them all up around 9 p.m. and everyone would go home and settle in for the night. The parents would wait for the children to go to sleep, and then make love in their upstairs rooms under moon visors that let the bright moon-light in.

All this and more seemed like it was going to happen, because Bob Stamps would have made sure of it. He would have made sure there were enough fish for everyone, and he would play tag with his kids all day. Linton himself would be in charge of dropping the fish basket in the deep fryer all evening long, while Kelly would keep the fish battered and ready for him. Lucy would be on the street drawing chalk pictures of crows and hawks flying over their rolling Hoosier hills.

Bob wasn't dead. He was still at Patoka Lake with his kids. They were fishing and having a great time. Bob loved his kids and he loved his town. He would be back on Monday. Everything would be all right. He just needed to wait and see.

Linton snapped out of his denial when he saw the red swirls at the bottom of the shower, dancing in spirals around the drain before they went down. Linton kept forgetting not to look, and the shower kept pouring over his face and body, and the Bob Stamps' blood just kept coming off. *Jesus! Why does it take so long to get clean!?*

Linton started scrubbing his body furiously with a soap bar, running his hands across his chest and ears, his face and legs. But the blood had dried on his skin and it caked off slowly, and Linton just could not rid himself of the image of Bob's blood-soaked eyes as the life drained out of him.

(Take this and feed your animal)

Bobby wasn't dead. He was waiting for Linton to come pick him up, and they would head out to do some Halloween stuff that night. Just a little pumpkin smashing, or maybe a little tee-peeing and

(some of these folks are old, they have bad backs)

they were going to have fun.. Just him and his best buddy. Bobby was going to have a blast and he was going to find a great lady tonight after the game.

But the blood continued to swirl around the shower drain, and Linton could not scrub hard enough or fast enough to get it off.

"Linton?" Kelly said from behind the shower curtain.

Linton couldn't answer. He was trying to hide all this blood — to erase the memory of Bob dying. If no one else thought he was dead, then he would never be dead. Linton scrubbed furiously.

Kelly drew the shower curtain open and saw his frantic scrubbing, trying to get clean. Linton continued to wash and didn't acknowledge her. She knew he was in shock, and he needed her.

She slipped her shoes off and stepped into the shower with him, fully clothed, and grabbed his distraught head. He had a hard time snapping out of it, but when he finally stopped, he leaned his naked body against her and exhaled laborious breaths, his arms pulled into himself like he was freezing.

"I think — I'm not sure why I'm here right now, but this seems like the only thing I can do for the moment. I have to just, I think — I think —" Linton said.

Kelly gently rubbed the back of his head and lightly shushed him. Linton emerged from his confusion, and as reality washed over him, he leaned against Kelly. He embraced her tightly and grieved the loss of his best friend.

* * *

Taking a shower wasn't exactly the soothing prospect that Sandra Stamps thought it would be. She had tried eating chips when she got home and had immediately vomited them back up. The next thing she thought of was getting the crusty vomit off her chest and relieving herself in some way.

But cleanliness was the last thing on her mind. She felt like she was starving, and even after she'd washed all the shit off, she still felt like she'd been hit by a truck. The last thing she wanted to do that night was go to a casino and wiggle her ass back and forth on some random rich guy while he howled and moaned. If she couldn't eat anything, then she just wanted to sleep. Of course, her mother had taken the first shower after they'd arrived home, and

Sandra was fairly certain she was asleep on the couch right about then. She had heard the phone ringing earlier and wondered who the hell would be calling her this early in the fucking morning. *It was probably that little bitch Ellen, wanting me to come bail her out of a boring weekend with her father.* Well, she had news for her and that was *tough shit!* It was her weekend without those two leeches.

Candy burst through the door.

"We have to go get Sebastian and Ellen. Apparently that worthless Bob Stamps got himself killed in a car crash," Candy said.

That momentarily shocked Sandra. She even felt grief wash over her, but then her stomach started hurting again. The hunger pains were getting worse.

"What? I haven't finished my shower yet, and I want to get some sleep."

"Go ahead and finish. We'll go get them on the way out of town."

"No way! I need to sleep before we leave."

"We're leaving as soon as you get out of the shower. And don't forget to pack them some pajamas to sleep in."

"We can't take them in the room with us!"

"We'll figure something out when we get there. Just get your fucking shower over with already. I want to case the place out and have everything ready for tonight."

"It's a fucking riverboat casino, Mother. There's a dockside hotel. What's to case out?"

"I have video equipment a friend is going to loan us. We're going to make this our last score of the year, baby. Now hurry the fuck up!"

* * *

The day was cold and the sun was barely shining in through the overcast sky. Any other time, this would be an ideal day to stay in. Noah and Joe both sat in Noah's upstairs bedroom, scared out of their wits. They needed to speak with Chief Derr.

"So what's the plan now, huh?" Noah asked nervously.

"I'm not sure. We can't tell your mom and we obviously can't leave the house. But I do have to go check on my mom and stepdad," Joe said.

Noah walked to his desk and pulled out some walkie-talkies.

"Just in case we need them for something. Not saying we will, but just in case."

"Why don't we just call the Boss?"

"Yeah, we could, I guess. But I have to make sure that my parents aren't around the phone."

The only phones in the house were in the kitchen and his parent's room, so calling anyone always risked someone hearing them.

"We could always go to my house."

Noah's door opened and his mother walked in.

"Joe, your mom's on the phone," she said.

Joe and Noah hopped up and ran downstairs. Joe's mother was always a little protective of him and Noah thought that had a lot to do with the possibility of Siders running off with him.

Joe picked up the phone.

"Hello?" Joe said.

"Joe, baby. This is you mother. We aren't feeling very well to-day and I think we have the bug that's going around," she said.

"You okay, Mom?"

"Yeah, we just need to rest and get some food in us. We're both really hungry, but we can't keep anything down. Some sort of fog got in the house last night and it made us really sick. Your dad opened the windows and cleared it out, but it had already gotten hold of us."

"Do you want me to go and get you some food? I can leave it outside the door for you and you can get it whenever you want."

"Well, I might have you do that later, baby. But for now, I'm going to try this soup and then go back to bed. I already spoke with Margie and she said you could stay there until we feel better. Just don't come over here. I don't want you to get it, too."

"Okay, Mom. I love you."

"I love you too, baby. Bye, now."

"Bye."

Joe hung up the phone, unaware that was the last time he would ever speak to his mother.

"How's she doing?" Noah asked.

"Huh?"

"How's your mom? My mom told me she was sick."

"I guess she's doing okay. She sounded sick. I've never actually seen her sick before. But I think she just always played like she wasn't."

"I'm sure she'll be okay. This is just a flu. You'll see. It'll be completely gone in a week."

"Yeah, I guess so."

8

Shane Duncan Siders had been wandering for half the night. After he dropped that body off in the mine tunnel, he had seen the mess made of the entrance. Someone had been there and had left while he was inside. The utility cabinets had been broken open and there was random crap scattered on the floor.

When he left the tunnel, he saw that whoever was there had left, too. The opening had been leaking that rancid water in. Whoever it was must have left in a hurry, because it had been sealed when Shane came in, to make sure that water didn't get in from the sinkhole. But they had scurried through the exit, which left just enough of the sealed barrier leaking a small stream into the tunnel. They probably also saw him pulling that little bitch's body through the shaft.

It wasn't likely to be any of the adults. They would have confronted him. So that left those teenagers and those wandering boys, one of which was his son, or so he believed.

It didn't matter either way. He was going to tie up loose ends, and he was going to start with the Jeffries up on the plateau.

Dead men keep the best secrets.

He wasn't worried about the situation, but the last thing he wanted was that *do-gooder* cop chasing him across the county or even down the river. He would have been out of his jurisdiction anyway, so he would alert the state boys in Indiana and Kentucky both. Shane would have to scurry all the way down to Cairo, Illinois just to make a break for it.

So why go through all the trouble?

He got all the information he needed when he stared those boys down. They had been there, watching him. The look on their faces when they saw him was enough to tell him that. They also hadn't gone to the Chief yet, or else Siders would've either been in cuffs or cruising down the Ohio.

They weren't going anywhere with all these idiots running around in the street. He saw what happened to them last night when he was scoping out the Co-op. This town had been bitten by the teeth of the Ohio and now they were all gonna suffer.

Sure, they'll live, but they aren't going to be playing basketball anytime soon.

Fucking Indiana! These fucks and their basketball. What the fuck is so special about that fucking game anyway? As his pops used to say, *'There aint't no niggers in that state worth a shit.' So all these white do-gooders scurry up and down the court like privileged assholes, proud of a sport they can't even play well!*

One thing he missed about his old man were those crude cracks at the expense of the underprivileged. He was an equal-opportunity hater when it came to that. They were always poor as shit and when they ripped off rich assholes, nothing really came of it. They nickeled and dimed those assholes who had thousands in the bank. Steal a boat here, maybe a car every once in awhile, then come back and they weren't suffering. They filled out a police report while tracking along in their caddy to the ninth hole on the golf course. What did they care, those fucking assholes?

Shane needed people to suffer. He needed to see them suffer. His old man, he could have cared less who suffered. He just wanted to make bank. That was one of things Shane hated about him. He took no pride in his work. He didn't take the time to stand back and admire what he had done. He just took the loot and he was off.

That was why he'd had to go. There was no honor in him. The pride and care it took to carefully construct his earnings, that's what made the life worth it. He always watched his ladies die. He took the time to see what they saw when the life drained out of them.

All these assholes that say your soul leaves your body when you die and you ascend to this magical place in the sky. He never saw it. Their lights just went out. Sometimes, they would close their eyes as they were dying and he had to open their lids back up. It wasn't ceremonious, it was just that he needed their eyes to tell him a story. What they were seeing and what they felt.

Shane doubted that whole God thing. He couldn't find it within himself to believe in something he could not see. But if the rumors were true, then he would trek his way to hell in the next life. No matter; though: He would be the first to mutinize that shithole.

He actually envied the people he killed. As for him, he was more than likely going to die of some long illness, like cancer or cirrhosis of the liver. He would suffer. But for them, it only took a few minutes. They should be thanking him for saving them from a debilitating death like the ones he might've endured.

He thought about a lot of things as he made his way through the north end of the Squaw Creek border of the TC. He would cut through the wilderness patch into Jeffries Plateau.

He'd had his arrangement with them for about two years now, and things went smoothly. But now that he'd been exposed, he couldn't let those leftover bones incriminate them. They would turn on him. They would either leave quietly or in a body bag. But either way, the Jeffries had to go.

* * *

The morning was in full swing when Siders reached the old farmhouse where he had first tied Ceril Jeffries up. There were a few scattered shacks throughout the area and some makeshift barns. But all in all, they were close enough that he could clear them out one by one in no time.

He made his way through the house quietly and saw that they were all still sleeping. Fifteen total in the house, but he wasn't sure if he saw Ceril. He checked the other makeshift shacks and found 11 more, and then the barn where he found two teenage boys sleeping naked beside a naked girl. They looked like they were kin to one another, which didn't surprise Shane at all.

He knifed them in the necks. The boys couldn't scream and the girl died after he jabbed the knife in her eye; one, two, three times.

He decided they all had to go in a blaze.

(Dead men keep the best secrets)

He trekked through the barn and found a hammer, some nails and a few pieces of plywood. He knew he was going to make some noise putting them up, but they had already boarded up their own windows *(paranoid fucking retards),* so all he had to do was board up the doors.

He finished with the doors and poured gasoline around the houses. When he lit the fire, he could hear them banging against the door. The line of blazes caught quickly and then he realized he had forgotten something crucial.

The cellar door!

Siders ran around the side of the big house and saw the door about to burst open. He jumped on it and nailed it shut as they screamed.

The blaze plowed through the homes quickly, and about 20 minutes later, the houses started to collapse.

I guess that takes care of the cellar dwellers.

9

Pete Brown was already up, drinking his morning decaf and doing a crossword puzzle, when the frantic knocks came at the door.

It was not uncommon to get visitors early at his house; Kelly and Lucy came over in the mornings before they opened the 'Bend.

But these knocks came in rapid succession, and they seemed to insinuate an emergency of some sort. He was still in his long underwear and robe from the night before, but that had never bothered him in the past. It also occurred to him that he felt a little guilty for having let those boys sleep out in the van last night, what with the weather turning cold so quickly after that unusual heat wave they'd had the day before. It didn't weigh on him too much, though, since he'd been wanting Izzy to come home and spend a few days with him. He missed his daughter.

Then he thought to himself, *What if they need to use the bathroom?*

When he opened the door, he saw Mickey and Jason standing there with their van parked in front of the house. He could see it was still running because the pipes were pumping out exhaust that was mixing with the cool day air. And then a rancid smell rushed in. At first, he thought it was the boys, but then he recognized the smell of the river. *Could have been because of the rain yesterday. That usually brings the smell out.*

It was a shocking sight, though, because when he'd seen those boys the day before, Mickey had been a tad overweight, while Jason had just about a normal build.

Now, their bodies seemed pale, fragile and a little sick. Mickey looked like he had shed ten or more pounds since the night before, and the guilt Pete had felt earlier that morning resurfaced.

Those boys got sick down there and it's all my fault. I could have let them in to stay on the couch, or even a cot on the floor. Anything would have been better than sleeping out in this cold, down in the Squaw Creek lowlands.

"Jesus, boys! What happened to you two? Did you both get sick?" Pete asked them as opened the door wider so they could come in.

Mickey wordlessly held a blanket around himself, shivering, and slowly walked in the house. Jason followed much in the same way. Pete noticed when they passed that their eyes looked a little off.

"A fog came through and hit us — hit everyone down there. It rolled in off the channel and there was — there was something wrong with it," Mickey said after Pete had shut the door behind them.

"What do you mean, something wrong with it?"

"He means that when it rolled through, it hurt us. It made us piss and shit all over ourselves," Jason said.

Mickey sat down on the edge of the sofa.

"We're lucky we didn't eat, or else we would've lost our supper last night," Mickey said. "It made us dry heave like a son-of-a-bitch though."

Jason sat down beside Mickey and they leaned into other to draw heat. This seemed a little off to Pete. It also made him feel awkwardly better about the whole situation, given that they would not be interested in bedding his daughter. He couldn't help but feel selfish for thinking that at the moment, though, since they were sitting in front of him with an obvious case of either the flu or poisoning. It wouldn't surprise him, since they said that fog rolled in off the river.

"Well, the first thing we need to do is get you down to the clinic and get you checked out. We may need to run you down to Jamison County though in Barrelton and get you admitted to the hospital," Pete said. "Geez, you boys look awful!"

"Thank you, Mr. Brown, but what we would really like to do is get back to Bloomington and go the hospital there. That's where Mickey's family is, and he wants to be closer to them right now," Jason said putting his arm around Mickey.

Pete realized that they were definitely gay, and that put an almost sympathetic smile on his face.

"Yeah, that's definitely what I would like to do. I don't want to end up like those people down at the dock," Mickey said. "I'm also really hungry right now. Sick and hungry, both. God, this sucks!"

People down at the dock? Pete thought to himself.

Pete wondered if Mickey was referring to the boozehounds that passed out by the 'Stow the night before, or if he was taking a jab at the working class with that statement. "What do you mean? What's wrong with the people down at the dock?" Pete asked. He pulled the drapes back from the front window and tried to look outside, but he couldn't see down the bluff beyond the 'Bend.

"The same thing happened to them. Everyone in the lowland area got sucked into that cloud, and we could hear them screaming before we passed out," Mickey said. "Then when we woke up this morning, we could see them all congregating, herding to the dock, looking just like we look right now. They all had blankets wrapped around them and were pale and weak — like us. When we left, we could see them drinking out of the river!"

Jason thought it would have been better to at least stay and see what they were doing. Maybe those people knew something about it they didn't. Maybe they knew how to deal with it, since it might not have been their first rodeo. He also remembered that alluring smell that had made him want to join them, but Mickey had insisted on packing up and leaving. He loved him enough to do as he asked. It seemed to be hitting him harder anyway. So they had just made their way up there to Izzy's old man's place.

Pete was a little perplexed at the notion, and at first he just thought maybe they were so sick they were hallucinating.

"Well, you boys can't drive all the way to Bloomington, that's for sure. Not in the condition you're both in," Pete said.

Jason gave him a pleading look. "We realize that, Sir, but there is no way we can play in New Albany tonight and we were hoping that we could get Izzy to drive us back. We could have Mickey's aunt bring her home . . . if that's okay?"

Pete loved the fact that they were asking his permission to do this, but it was not necessary. He had let Izzy out to travel with them all over for months. She was old enough to make those kinds of decisions herself.

"Well, sure she can, but you'll need to ask her first."

"Ask me what?" Izzy said, walking into the room. She had a case of bedhead and looked sleepy. She was wearing a pair of shorts and a short shirt that exposed her midriff. The black lipstick had been smeared off in a hurry the night before, and her makeup was still sticking to a few parts of her face. She stretched and yawned before she could get a good look at Mickey and Jason.

"Oh, my God! What happened to you?" Izzy exclaimed. She sat beside Jason and ran her hand through his hair like she was checking its temperature, but he jerked his head away.

"The boys got sick last night; some sort of fog cloud rolled through and messed them up. Not sure how, but it really did a number on them," Pete said.

Izzy turned her attention back to Jason and Mickey with obvious sympathy.

"Can you drive us back to Bloomington? Mickey really wants to see his own doctor," Jason said.

"Of course," Izzy said. She went to her bedroom to change.

That was one of the things Pete loved about his daughter. She had always been one to care about the people in her life, including him. Not having a mother might have forced her to grow up too quickly, but she was a kind-hearted young lady and he couldn't have been more proud of her.

"There'll be no need to have your aunt drive her back. I'll just follow you guys in my car and bring her back myself," Pete said.

"Thank you, Mr. Brown," Jason said.

Although Pete wasn't complaining, he couldn't help but be a little surprised that they kept calling him Mr. Brown. It was just last night that they were up on stage thrashing out that young new-age rock music that was so creepy. They gave off the impression that they could care less about the formalities of American society. But he liked the fact that they had a tamer side. It made him feel better about sending his daughter on the road with them.

10

Candy Odair and Sandra Stamps were making their way through town while Sandra was still drying her hair and applying lipstick and other makeup to cover up her pale, sickly skin.

Their Caprice still stunk from all the human waste from the night before. Candy had tried to vacuum most of it out while Sandra was in the shower, but she did a lackluster job and she knew the kids would complain.

No matter, they'll just have to put up with it. There's too much at stake tonight, Candy thought to herself.

Sandra was having trouble getting her makeup just right. Once they crossed onto Locust Street, the potholes caused her to smear the makeup on her face. She was so tired and weak that she almost didn't care, but her mother had insisted on this escapade and she had been living with her long enough that she knew better than to go against her. All Sandra really wanted to do was find something to eat and go to sleep.

When they reached the rear side of the Co-op, Candy could see that Ellen and Sebastian were upset. Ellen was on Burnley's lap with her face buried in his chest, while Sebastian sat alone on a hay bale, not saying a word.

"You go up there and get our baby girl off that nigger's lap and see that she doesn't get in crying the whole time," Candy said.

Sandra rolled her eyes and started to get out of the car when Candy grabbed her arm.

"And you see to it that nigger never comes around her again, you hear me, bitch?" Candy said.

Sandra gave her a dirty look and jerked her arm away.

She made her way up to Burnley, but Sebastian stopped her before she could get there.

"Can't you just let us stay here a little bit longer? We need to make sure Dad's okay," Sebastian said.

Sandra smiled and ran her hand through his hair, almost seeming to care about his feelings.

"Oh, Sebastian. You know I can't do that. Your dad is dead."

Sebastian turned sideways, not convinced.

"He's not dead! He just needs a doctor."

Sandra giggled, took her hand off his hair and walked away to get Ellen.

Burnley was eyeing her like he'd just seen a serpent emerge from the ground. He had heard what she had said to Sebastian and it almost made him sick to his stomach. He wondered if anyone would miss those two ladies if he knocked them out with a tire iron and threw them in the Ohio.

Let the river wash away their polluted souls!

Sandra reached down to grab Ellen out of Burnley's lap without even saying a word to him. He had no choice but to give her up, but Ellen held onto him and did not want to go.

"I'm sorry, sweetheart, but your momma's here and she needs to take you with her," Burnley said.

"No, Burny, no. I want to stay here with you," Ellen said, grasping onto him more tightly as her mother tried to pull her away.

"Come on, little woman, it's time to go," Sandra said and jerked Ellen away with enough force to break her grip, snapping them both backward.

"Careful, now!" Burnley said.

Ellen was reaching back for Burnley when Sandra turned her around and faced him herself. She tried to speak so Ellen and Sebastian could not hear her, but that was not possible.

"You'll keep your nigger hands off my daughter if you know what's good for you," Sandra said, but in a more hesitant tone than her mother's.

Burnley just stood there, speechless. He was not sure what to say back to her that would not come back on the kids a mile or so down the road, so he just said nothing.

Sandra walked off with Ellen in her arms and pulled Sebastian along behind her. After they got in the car and drove off, Burnley snapped his hands backward and punched the hay bale a few times, and then jerked around to see if he could still see them driving away.

Some day, ladies, karma's gonna come-a-knocking! And I hope you're scared when it does!

* * *

They'd made it less than a quarter of a mile down the road when they came across the wreckage of Bob Stamps' Wagoneer. Teams of emergency workers maneuvered around the vehicle. Bob had already been taken from the wreck and transported down to the Jamison County morgue.

Sebby and Ellen were glued to the driver's side window in the back seat of the Caprice. Air and wet road residue was coming in through a rusted hole in the floorboard, but they did not pay any attention to it. The only thing they wanted to see was if their dad was okay.

The Caprice made its way west, out of town and toward Barrelton, as the image of their Dad's Jeep receded in the back window.

Candy and Sandra were not looking, but rather were paying attention to the road and each other as they approached Derbie.

"You get that makeup on, now. The road is clear ahead and I want you to be ready as soon as we get there," Candy said.

"It's still an hour and a half up the road. I'm sure I'll be ready by the time we get there. But even still, it's early and there'll be no one there," Sandra said.

"You let me worry about that. When we get there, I want to set up this VHS recorder in the room so he won't be able to see it. It's Saturday, so he will get to the Riverboat by noon and he should be good and loaded by around two in the afternoon."

"How did you find out about this guy . . . and who is he?"

"Not that you need to worry about that part, but he is the chief executive for a pharmaceutical company down there. His wife and kids are up in French Lick for the weekend so he will be an easy..." Candy slowed down to choose her words wisely around the kids. "T-A-R-G-E-T."

Sandra sat back in her seat and moaned under her breath. She was so hungry that it was driving her insane. Her whole body hurt and her vagina was rubbery and tender, like the skin of a mushroom. She wanted to make the score, but there were other things on her mind at the moment.

As they made their way along a scenic path on the Ohio River, the smell that Sandra craved still hung in the air, although it was much fainter than before. That eased her hunger a bit, but she still wanted to sleep. Her muscles felt like they were deteriorating.

"God! When are we gonna stop and eat?! I'm starving!" Sandra said.

Candy looked at her with wicked eyes and then looked away. She knew how Sandra felt, because she was feeling the same way. But she was focused on the task at hand. She had been planning it for a week now, after she'd received a tip on the matter at hand. If their plan fell through, she was going to knife the man and take whatever he had on him. Either way, she wasn't going to walk away empty-handed. At least they had Bob's life insurance to fall back on. *If the bumbling idiot remembered to pay it.*

11

Sandra and Candy had already been to the hotel and rigged the room with cameras for their new score. It was their intention to get Larry McConnell to come back to the hotel room with them after he was good and drunk from the riverboat.

But it would be another seven hours before he showed up at the riverboat, and another three hours of drinking and debauchery before Sandra would be able to convince him to get him back to the room with her.

She had laid it on thick with Larry. Candy was standing beside the bar directing her every move. But he had finally given in and tickled her rear end as they walked off the Riverboat and crossed the street to the hotel. Candy followed them into the hotel room, much to Larry's surprise.

When they got into the room, Sandra kissed him and loosened his belt. Larry cupped her rear end while trying to pull her pants down.

He was a little skittish at the idea of having her mother in the room with them while they were in the early stages of a sexual encounter, but he was also intoxicated enough that it did not stop him.

Sandra slammed him down on the bed and pulled his pants off. He pulled his shirt over his head and Sandra started undressing in front of him — along with Candy.

Larry's squeamish feelings about Candy's presence intensified, but he decided to just not look at her and only focus on the hot little number in front of him so he could get his rocks off and get the hell out of there.

Who cares what kind of sick twisted shit they're into? One good fuck and I'm out. I'm not touching that other lady, Larry thought to himself.

Sandra crawled on top of him and got right down to business, positioning his penis just right for the soft entry. An all-out sexual frenzy ensued.

Candy had walked around the side and stood behind Sandra during the sex, cupping her breasts and giving her rear leverage.

* * *

Sebby and Ellen had been in their mother's car in the parking garage for hours now. They had both gotten into their pajamas about an hour before and they were still upset about their dad.

"I think we need to just go live with Dad after we get home. He's going to be just fine. Don't listen to Mom," Sebby said.

Ellen cuddled in close to Sebby and nodded her sad head. She was shivering cold. Sebby was cold too, but he only worried about her.

"You cold, sis?"

Ellen nodded again and scooted closer to him.

"Okay," Sebby said. He crawled into the front seat and pulled the spare key out of the sun visor.

"What are you doing?" Ellen asked him.

Sebby didn't answer right away, but started the car and turned the heater on. He returned to the backseat.

"There, that should warm us up soon," Sebby said.

They huddled together. Their mother may have remembered to bring their pajamas, but she hadn't brought any blankets or pillows for them. He was also angry that their mother and Candy got to go inside and sleep in the hotel while they had to sleep in the car.

He'd had similar feelings before, and he'd been thinking about living with his Dad a lot lately. His dad may not have had much, but at least he cared enough to pick them up every weekend, and he was always there to do stuff with them. He even played with them, even though Sebby knew that he was tired from working all day.

He was saddened by the fact that he had wanted to leave Patoka this weekend. He hadn't been able to help himself, though. He had been bored; being up there was nothing like what he'd expected. But he knew it wasn't his Dad's fault.

Ellen started to nod off and Sebby put his arm around her. Something that he also realized was that he couldn't have just left his mother to live with his Dad without Ellen. She depended on him, and his mother would not allow her to go. She may not even allow him to go, but he was going to give it a shot anyway. He didn't want to live with his mother and grandmother anymore. They weren't nice people, and he knew it.

"So it's settled then, right?" Sebby said.

"Huh?" Ellen said, half asleep.

The car was starting to warm up enough that Ellen wasn't shivering anymore. They could both feel the warmth coming in from the hole in the floorboard. Sebby assumed it was from the warm gears below, but it was actually the noxious mixture of exhaust coming from the engine's tailpipe. That hole had been a nuisance to them the whole drive up there, letting in the water and crud from the road. But now, it was sending a little warmth their way, and that was good. He didn't like it when they were cold.

"We're going to live with Dad when we get back?"

Ellen opened her eyes enough to look straight into her brother's eyes. She nodded, and then closed them again.

Sebby just smiled. He was proud that they had both decided to do it together. He knew it would make his Dad so happy for them to come and live with him. He couldn't wait to tell him.

The longer he lay there and thought about it, the more tired he grew, and as the car started to fill up with carbon monoxide, Sebby and Ellen drifted off to sleep . . . and went to live with their Dad.

* * *

The time was approaching 7:30 p.m., and Sandra was trying to finish off Larry McConnell at about the same time her kids were dying of carbon monoxide poisoning outside in her car.

Candy had walked back around them while Sandra straddled the white-collar misogynist. She'd shed her pants, but she was still wearing a shirt.

Larry was slowly approaching his climax when Candy walked up beside the bed and took his hand off Sandra's waist and placed it between her own legs.

Larry could feel the battered remains of what he could only assume used to be a vagina, but now felt more like a rotten eggplant.

He yanked his hand away and threw Sandra off him. He sat up on the bed and Candy was taken aback, even a little frightened, at his sudden action.

When Larry wiped his hand across his nose, a rancid smell overpowered him and he gave a contorted, frenzied look. He jumped off the bed and went straight to the bathroom to scrub his hands clean.

His comical, frantic response gave Sandra a chuckle, but Candy had been deeply offended by his actions.

She drew her knife and pointed it at the laughing Sandra, whose own demeanor quickly turned.

Candy's hurt and desperate eyes stared at Sandra for a few moments, and Sandra looked back at her in fear. Candy lowered the knife and walked into the bathroom.

Larry stood over the sink, furiously scrubbing his hand, when Candy entered the room. He didn't even look at her; he just kept on washing his hands.

"At least one good thing will come of this," Candy said.

Larry looked over at her and had no time to react before she jabbed the knife into his neck.

He jerked back against the wall with his hand over the gaping wound on his neck. Candy approached him again and jabbed his neck two more times, and then jabbed him in twice the gut.

She stood back to watch him as he slid his back down the wall, trying to hold his wounds, unable to scream or cry for help.

Sandra entered the bathroom and stood beside Candy, watching the man bleed out on the floor. She slowly took the knife out of Candy's hand and calmly placed it on the sink. Sandra gently patted her back and told her everything was okay, but Candy could not look away from Larry as the blood sputtered out of his neck and abdomen.

Candy's eyes were fixed on him, nearly hypnotized to the sight of the gushing blood. She was not ashamed of what she'd done. Sandra was also staring at Larry's bleeding body.

He was fighting to stay alive, withering on the floor. Tears leaked from his eyes and anxiety caused his blood to flow more rapidly out of his body.

Sandra slowly kneeled down beside him and he reached his hand out for help, She gently caressed it and then placed it aside. She couldn't think of anything else at that moment. She did not have the capacity for emotion. No love. No compassion. No sympathy. There was only one thing on her mind — hunger.

To his surprise, she pinned his weakened body against the wall. He let her, thinking she was about to help him in some way. Her own weakened body would not have been able to do it otherwise.

She could smell his blood. She could smell his body dying and the sweet allure of his soon-to-be lifeless corpse pleased her. She was not sure what she wanted to do with him. Choke him? Help him? Hold him?

Bite him.

It was suddenly so clear to her. She had known all day long that she did not want a bologna sandwich. She did not want chips or olives or crackers. She wanted meat.

Larry started to lose consciousness. Sandra squatted lower and opened her mouth around his wounded neck. Her tongue touched the blood and absorbed it. The hunger was being satiated as she licked more and more of the blood. She sucked and sucked until the blood just wasn't enough. She needed something more, so she started to close her teeth in on Larry's wounded neck. But as she bit down, his strong skin muscle did not budge. She kept trying, but instead of biting a chunk of meat out of Larry's neck, her two front teeth broke off and gave her excruciating pain.

She fell backward, holding her mouth, and Candy came out of her own trance to see what happened to her.

Candy kneeled down and saw her teeth had broken off. It bewildered her at the moment to see that Sandra couldn't have cared less about the pain in her teeth. She was, however, partially satiated by the blood and her body hurt less. Nevertheless, her two front teeth were still dangling from her upper jaw.

They both had a new biology, a taste for humans. But their bodies, their mouths and their own teeth, were too weak to eat fresh meat. They needed something more tender, something brought on from — decomposition. The kind of meat that comes apart from decay or from soaking in water, although neither one of them knew that at the moment.

* * *

After Candy satiated her appetite with Larry's blood, they both left the room in a hurry. The exhaust had already filled the car and they gave it a second to air out before they got in.

That's when Sandra found her children.

A sudden jolt ran through her body and she felt the kind of grief she thought she had been immune to. Her children were dead and it was her fault.

Sandra held a hand over her mouth to keep from screaming.

Candy grabbed her.

"Pop the trunk, sassy; we need to put them in the back. The police will hold us responsible, and we need to take them somewhere else," Candy said.

Sandra was slow to respond, still grief-stricken, but popped the trunk while her mother put Sebby and Ellen in the back. They made their way out of the garage and out of Indiana.

They completely forgot about the hidden camera they had left in the hotel room.

CHAPTER 5
RISE OF THE CREEPERS

1

IT WAS ONE OF THE THINGS that made them different from the other animals in the kingdom: the desire to preserve their species and eat those lower on the food chain. Not for pride, but more out of a sense of duty to their fellow humans, the thought that eating their dead would be considered a crime They had built a society that sustained them and now, they didn't have to resort to such primitive means as eating the bodies of their dead, consuming their brethren for sustenance.

But in the mind of Harry Keethers, his own life and the lives of people he knew — the people he cared about — were about to set themselves back thousands of years on the evolutionary scale. Trying to figure out a medical explanation for what had happened to him and what they'd done was out of the question. The fog rolled in from the river and there may have been noxious chemicals mixed in with it from the polluted river, but that didn't help him figure out why they had changed.

It had become apparent to him that they weren't in the midst of some disease or epidemic. As incomprehensible as it was, they had become the monsters of legend. The Living Dead. Ghouls.

He couldn't find any way to make sense of that, either, because he could think perfectly fine, and he did not aimlessly wander the streets moaning and stumbling. He did not feel the need to kill people, nor did he want to see people in pain.

One thing was certain: He had to eat human meat, to drink out of a polluted river and scratch the tips of his itchy fingernails along stony surfaces just to get by.

He had scratched so much at that point that his fingernails had become sharp as those curved, pointed paring knives. His body was considerably weaker, but his nails could cut through the deck planking outside on the dock with little effort.

He had already seen what his own eyes looked like in the mirror, and had seen that they matched the eyes of everyone else who had come to the Stow and sipped from the channel. The whites had cleared away and taken on a translucent quality. He could see the vessels that were attached to the pupils and the eyeballs.

It was both scary and remarkable. A glimpse into this changing new biology that no one could have ever predicted. But when he closed his eyes, that's when the really extraordinary part hit him.

The view was just as clear, if not more defined, with his eyelids shut as it was when they were open. Not only could he see through his eyelids, but he could pick up heat signatures. He could see the biological elements that clung to the walls and floors of the Stow. He could see where people had spit on the floor and where fights had broken out and left blood on the walls. He could see areas where people had drunkenly pissed on the floor and other parts where people had had sex, or maybe fooled around in the back behind a table. They were, of course, invisible to the eyes of a regular human being, which was a good thing because they were disgusting, even to him and his new existence. But now, his new biology had given him this gift.

But with every gift, there is a price to pay. He would never eat a burger or a slice of pizza again. He would never be able to sit down to a Sunday dinner and enjoy a pot roast with rolls. He would never again be able to savor the carved turkey at Thanksgiving with his friends, or sip on eggnog on Christmas Eve.

He would be confined to the background of people's lives and forced to feed in the shadows of a graveyard, or even in his own laboratory back in Barrelton, as the county coroner.

That was something he knew he could do to take care of himself. But that did not solve the problem for everyone else who had congregated at the Stow, anxiously awaiting someone like him to help them, or guide them to better health. They did not fully comprehend their new biology, but Harry did.

When all was said and done, Harry surmised that he would not be able to help all those people. Most of them would either perish from starvation or be euthanized by a fearful town — once the townspeople had found out, of course.

It was Harry's duty to make sure that he took care of his own. That meant the original four, which included himself, Perry Dupont, Erin Mills and Arn Simmons. He would have also included those two boys from Izzy's band, had they not taken off. But Harry had to stick to what was in front of him.

* * *

After a commotion outside of the Stow, Harry was stirred enough to make his way to the dock, followed by Perry and Erin.

Arn was in the kitchen sulking and Harry was afraid he was going to do something to himself. That had always been the thing about Arn. He may have had a gruff, tough-as-nails exterior, but on the inside, he was a man who cared about everybody and everything. There was no capacity within him to do wrong. Arn saw his body as a curse now, one that might cause him to kill someone once his pain and hunger returned, and Harry wouldn't put it past him to off himself just to avoid it.

Once he got outside, though, he could see that his prayers, the ones he had never actually spoken, had been answered. There were at least seven dead bodies floating in the channel, one of which had arisen from the depths of the water when he first arrived.

The people were scared but also soothed by the thought that they were finally going to get something to eat. Something, in all its horrible glory, that would make their pain go away. A pain that had now been equated to their own bodies fading away. Decomposing while they were very much alive. The pain that people only feel when they are prisoners in their own bodies.

That made the situation even worse for them. They had human souls. Emotions and feelings. Bodies that reacted to their consciences, and they had to merge that with their need to survive. The process was a horror that did not jump out and say *"BOO,"* but rather a *"slow burn"* that ate away at them, mercilessly, with no emotion.

Now that the rotten bodies had emerged from the water and the people, cloaked in their blankets, their faces gaunt, clung to the edge of the dock. They reached for the floating bodies of people who had been long dead, probably killed in some city up the river in places like Louisville or Pittsburgh, maybe somewhere in between, and dumped in the river. These same bodies that had somehow made their way downstream to dock in their little channel that ran nearly half a mile inland from the Ohio River.

It was a guarantee, in Harry's mind, that this was not some biological coincidence. He and those people had not just fallen victim to the malicious fog that arose out of the polluted river; rather they had been reborn into a life that had chosen them.

As is the case with any mother who bears a child, she did not do so without a nipple to feed them. The Ohio River had not changed them; it had given birth to them, and now, their mother was feeding her young, who anxiously awaited her nourishment. They would now answer to one parent who would not take no for an answer. They now answered to the river, as horrifying as it may have sounded. They now enforced the will of the river.

* * *

They started hauling the rotting bodies inside the Stow. After each trip they made, another body would emerge from the channel's dark depths.

When they finally filled the Stow with starving patrons of the Squaw Creek horror, there were a total of eleven dead bodies feeding nearly a hundred people. Men and women all feasted in horrified delight on the rotten flesh. Kids cried as they watched, but dared not interfere. Women forced the rotten, water-softened flesh into their children's mouths and they ate it. They swallowed, and as time passed, they began to feel the relief they had all wished for.

Their bodies were not getting any stronger, and their faces still appeared gaunt, but they were free of the pain. The same pain a body might feel that was alive in a coffin, rotting away as the Earth slowly reclaimed its biological elements. The pain that can only be described as a slow burn.

Harry also had his fill and as he was eating, his nails sliced through the flesh with considerable ease, cutting off portions that were easily digestible. When he finished, he slowly descended into depression, dismayed at how easily he had accomplished this task. How he had been able to do it with no remorse. He had eaten like it was just another meal, minus the forks and spoons. He did not need the silverware anymore because his new, natural state was primitive and horrifying.

Far be it for him to give it a name or a classification. If he was seeking the classic term, the classification derived from popular fiction on TV, film and comic books, then he could not quite put his finger on it.

He was not the Living Dead. He still had a heartbeat. He could still think. The same reasoning applied to a zombie, which he was able to rule out. But it was the ghoul that caught his attention. The classification seemed right in all aspects, but in most stories ghouls were not humans, but rather doomed creatures from hell, forced to walk the Earth. They feasted on the living and dead both. They were scavengers and most of those would apply to what he and his new comrades were doing right now. But still, ghouls operated with indifference, with no remorse or empathy for their victims. Harry and all his people in the Stow did this out of necessity, and they mourned their actions during the feast.

So he could not call himself or the others that, and he thanked whatever God he could that he was able to rule it out. Just the sound of that name was displeasing, and he did not want the classi-fication. He also did not want the world to find out about them, but he knew that it was inevitable.

There was one name that stuck in his mind. One that was not clearly defined in any area of folklore, but rather loosely defined in many cultures. The name struck fear in the hearts of men, women and children alike, but has no basis in reality— until now, of course.

Creeper.

It fit the bill just about right, no matter how much he disliked the name. They were not quite zombies, not quite ghouls, but a loose variation of the living dead. Their bodies were decomposing, or experiencing the awful pain of the "*slow burn*" that forced them to eat or wither away in torturous misery.

We're creepers. We're tortured souls and some, likely most, of us will die at the hands of our own townsfolk. There will be no tolerance for what we must do to survive and we'll be extinct before Tuesday.

There was a good chance he was right, but then again, Linton Derr could likely find a different solution to this. He and his family had always been known to show people a certain amount of tolerance.

2

About the same time Harry Keethers and his people were dragging dead bodies into the Stow, Lucy Doss was playing jump the hay bale again with Burnley behind the Co-op. This was also about the same time Sandra Stamps and Candy Odair were pulling their car into a parking garage next to a hotel, expecting to pull off a scam on a white-collar gambler.

Carolyn Weyerbacher-Derr watched Lucy and Burnley play while she leaned against her old Ford pickup truck. She couldn't help but worry about Linton. She wanted to go up there and check on him, but that was Kelly's job now. Carolyn knew Kelly would be Linton's wife someday. She was sure if it. So she had to sit outside and wait. She could keep an eye on her little Lucy, but the torment of losing *poor little Bobby Stamps* caused her heart to miss a few beats. She wanted to cry right where she stood, but she did not want Lucy to see her cry. Although Lucy was going to find out sooner or later, Carolyn would rather wait to tell her when she herself was not so emotional. Really, it was her momma's job to tell her, but Kelly might need some support. Anyway, there was nothing to gain by telling her then.

My God. Poor little Bobby.

Carolyn remembered when Linton and Bobby Stamps were young. They would invite him over to the reservation and those two boys would swim in the lake all day and chase turtles around. They would go out to the side of the highway and carry the turtles across to the edge of the river. She hated when they did that, but she loved the fact that they cared so much for living things.

They would run beside the river with their shirts off, playing pirates. Little Bobby made two eye patches for himself and Linton out of some old hemp string Carolyn had forgotten about in their barn. That made her chuckle.

And Bobby looked out for Linton just as much as Linton looked out for Bobby. When they were walking alongside the highway with sparklers one evening, a car had veered off the side of road. Carolyn had always told Linton to walk on the side of the road that had the traffic coming toward him. *You always have to see what they are doing.* But this time, they were walking alongside the highway and the traffic was coming from behind them. It was little Bobby who had turned around and had seen that car coming toward them off the side of the road, and it was he that grabbed Linton and leaped into the ditch. Bobby had saved her son's life and they would forever be more than just friends. They were brothers.

This forced Carolyn to walk around the side of the building and break out in a frenzy of tears. She felt as though she had lost her own son. The young boy who had grown up to become a great man. Such a good heart that had been lost to this world.

She could do nothing right now with Linton, anyway. She felt too torn up about the situation, and he was no doubt even worse off than she was. Kelly was up there with him, and Burnley had an eye out for Lucy, so Carolyn just walked through the alley and in front of the Co-op.

That was when she saw it. The sight that would make her wonder what the world was coming to.

Flakes of ash were falling on the street like snow in winter. At first, Carolyn thought that someone had just started a fireplace and was burning off the old soot from the year before. Probably using a chimney cleaner to burn it all, maybe mixed in with some newspaper to get the fire going. But there was so much that it became apparent that it was not just a fireplace. There was a fire.

She could smell it. She stepped into the street and looked around, then spotted the glow in the distance. It was easy to see against the overcast sky.

It wasn't in Fogstow, but rather up in the plateau. It was the Jeffries plateau, and there was no easy way to get there. They had formed their small community up there and never built an access road to it. County funds for the road were diverted because Ceril Jeffries had raised hell with the council several years before when they started planning it, and several people had their cars vandalized. No one could ever prove the Jeffries did it, and they were crazy enough to keep on doing it, so the council just dropped it.

There was a muddy path of water runoff ridges, but she didn't think a fire engine would be able to make its way up it.

She had been up there when she was younger, and those people were some of the weirdest she had ever met. They didn't seem to have any respect for human life. They lived like animals and ate anything they got their hands on, including roadkill and snakes. She had heard all the stories about them being cannibals, eating people who died in the National Forest. Of course, those were just stories, and there was never a shred of evidence to prove it, but she believed it. From what she had seen up there, it certainly seemed like something they would do.

Carolyn made her way back to the alley and climbed the stairwell. She hated to do it, considering what Linton had gone through that morning. The last thing he needed was to be fighting his way up Pine Hill just to put out a fire for a group of people that couldn't care less about the town or for them being there to help them. But she had to.

As soon as she walked in the door, she saw that Linton was lying on his back and his head was in Kelly's lap. She was rubbing his hair and he seemed to be okay for the moment.

"I'm so sorry to bother you with this, son, but we have a situation," Carolyn said.

Linton bolted up and turned toward her.

"What's wrong, Mom?" Linton asked.

"There's a fire. I could see it from the front of the Co-op, and it appears to be coming from Jeffries hill."

"Oh, shit."

Linton rose and buttoned up his shirt.

"Kelly, can you get on the horn with Barrelton? I need Kramer to send a couple of deputies out — and have them send their fire engines."

"Of course," Kelly said, and tried the radio in his office.

"Mom, can you keep an eye on Lucy for Kelly? I need her to run point from the office while I roll down to Gil's and see who can lend us a hand with their four-wheel drives," Linton said.

"I sure can," Carolyn answered. She turned to Kelly. "Do you want me to keep her here in Fogstow, or do you want me to take her to the reservation?"

"Either way is fine. You can take her down to the 'Bend if you want or she can play with Burnley. Just let him know that I am in the office running the comms," Kelly said.

Linton had already made his way out the door toward his Bronco. Lucy was coming along in the alley with Burnley.

"Hey Win-ton. You okay (*yaokay*)," Lucy said.

Linton turned toward her and the thought of losing people he loved overwhelmed him. He picked her up and looked her in the eyes before he gave her his best hug. She reciprocated and patted his back, although she hadn't been told yet what was wrong. Lucy always knew when someone needed a hug. Especially her Momma. And now, especially her Linton.

"It's okay (*isokay*). It's okay," Lucy said.

Linton gently pulled her back and gave her a proud smile before he let her down.

"I am now," he said.

He looked at Burnley and pointed at the office door.

"Mom will be keeping an eye on Lucy today. Kelly has to run comms for me."

Burnley did not want to ask in front of Lucy, but he wondered what was going on. Linton could tell he wanted to ask, and he pointed up the stairs again.

"They'll fill you in."

"Okay. You go take care of business," Burnley said. He gave Linton a quick pat on the shoulder about the same time Stark came riding up on the three-wheeler.

"Did you see . . ." Stark said before Linton cut him off and nodded his head. Stark took one look at Lucy and realized. They both left for the Bronco.

*   *   *

Linton pulled up at Gil's Taxidermy Shop and Filling Station only to be greeted by an empty parking lot. Gil Boyd had not even opened up shop that morning, despite the fact that he lived right behind the station, and it made Linton worry. Today was a big day for the town.

"What in the world is going on?" Linton said.

"Where the hell is everyone?" Stark asked.

"This place should be full of trucks and three-wheelers by now. Hell, even the soda fountain and the snipe hunt should be starting by this time."

"You think Gil called it off?"

"No chance. He would have to be deathly sick to call this . . . oh, shit! I guess I better check on him."

Linton knocked on his door several times.

"No luck?" Stark asked from across the lot.

Linton shook his head and banged on the door three more times. Nothing. Three more times and nothing again. What he couldn't understand was why, if everyone had shown up there and found the same thing earlier that morning, they didn't come and tell him. Why wouldn't they have at least told someone? At the very least they could have told Dr. Strange.

Linton tried three more times before he opened the door and jimmied the lock open.

Gil lived in the back of his shop and Linton just needed to be sure he was okay.

Stark made his way over, looking around to make sure no one had seen Linton forcing his way into Gil's, and then walked through the door behind him.

The smell almost knocked them down. It was the combination of the stench coming from the channel, which they had gotten so used to by now that they didn't even notice most of the time, and something even worse.

Linton had a pretty good idea that they were about to find Gil sitting in his La-Z-Boy recliner, dead of a heart attack, or whatever else that gets you when you least expect it. Gil had been sitting there eating a pot pie and a bag of Grippos when it hit him. He'd grabbed his chest and the phone beside him on the portable tray, but by the time he got it to his ear, he was already gone.

(*SORY*)

But when he got into Gil's living room, Linton didn't find anyone. He picked up the phone on the tray and heard a dial tone, so it wasn't recently off the hook.

He made his way toward the bathroom where he envisioned Gil on the toilet seat. It was no easy task for these overweight old-timers to do their business when the fried brainers made their way through the digestive system. Gil was probably trying to force the task (*no constipation is gonna keep me down*) when it was just a little too much strain. He was dead before he could stand up and get help.

Linton opened the bathroom door and found that the smell was not coming from in there. It was clean as a whistle, just like they trained him back before he went to Korea.

(*I'm taking the kids to Patoka this weekend.*)

Stark had already checked the rest of the tiny dwelling and had found no sign of Gil. They both made their way back out and Linton tried to undo his jimmy on the lock, which he was having no luck with.

"Are we in the frigging Twilight Zone? What the hell is going on?" Stark said.

Linton hopped into the Bronco and fired it up. On the backside of Gil's, he could see Shane Duncan Siders walking through the parking lot, crossing the gas islands and making his way up Locust from the opposite end. He seemed to be minding his own business.

"Today is gonna be one for the history books. That's about all I can . . ."

Linton was interrupted by Joe Terrance and Noah Buchanon spouting out frantic words in his ear through the side window of his Bronco. It gave Linton quite the shock, and for a moment, Stark rested his hand on his gun, but he quickly let go and pretended he hadn't done it.

"Boss! Boss! Listen to me, there's something I need to tell you," Joe said as he approached.

"Jesus Joseph Harold Terrance! Don't you know you can give someone a heart attack sneaking up like that?" Linton said.

Joe pulled back a little bit and the tension in his face seemed to break. He frowned and continued.

"Sorry about that, Boss."

"And that's another thing. Call me Chief or call me Linton. Don't call me that anymore."

Joe started to a look around nervously, and he had only partially heard what Linton had said.

"Yeah. Yeah, no problem. Listen, Boss, we did something that we shouldn't have and I . . ."

"I don't have time for your confessions right now, Joe. Either cut to the chase or I have to go. Now."

"We went into the sinkhole."

"The one out by the park?"

"Yeah, we went in there — and there was a cave, or more like a tunnel that was part of the coal mines because we saw all the coal tracks and stuff and . . ."

"Listen, Joe. You kids stay out of there and I will deal with you later," Linton said and put the Bronco in reverse. "I have pressing matters to tend to right now."

Joe grabbed the window as if that could make the Bronco stop. Linton let off the gas and put the truck in neutral.

"What's gotten into you, Joe?" he asked.

"That's just it. I don't make it a habit to rat myself or my friends out. But we did see something down there and you really need to know about this."

Linton put the Bronco back in park and turned the ignition off.

Noah was standing behind him and looking around while Joe talked. It only took another second before he saw what he was looking for. Shane Duncan Siders had walked around the corner and was approaching the Bronco.

Noah frantically tugged on Joe's shirtsleeve, frightened out of his mind. The tall dark man approached with no emotion on his face. He took long, seamless strides, and to Noah, he looked a lot like the man that could kill you in a crowd of people and walk away like he was just passing through.

Joe had already turned to see Siders approaching and he became speechless, scared out of his wits.

"Come on, Joe! Let's hear it," Linton said impatiently.

Joe turned back to look at the Bronco and Linton could immediately see the fear in his eyes. It was the kind of fear that makes a young man wet himself in public. The kind of fear that makes a child freeze in front of a speeding train.

"Joe, it's okay. You can tell me, son."

Joe looked directly into Linton's eyes and said the only thing he could.

"Don't trust him. Don't believe a word he says." He took off running with Noah in tow.

The boys were out of the parking lot and across Squaw Creek. They ran more quickly than he had ever seen a kid run. Linton was about to put the Bronco in gear to go after them when he saw Siders approaching.

That was one encounter that Linton could do without. He had spoken with Siders on maybe a handful of occasions and each time had sent a chill straight to his bones.

"Chief," Siders said as he approached.

Linton turned around and took another look for the boys, but they weren't in sight. He knew they had to tell him something about Siders, but the man had just put an end to their confession by approaching.

"What can I do for you, Shane?"

Siders pointed at Pine Hill and the fire in the distance.

"I just thought you could use some help with that situation."

Linton turned around and looked at the glow of the fire over the treetops and realized he had to get back to square one. He was also down several volunteers since no one was at Gil's, and he did need help.

Linton found this disturbing, though, because he had gotten a sense of who Siders was several years ago when he was a deputy under Marvin Kramer.

It was in the summer of '87, if memory served him correctly. A call had come through about a boy who'd gone missing on the east side of Barrelton, and Linton was the responding officer. He took the statement from the worried mother who looked like she was just about to break down. The boy hadn't come home the night before and he had been out all day the previous day. It filled her with guilt, thinking that she hadn't realized the boy had gone missing until that night. She had let him roam the streets and the area around the old stripper pits all day while she worked. He was fifteen years old and her husband and she both agreed he was old enough to mill around the area while they were busy making a living.

A day turned into two days and two days turned into a week. Search parties had been formed and they combed the old stripped mining areas where the coal companies had been. Whatever happened to the boy was soon coming to closure.

Siders had joined in on the search party and it was he who came walking over a hill that obscured the old ventilation shaft from one of the original Oarshire installations in the area. The shaft had been decommissioned years before and someone would've really had to be looking for it to find it, because it was covered in wild brush and vines.

Siders came walking over the hill carrying the lifeless body of that young boy. He had told them he had pulled the boy out of the shaft and it had appeared that he had fallen into it, and that was what had killed him.

Linton had given clear instructions to everyone in the search party not to move any body they found, but rather to call them and they would tend to the remains. He knew that Siders knew it, but he had pulled him out of that shaft anyway, painting himself as a hero.

But it was immediately apparent to Linton that Siders couldn't have cared less about the hero status. There seemed to be something more rewarding in it for him than the fame or the glory. He just stood there while Linton questioned him about removing the body from the shaft. He didn't move his head. He never even blinked.

His eyes were what bothered Linton the most. He could have sworn up and down that if he had poked one finger into Siders eye, he still wouldn't have blinked. To Linton, Siders seemed almost like a dummy, the kind that ventriloquists used. That's what Siders eyes reminded him of.

It was only later, when they set up a perimeter around the shaft, that they found another body inside. It was the body of a boy that the original boy had been fighting with in school. The rumor was that they were enemies because of a girl, but others had told him that the mutual hatred went further back.

The investigation concluded that they had both agreed to meet in the area and settle their differences. It was presumed that they had fought at some point and both went down the shaft. But for Linton, the fact that Siders found the boy in such an obscure place, the fact that his demeanor seemed almost lifeless, as if he did not have a conscience, gave him the chills any time he saw the man.

But at that moment, he couldn't be too picky about who was allowed to help him go up to the Jeffries plateau and potentially save some lives.

He turned around and opened the back door of the Bronco.

"Hop in," Linton said.

3

Joe and Noah peeked around the corner of councilman McCallister's house in Squaw Creek and saw Siders getting into Linton's Bronco, then heading north to what appeared to be the fire up on Jeffries hill.

"This may be our only shot at going back and bringing that body back out. Otherwise, we're sure to get killed by that maniac. We have to prove he's guilty," Joe said.

Noah looked worried.

"Let's just do this quick!" Noah said.

They took off from the councilman's yard. They had no idea that Roman and Patty McCallister were inside their home, decaying. Their bodies hadn't been able to handle the fog cloud and all its gifts. Roman's heart had given out first. Patty had lain over him and mourned, and then had followed him out of this world.

* * *

When they reached Dean and Mark Chapman's house, they found Mike Brownsman's big truck in the driveway. Rush Amiano and Carrie LeBalte had driven it there and were knocking on the door. Rush was holding Mark's jambox.

Joe and Noah both approached the front door out of breath.

"Jesus, boys. Did you run all the way here?" Carrie asked.

"We have to get Dean and Mark and head back out to the sinkhole," Noah said while Joe caught his breath.

Rush handed the jambox to Carrie.

"Why?" Rush asked.

"We found something down there. Something awful," Noah said. Joe smacked the back of Noah's shoulder.

"What did you find?" Carrie asked.

"I'm not sure we should say until we pull her out," Joe said.

Carrie gasped and dropped the jambox. Rush put his hand on Joe's shoulder.

"Just slow down a minute and tell us. What did you find down there? Did you find a body?" Rush said.

Noah and Joe traded looks and decided to give in and tell them.

"We saw Shane Duncan Siders down there yesterday. He was

pulling along one of those big grain sacks they used to use at the Co-op, and we could a see a girl's hand hanging out of it. We think he killed her and took her down there to dump her body," Joe said.

"Did you tell the Boss?" Carrie asked.

"We just tried to, but when we caught up with him down at Gil's, Siders came walking up and we bolted," Noah said.

"Holy shit! Did you come straight here?" Rush asked.

They all heard a racket from the side of the house. They could hear empty aluminum cans rattling around. Brad Oxley was barking orders at Mark from the front side of the house.

"Just squeeze them all in there and make sure the tailgate closes. We need to get to Derbie before three," Oxley said from the side of the house.

Joe held a finger up to indicate silence to Rush and Carrie. They both stayed quiet and gave a jolt when Dean opened the front door to answer Rush's knock.

"Hey guys. What's up?" Dean said as he walked out to give Joe a high-five, but Joe was less than enthusiastic about it.

"We have to get back out to the sinkhole today and take care of a little business," Joe said, trying to keep his voice down.

Dean took a quick look around the side of the house to make sure his stepfather wasn't listening before he responded.

"I would, but Brad is making Mark go with him to Derbie to drop the cans off at the recycling center. I don't want Mark to go alone," Dean said.

Joe whispered into Dean's ear and told him about the girl's

body and how he didn't want Mark with them when they went. It was the perfect opportunity to do it, since Mark going to Derbie. Dean worried about Mark when he was with his stepfather, but he knew the worst that could happen would be for something of his to get broken. He wasn't too afraid of Brad physically harming his brother.

Dean agreed to go and went back inside to get his jacket.

"Listen, boys, I don't want you three going out there alone," Carrie said.

She looked over at Rush and he went along with her idea without her having to say a word.

"Okay. You walk over to the 'Bend and I'll drive them out there. We'll take care of it," Rush said to Carrie.

Carrie beamed and rose onto her tiptoes to kiss him.

"Don't be long," she said as she wiped the side of his mouth off and turned to leave for the 'Bend.

The boys got into the truck with Rush about the same time Brad Oxley was backing his old truck out of the driveway with Mark in tow. They puttered down the highway toward Derbie.

"Are you boys sure about this?" Rush asked.

"Yeah. One hundred percent," Noah answered.

Rush put the truck in gear and went through the Chapman's back yard and toward the sinkhole.

4

Linton had driven all over Fogstow and could not find anyone with a four-wheel drive truck that could get some man power up over Pine Hill to help with the fire. This frustrated him. Of all days that people would sick or go missing, it had to be the day that his best friend got killed and he had to deal with a massive fire on a hillside full of inbred cannibals.

He was ashamed of thinking that way. It almost made him feel guilty to be so selfish. But he didn't care at the moment. He pulled the Bronco up behind the Co-op and parked it. He needed to go upstairs and see if Kelly had reached the county for the units and fire trucks.

As Linton pulled up, Siders could see from the back seat what Joe and Noah were up to. They were getting into a truck with that Amiano boy and heading back toward the sinkholes. He was going to have to blow off Derr and go take care of this himself.

It also seemed to Siders that Derr was giving him the run around, like he was stalling for time or something. He probably sent those boys out to the sinkhole to pull that girl out, all the while keeping him within his sights so that he could arrest him as soon as he had hard evidence.

He could get out and walk away from Derr and Stark right now and they wouldn't be able to do anything. They would also be too tied up with the fire to be able to deal with him as well. Right then was the best time to take care of business, while Derr and that deputy were preoccupied. He would take care of this now, and take care of Derr later.

Linton got out of the Bronco and sprinted up the stairs. Stark sat in the passenger seat and waited for him.

Siders opened his door and got out of the Bronco. He didn't say anything to Stark when he walked away. Stark just stared at him as he made his way across Locust out to the caddy-corner. For Stark, Siders' weird departure was a blessing.

* * *

As he watched Siders walk away, Stark saw the fire trucks wailing in from the highway. The deputies were close behind. They brought all the manpower they could muster, but it was going to be a battle just getting the fire trucks up the muddy hill.

Linton came hurdling back down the stairs and ran toward the fire engine. He and the driver talked over a plan of action and drove off down Locust onto Main Street, then Highway 66 ,to the only known turnoff for Pine Hill that could lead them up to the Jeffries' plateau.

The fire was starting to die down when they reached the hillside, which was so slick there was no way they could get their fire engines up it.

Linton decided to cram as many firemen into his Bronco as he could, and they barreled up the hill. Several deputies followed them on foot, but by the time they got there, the houses were mostly burnt down and it didn't look like there were going to be any survivors. They started searching for anyone who might need medical attention.

What a mess! Linton thought.

5

Carolyn and Lucy had made their way into the 'Bend for ice cream when they met up with Carrie just outside the door.

"Hi there, Carrie. What brings you out here today?" Carolyn asked.

Carrie kept her hands buried in her vest pockets and smiled at them.

"I was just hoping I could hang out here until my boyfriend gets back. He ran the boys out to the sinkhole to . . ." she wondered if should say anything just yet and decided against it, ". . . to see if their bikes were still out there."

Carolyn unlocked the 'Bend and motioned Carrie and Lucy inside.

"Okay," Carolyn said, and decided not to press any harder. If nothing else, she could use the extra company.

After Carrie walked inside, Carolyn heard a commotion down at the docks. She walked across the street and looked down the bluff and could see all the people congregating around the Stow. She saw blankets wrapped around them; they all appeared sickly. Their skin was pale, their bodies looked frail and they were hunched over as if they were in pain. That was enough to worry her. It appeared as if there was a bug or something going around, and her first thought was to get Lucy, Kelly and herself out of town before they caught anything. She would go ahead and take Carrie with them if she wanted to come.

Carolyn made her way back to the 'Bend, asked Carrie to keep an eye on Lucy, and walked up the stairs in the alley and went into Linton's office. Kelly was sitting at the desk waiting on Linton to call in on the comms.

"Kelly, I think we better get out of town."

This startled Kelly. *Surely Carolyn didn't think the fire was going to reach all the way down the hill and spread across the town.*

"I don't think the fire is that bad," Kelly said.

"It's not the fire that I'm worried about," Carolyn said. She walked across the room and opened up the window that overlooked Main Street in the Highland district and gave them a view straight down the bluff and onto the docks.

Kelly got up and looked out the window and saw what Carolyn had been talking about. The people weren't just sickly; they were drinking out of the channel! She was both scared and disgusted. Some of them were furiously scratching their fingertips with rocks and others were drooped over like they were about to pass out.

"Oh, Jesus. What's wrong with them?"

She noticed several who looked like they had lost ten pounds overnight. It was frightening to see such an awful thing happening to her own people, but Carolyn was right. If they stayed, they could catch it, too.

"I can't say for certain, but it looks like an epidemic of some sort. All I know is I want to get you and Lucy back to Derbie before we catch anything."

Kelly nodded and got on the CB with Linton. She told him they were heading to Derbie. She would call Amy Strange when they got back to the Reservation and let her know what was happening. Someone needed to get down there and help them. They didn't deserve to suffer like that!

Carolyn had already grabbed Kelly's jacket and they both left to get Lucy from the 'Bend.

Carrie had decided to stay there and wait for Rush and the boys to get back. She had taken a liking to the boys, and she wanted her own family. She and Rush were both eighteen and they had graduated high school last spring. It was time to start their lives, and she really hoped he felt the same way.

Kelly let her stay in the 'Bend, and Carrie promised to lock it up when she left. But she couldn't help but go across the street to see what they had been talking about. She could see at least 50 people down there, just as Carolyn had described.

Carrie rushed back to the 'Bend, shut the door and locked it. That had been one of the creepiest things she had ever seen. When Rush returned, she would insist they get out of town. Maybe go stay with some of their friends down in Barrelton or take one of the cabins at Carolyn's reservation, if she would let them. But Carolyn Weyerbacher-Derr had always kept those cabins closed off to the people around here.

6

About the same time everyone in Fogstow was waking up to the new Hoosier Dawn, Cam Wright was taking a johnny from the Bucky Cole barge over to Rocky Pointe Marina just outside of Cannelton. He wanted to hitch a ride back into Fogstow. The captain had given him leave so he could go back and check on something. Cam hadn't told him the real reason why, though. He'd made up a story about his grandmother being sick and all alone. He had said he wanted to go check on her.

He had made his way off the barge and had said he would come back to Rocky Pointe later in the day to pick up the johnny and rendezvous with the Bucky Cole on its way back up the river.

When he got to the Marina, he met up with a guy driving short hauls on a milk tanker. He said he could get Cam as far as Derbie, but his route cut off there and circled back around to Ferdinand, out by the interstate. Cam shook his hand and climbed in. He could easily find a ride into Fogstow from Barrelton.

The truck dropped by all the local farms to pick up the milk. After the driver's route was complete, he would take it to the dairy plant in Holland. The guy was an independent contractor for the West Dubois Dairy Company, after they had cancelled their contract with Cliff Holder's trucking company.

Cam actually enjoyed the ride. They didn't have to make many farm stops as they cruised along the scenic byway of the Ohio River. He'd seen a lot of the river on the barge, and he couldn't have cared less about watching it at the moment. The sky was overcast and the day was dark. Not much sunlight was going to spill through, so Cam just leaned back in his seat, pulled his UMWA hat over his eyes and took a nap.

* * *

Once they reached Barrelton, the driver woke him up and dropped him on the square in front of the Five and Dime Store. He gave the man a wave and the driver blasted his horn as he drove away.

Cam walked down to the filling station, about two blocks from the square. He was glad that he had remembered to wear his long underwear under his vest. The day was cold and his ears were starting to hurt. He bundled his jacket up, and when he walked inside the gas station, he bought a cup of coffee and looked around for anyone he might know, preferably someone who lived in Fogstow and with whom he could catch a ride.

Although he knew no one inside the station, he did see an extended-cab truck wheel by with Cliff Holder behind the wheel and Bret Holder in the passenger seat. Even in a residential area, that wealthy old man still trucked through like it was his own personal racetrack. He always drove like he was in a hurry, and people had a habit of simply getting out of his way. He was cantankerous, ornery and downright greedy. He had his hand in just about every lucrative business in Jamison County and Cam had about as much use for him as he did for a tampon.

Although he had expected a lot of people from Fogstow out and about in Barrelton today for deer season, he would wait there another hour and a half before he would find a ride back into town.

It was Russ Morgan who finally pulled through and picked him up. Russ had his gun hitched on a rack behind their heads in the truck, and Cam noticed it when he hopped in. Can saw there wasn't any dead game in his truck bed.

"No luck today?" Cam asked.

Russ wondered what he was talking about, and then realized Cam thought he had been hunting.

"Oh. No, I don't hunt. Me and the old man just go out and shoot the guns on opening day."

"Speaking of the old man, where is he?"

"I'm not one hundred percent sure, but he left the Elk's dinner last night with Alice Konicke and never came home. I wasn't brave enough to go to her house this morning to pick him up for the trip, so I just went alone."

They both shared a laugh. There was no doubt in their minds that Allen Morgan got lucky last night and it was going to be a scandal, especially when Burnley found out about it. Not that Burnley himself hadn't had a few one-nighters with Alice in their golden years as well. She loved both of them. But that was just their speculation, of course, and they stayed out of it.

7

The pain was back! Harry Keethers had already eaten twice today and now he wanted more. He had scratched his fingertips and his toenails to the point that they were sharp as paring knives. Everyone inside and outside the Stow had done the same, and they were all feeling the same pain. The pain was lurching up inside of them, and judging by the smell, there was no more bodies coming anytime soon.

Harry walked outside just to check, but he was right. The river had not sent any more bodies to feed them. Not that he should have expected it to start with — but he also did not expect to be turned into a monster on a cold October morning in 1993.

He wasn't going to roam the streets and kill people, so what else could he hold out hope for? He expected this beast of a river to feed them. It changed them, so now it could feed them as well!

Suicide.

It wasn't the only thought that was going through his mind. He did not want to do what he was craving at the moment. Killing people was not in his DNA. But his body felt the pain and the hunger much in the same way a lion would when it saw a gazelle grazing on the land.

He thought back to all those vampire movies he watched on TV or in the cinema over the years. He remembered thinking to himself, *why can't they just* not *kill people? They're immortal; it's not like they can die. They can just not kill people and keep on living.* But the movies always explained it like the vampires were driven by the hunger. It overpowered their consciences. Or when they became vampires, they lost their souls and they didn't care if people died.

But he knew, then. It was naïve of him to have ever thought that way. It was in their nature to do that, just like it was in a lion's nature to hunt down its prey and destroy it. But he couldn't bring himself to do it.

Not only could he not will himself into it, but he was physically unable to do it. His body was too weak. All of their bodies were weak. All the people at the Stow looked like patients in a geriatric ward.

Harry leaned against the wall of the Stow with his hand and when he squeezed it, he didn't even realize that his nails cut through the wood. They were so sharp that it required no force. They just cut right through it, like a knife through hot butter.

He took a long look at his hand and those nails. There was nothing natural about them. He felt the tip of his index finger with his left hand and it immediately drew blood.

"Help us!" a voice said from behind him, causing him to whip around.

It was Connie Brown, whose husband Darvin was leaning against the wall behind them. Neither one had eaten anything that came off the river that morning and their bodies were so extremely fragile and malnourished that they could easily be mistaken for a picture of people suffering famine on the cover of National Geographic.

Harry was startled, but relieved to see it was them and not Linton Derr. He reached up to put his hand on her shoulder and gasped a sigh of relief, not realizing he had squeezed her shoulder.

She had the same look of pain on her face. She started to squeal in pain and when Harry pulled his hand back, it was covered in blood. Blood started filling her shirt. Her squealing stopped and slowly, she started to lose her footing and fell. Harry tried to grab her but he was to weak and she fell all the way to the dock planking.

Connie Brown was dead. The wound that his nails made on her back had caused her so much pain that her heart had given out.

Darvin Brown made his way over to his wife as quickly as he could, but it was slower than the average granny. His body was weaker than hers and he kneeled to retrieve her. He hadn't realized that she was dead. He just sat there and held her. Quietly. Like there was no surprise in the matter, just grief and anxiety. Her passing slowly crept over him, but he wouldn't let go. He did not cry or yell. He wished he could simply slip away with her.

Other people were starting to crowd around them on the ground, forming a huddle of sorts. They wiped the snot from their faces and the tears from their eyes. Their bodies were reacting to the pain rapidly, and some were even slobbering. Their blankets were wet from bodily fluids, and their symptoms looked like the combination of a cold, a flu and chickenpox, with deeply pale skin and red blotches.

Then it just happened. They all descended on Connie Brown at the same time. They tore Darvin away and he whimpered like a little boy being pulled from his mother on the first day of kindergarten. He screamed the best he could, but his body was too weak. A man tried to bite Connie, but his teeth just broke off on her flesh. They were too weak and her body had not been tenderized by decomposition or the river.

Everyone stopped at the same time, watching the man hold his bloody teeth in his hand as if he had just been punched by the varsity quarterback. They looked at him in shock and felt their own teeth. They wiggled them like little kids do just before they lose their baby teeth. They were all loose.

The small crowd sat there on their haunches and wondered what they were going to do. Darvin Brown tried to muscle his way back through them, making about as much progress as a rabbit does in the contortions of a boa constrictor.

Harry Keethers squatted down beside Connie and checked her pulse.

She's dead. There's no doubt about it.

Then he reached down and ran his fingernail along her abdomen slowly, as if he were performing a medical procedure. The others started to do the same and soon, there was a frenzy of slashes that broke away what little meat was left on her body, and they didn't have to bite. They just put it in their mouths and swallowed. Chunk after chunk slid down their gullets, the same way a seagull eats fish.

When it was over, her bloodstained bones and tendons were the only things that remained. They had eaten her whole. Her skeletal carcass lay there in a pool of blood on the dock planks. Some were licking the blood off the deck, but the stain still remained.

A man pulled her remains off the dock into the channel and she slowly sank to the bottom, disappearing in the murky river water.

That's when another dead body floated to the surface. It was another drifter. A floater who had just arrived in town for processing there at the all-new Stow Bar & Meat Processing Plant.

Under his breath, Harry cursed the river with all his vigor. It was playing games with them. Maybe it was trying to teach them how to survive. How to hunt and kill for themselves. If it had floated that body fifteen minutes earlier, Connie Brown would still be alive. He would not have the blood of the living on his hands and he would not have the death of a good person on his conscience. But that ominous river had tricked them into killing. It had forced them to pursue their true nature and just like in the animal kingdom, only the strong would survive. That was going to be the theme moving forward and Harry knew it.

He looked back and saw Darvin Brown lying flat on his back with his hand over his chest. His heart had given out and he was dead now, too. Darvin was dead and Harry was the one responsible for him. He had murdered two innocent people and there was nothing that could change that now. Harry was a monster. Even worse, he was a *creeper.*

8

Rush Amiano had parked the big four-wheel drive truck on the edge of the sinkhole and he followed Joe, Noah and Dean down the steep hill to the entrance. They pulled away the clay and drift-wood and hurried through the entrance before putting it back. The water rushed in furiously until they re-plugged the hole. It was more rank this time than they remembered. It smelled like rotten fish and overbearing mildew, mixed in with a coppery odor.

One thing that Joe knew for sure was that they needed to get in and out fast, before Siders circled back around. He may not have known they were down there at the moment, but he would see the truck when he made his way back to his houseboat and know for sure. If that happened, then they were goners.

Joe led the way with a flashlight from the busted storage bin. They did not have their helmets from last time because they had stashed them on the backside of Floating Asshole. It didn't really matter, though. They were expecting to be in and out of there in no time at all.

They made their way down the steep shaft track in the mine. It wasn't very high, so Rush had to squat as they descended it. The bottom of the coal tunnel was nearly half a mile, so the walk was quite uncomfortable for him.

Once they hit the bottom, though, they faced a new challenge. The bottom of the mine was filled with nasty water that had seeped through the sinkhole. It was going to be a mess trying to find the dead girl in there with only one flashlight in the stone cold dark-ness. The smell of coal was the only thing that overpowered the rancid odor of the water. That, and the mildew emanating off the walls of the long-forgotten mine.

"Now where do we look?" Noah wondered.

Joe looked around with the flashlight to try to find a likely spot where Siders could have left her. He saw the old elevator compartment, but nothing was inside of the open doors. The elevator shaft had been filled in and sealed off from above, so there was no way Siders could have stuck her in there, either.

They waded through the water and walked just far enough to try to find some obvious areas where he could have hidden the girl's body, but she could have been anywhere in the enormous mine that was once a staging area for the old Oarshire mining operations.

A sign on the wall read: "OARSHIRE MINING COMPANY WANTS TO REMIND ALL OF ITS EMPLOYEES THAT SAFETY IS OUR NUMBER ONE PRIORITY."

That's when they heard a thunderous crash that sounded like lightning hitting a large steel building. It shook the walls of the mine and several boulder-sized rocks fell from the high ceiling in the staging area. The crash, whatever it was, had shaken the entire area.

Joe shone the light up the mine shaft track, and they all saw water running down it in a slow stream that started flowing faster and faster. The walls of the mine started making noise that sounded a lot like the metal of a tall building bending and stretching, as if it were trying to get comfortable.

More rocks started falling and an area directly behind them suddenly crashed in.

Rush scooped the boys up and started running toward the old elevator compartment. He dropped Noah and Joe but they caught up with him and Dean.

"Get to the elevator! This mine is coming down and the whole TC is going to cave in!" Rush yelled at the boys.

"Okay!" Joe yelled back at him as he struggled to wade through the water. It had filled the area to their chest and they were half-running, half-drifting toward the elevator capsule. Only about 50 more feet.

Another collapse toward the middle of the mine's staging area. It threw Noah and Joe off balance, but they quickly regained their footing after the near-miss of a gigantic, coal-stained stone.

The water was up to their chins now and they weren't running, but rather swimming in the foul flow of rancid water.

More rocks fell from the ceiling and another loud crash indicated that areas of the mine's upward track tunnel had stretched to fill in with sinkage.

Judging by their proximity underground, Rush estimated that they were directly underneath the East Jamison High School, which educated the teenagers of Fogstow and Derbie both on the west side of town, just off Highway 66.

Oh, what I wouldn't give to be on top of this mess right now! Rush thought to himself as he furiously made his way to the open elevator shaft.

He still had Dean in his arms and the last time he turned around, Joe and Noah were not far behind.

Almost there!

Another crash followed by another. Again and again! The mine was collapsing in on itself. Not just one section, but the whole damn thing! It ran all the way from the sinkhole on the southwest side of town, directly under the high school on the west side and bypassed the Highland district altogether. But it still ran the entire length of the TC, at least to the north side of the TC were Rush last saw the old airshaft that he and his friends went down when they were kids.

He finally reached the elevator shaft and sat Dean down. He didn't realize at the moment, but Dean was in such a state of shock that he was completely unresponsive. His claustrophobia had stricken him into a panic and his breathing was labored.

Rush turned to look back for Joe and Noah and they were fighting the water to get to them. The surface of the elevator capsule was elevated and the water level inside it was considerably lower.

Noah was in the lead and Joe was directly behind him.

The slow cracking sound made an easily identifiable flexing sound, and all at the same moment, the entire mine caved in. Rush was looking at Noah and Joe swimming toward them, Joe's light fluttering with the movement of his little arms as he tried to keep his head above water. The next moment they were gone. In their places were boulders the size of small cars.

Dirt filled between the boulders that buried the two boys and musky odors sprayed out of them. The cave-in caused the water level in the elevator compartment to rise almost to the top of its ceiling.

Rush screamed for Noah and Joe over and over again. He floated to the top of elevator capsule. He reached down for Dean and finally found him, pulling him to the top of the capsule.

They had less than six inches of area to breathe in. It was completely dark and Dean was unconscious. Rush couldn't even tell if he was breathing. He wrapped him in his arms and kept trying to feel for a breath, all while holding him above the water.

"Stay with me, man! Dean! Stay with me!" Rush screamed at him while he fought to catch some air himself. It was almost completely dark inside the capsule. The only exception was a small light above it that was peeking through.

Rush struggled violently to keep himself and Dean both afloat in the elevator capsule. The top of the elevator and the shaft had been filled in after the mine closed, so there was little hope of escaping through it.

He was tiring out quickly. He needed something to brace himself against so he could rest while he held them up. But there was nothing.

When he had thought before about a moment like this, when there was little to no hope for survival, Rush had once imagined himself praying to God. But that is not what occupied his mind at that moment. All he could see was the image of little Joel and Noah being crushed by boulders. It kept playing over and over in his mind as his fight to stay above the water level, just six inches below the ceiling of the elevator capsule, started to weaken. They were trapped.

There was no hope for escape. They were all going to be entombed in that mine. But still, the image of Joe and Noah kept running through his mind. He did not want to let Dean die, but a certain feeling of inevitability was creeping into his mind as the mine crash continued to roar thunderously from above.

He would have given anything to have had a fighting chance in the TC with these boys instead of being buried alive in this coal mine

9

Shane Duncan Siders had made his way to the sinkhole, directly behind the truck Rush Amiano and the three boys were in. He hadn't quite kept up with them, but he would find out soon enough just where they were going.

As if it wasn't enough that he had given that Joe Terrance kid life. That little pissant had to meddle in his affairs and become some sort of small-town hero. He knew all about Joe and his friends. He had watched them all from a distance for years. But now, that little bastard had betrayed him and he needed to see that things got taken care of.

It took him nearly fifteen minutes to reach the sinkhole, and sure enough, that truck was parked right at the edge of the damned thing. None of the boys were around, and that could only mean one thing. They were down in the mine. Down somewhere they didn't belong.

Siders approached the edge of the sinkhole and pondered what the hell he was going to do to take care of this. If he went down there, he would have to kill all four of those boys, and it might not be an easy task. There's no telling what those little assholes were armed with and the situation might not end in his favor.

He took a seat at the edge of the cliff and thought over his options. He looked around at the gray sky and thought to himself that today was just like any other day. How could he have let it go so far? How could he have let it get so out of hand? He had never been this careless before.

Deer ran across the opposite side of the sinkhole on the open land. Hunters were out in full force and the deer would be scattering all over the place, which usually meant more roadkill for people to pick up.

The Jeffries.

It would be a cold day in hell before their kind would get another shot at living in these parts. He had already taken care of that.

He stood up, turned around and saw a few wild rabbits scuttling around the brush at the edge of the bluff trail in the distance. Then it occurred to him. The answer was right in front of his face.

He opened the door of the truck and looked to see if the keys were in it.

Nothing.

But the nice thing about these older model trucks was that you could jam the steering column and unlock the safety switch to put it in gear.

He pulled the gear lever down and stepped out of the truck. That damn thing might have weighed a ton or two, but he was able to push it, just a few feet at a time. He had to reach high to keep hold of the steering wheel, but eventually, he was able to get it to the edge of the cliff.

One more push and that beast of a truck was going to take a plunge right down the sinkhole, directly on top of the mine entrance.

A smile spread across his face and he gave it one last shove.

The monster truck with its enormous mud tires trailed hastily down the sidewall of the sinkhole and when it crashed into the entrance, it went directly through and plowed into the mine, opening up a gigantic hole. The pit water rushed over the sunken truck like Niagara Falls and damn near emptied the sinkhole.

"*Sayonara*, you little shits!"

He heard the breaks in the mine walls tearing through, and he started to realize that this little event was going to swallow up a significant portion of Fogstow if it kept going.

Sure enough, the land above the mine started to cave in. It looked like a giant monster was making his way through the ground in a straight line as Siders watched the land fall directly in a line toward East Jamison High School.

Well, I guess that takes care of that problem.

But then he thought about Linton Derr. What had those boys told him?

Siders wrinkled his nose and snarled under his breath as he made his way back to the river to board his houseboat.

I guess I'll have to show him some love as well.

10

Linton Derr made his way back down the muddy hill with the firemen and deputies in his Bronco. They needed to get a helicopter in there for the Jeffries plateau, as well as an investigator to see what had caused the fire that had taken them out. Linton suspected arson. It raged for about an hour before the mist took care of the rest. There was little more they could do at the time, so he took a load of emergency personnel back down to the highway and the county fire inspector stayed behind to look over the remains.

Several of them had to get back to Barrelton to stay on duty. They had their entire squad out on the Jeffries plateau and now that the fire was out, it was time to be ready for other emergencies.

Linton took the muddy hill quickly, sliding through the runoffs and straddling the ruts to avoid getting hung up. Once they hit the bottom, which was basically a portion of Highway 66, they slammed down on the surface like they had just jumped the hill. Everyone in the Bronco had enjoyed the thrilling trip, but they were filing out of it and loading up on their fire engines.

Startling loud crashes were coming from just inside town, apparently from the TC. They could see the ground dropping out from under the TC in a straight line. The firemen jumped into their engines and fired them up, racing toward the scene of the disaster. The deputies followed them in their cruisers.

Dust and water sprayed from the ground as the cave-in broke through utility lines. The telephone poles were vanishing, homes sinking and disappearing. The ground was giving in. Sparks were jumping from downed power lines and the entire TC was a straight line of disaster.

The fire engines raced along the highway to get a better look at what was happening in the TC, and the line of sinkholes trekked its away across the area, quickly approaching the highway.

The fire engines stopped to see where the line of disaster was headed, and no sooner could they get a good read on it than the ground below them gave out and swallowed all four fire trucks and five deputy cruisers.

Linton pulled up directly behind them in his Bronco. He jumped out, with Stark close behind. They stood at the edge of the cave-in, seeing if they could see the brave men. He saw the engines being swallowed by the earth below them as soil quickly rose over the tops of the fire ladders. The deputy cars were underneath the trucks in the mess, already gone from sight.

Linton could hear them screaming from inside their mobile tombs, trapped and yelling for help. But there was nothing they could do.

Stark tried to crawl down what was once the edge of Highway 66 in a desperate attempt to reach them, but Linton stopped him and pulled him away from the edge.

There was no sense in Stark losing his life on a long shot at reaching those men. They were gone. The rest was just the added torture of hearing them scream as they raced toward their fate: to be buried alive, much the same as Joe Terrance and Noah Buchanon.

The edge of the cave-in was unstable and started to give away. Linton had to force Stark to move back as the ground below them started to crumble. He pulled him all the way back to the Bronco, and for the first time, they had a real chance to scope the carnage that lay ahead of them. The entire TC was gone. It had swallowed the whole area in what seemed like less than a minute.

To top that off, the town was sealed off. There was no way into Fogstow from the northeast end. Highway 66 was the only route in, and an entire section of it was missing, along with nearly all the emergency personnel in Jamison County. The only people left in the county for emergency services were Linton, Stark, Sheriff Kramer (who was still in Barrelton) and the Barrelton City Police Force.

"Listen, Stark! I need you to get on the horn with Kramer down in Barrelton. Update him on the situation and have him send immediate help into town! Do it now!" Linton shouted.

Stark could only stare at the disaster for a moment in total disbelief, then he nodded and slowly made his way back to the CB in the Bronco

Linton tried approaching the disaster line, but the ground was too unstable. He went back to the Bronco and pulled it further north up Highway 66.

Stark was on the CB with dispatch down in Barrelton, and when Kramer got on the line, he thought Stark was pulling a gag on him. Then Linton got on the radio and confirmed the mess. He requested immediate emergency services to come into Fogstow on the southwest entrance and to follow up with surrounding counties for assistance on the northeast side of what was now ground zero for his small community.

Although Linton did not know it at the time, the southwest end of Fogstow had also collapsed along with Highway 66 just before it hit the TC. The high school was gone and the town was completely sealed off from emergency personnel. The town of Fogstow was now lawless, with a bar full of hungry *Creepers* waiting to prowl.

Chapter 6
The Fall of Fogstow

CARRIE LeBALTE WAS STARTLED OUT OF HER CHAIR when the disaster line started to thunder across the highway into the TC. It sounded like they were being air bombed. She was too young to remember what it was like when Oarshire was operational. They used explosives to blast out areas for surface mining before they breached the upper line and built tunnels below. The sounds of the disaster were much like those when they were first stripping the area.

She ran outside to see what was going on. Nothing. She approached the side of the bluff that looked down on the docks, and there stood legions of desperate Creepers, looking up at her with immense pain in their eyes. They were still shrouded in their blankets.

She saw Harry Keethers walk out of the bar. He did not look

quite like the rest. They all had slim, skeletal features, and they looked weak and sickly. But not Harry Keethers. He looked like he was made up of nothing more than skin, bones and ligaments. And those eyes! There was no humanity left in them.

Oh my God! His fingernails!

Carrie wanted to race back into the 'Bend. Never in her life had she seen such a terrifying view of people. They weren't even people anymore. They looked more like monsters.

They're drinking out of the channel!

She turned to run back toward the 'Bend, but that's when she saw the cloud rising over the west side of town. It reminded her of those documentaries she used to watch on PBS when she was a kid, the ones about the dust bowl in Kansas, or somewhere around there.

She knew she shouldn't leave her back turned on Harry and those things down at the Stow, so she made her way directly back into the 'Bend and quickly locked the door. It should have been safe enough, but they could break through the glass if they saw her inside. She needed to get farther back, somewhere inside the kitchen, and hide. Somewhere she could still see outside, but they wouldn't be able to look in and see her.

* * *

Harry Keethers and his people looked at the dust cloud rising out of the west. He knew that something was going terribly wrong there, and his phone in Barrelton would be ringing off the hook. By the looks and sounds of the carnage, there would be dead bodies all over.

Carnage!

It was everything that his kind would be looking for now. They needed to feed to get rid of this pain. That indescribable feeling, like their bodies were dying. That was the only way he could think of it. The pain of dying. It was going to be either those people or his people and in the end, it would come down to making a choice. Eat and survive, or wither away and die. Not just die, but endure one of the most excruciating deaths imaginable. That *slow burn* eating away at their life force.

"That's not going to happen," Harry said out loud as he thought about it.

We're going to live. We're going to feed and we're going to live. Only the strong survive!

There were no more bodies in the channel and his people were all fading away. They had already started turning on each other and the macabre dance was playing out inside the Stow as he stood outside with others, watching the dust cloud in the west rising over the city. The day was darkening, and if there were ever a time to strike, that would be it.

Harry walked to the edge of the steps that led up to the Highland district, and on his way, he yanked blankets off people's shoulders and threw them in the channel.

He reached the third step and turned around to address his people.

"There were about a hundred of us out here this morning when we woke up and made our way to the channel. Right about now, I would estimate there's about half that number. Some have been dying off while others have turned on our own kind, whatever our kind may be. But one thing's for sure! We know what we must do to survive. Some of us have had a hard time coming to terms with it. But that doesn't make it any less true.

"It's time we accept our nature. It's time we come to terms with our fight and what we must do to survive. I know that some of you won't be able to do it, and that's just fine. But for the rest of us, we're going up there and we are going to take this town for our own."

Harry turned and pointed at the gigantic dust cloud that appeared over the horizon.

"You see that cloud up there? Now I can't say for certain at this time, but I know for a fact that the Oarshire Mining Company sold off all that reclaim land dirt-cheap for a reason. It was because they wanted to get out from underneath it and make it someone else's problem. They had already stripped our land to the skeletal roots and they wanted to be done with us.

"That cloud you see up there is the result of a greedy corporation that did not want to pay to have those mines filled in. Instead, they just left them there to rot. Their supports may have lasted a good decade or so, but eventually they would give out.

"We all saw what could happen when that sinkhole out by the bluff park caved in and now, the rest of that mine has gone under. That dust cloud you see up there, that wasn't made from a dynamite stick. The mine has caved in and the land has been reclaimed by the Earth.

"Does anybody know what that means?"

The people in the crowd shook their heads.

"That means this town has been sealed off. That means no emergency personnel can get in, and nobody can get out."

Their eyes started glow as the lights turned on in their heads. There was a lot of truth to what Harry just said, and to them, that only meant one thing. It was dinnertime!

He knew that he had rallied a sleeping monster.

He thought to himself, *Why did I do that?*

He had not wanted to in the beginning, so why now? Why not just take care of his main four and let the rest figure it out for themselves? It would have after all meant less of a body count and more security for their kind.

He tried to reason it out with himself. It was the disaster. It was nature's way of giving them a push toward sustaining themselves. It was the river that had come upon them and forced them into this and set the conditions just right so that they would embrace it.

It was no surprise to him that his people had been charged by his speech. It was as if the lights had finally come on in their translucent eyes and had given them the will to live. The will to kill and the need to be pain-free. They were all about to become merciless killers and it was those itchy fingers that gave them their most dangerous advantage.

2

Harry led his people up the concrete steps to the Highland district, just as others were leaving their houses on Locust Street and Main to get a glimpse of the disaster that was taking place. They did not even see them coming.

One lady held a cat and shaded her eyes with her hands as she watched the dust cloud rise. There was no sunlight smashing through; it was just a knee-jerk reaction to a cloud of dust. She wore a sweatshirt that read *Indiana Hoosiers* across the front and had crimson candy stripes down both shoulders. She was about fifty pounds overweight and all alone in the world after the death of her husband at the age of 46. Her son had left home three years ago and had never come back, taking up work in Louisville before relocating to Portland, Maine for a permanent position. He called her the first two years over the holidays, but he'd forgotten this past season. She had no other family.

It was Harry himself who walked up behind her and dealt the first blow of the war that would eventually lead to the end of Fogstow.

One swipe across the lady's back and her shoulder split open, a layer of bloody fat rolling out of it. She never even had a chance to look back at who struck her. She fell to the ground and landed on top of her cat.

The fall killed the cat, but she was still very much alive. Although she could feel the pain, she could not move her body. She was paralyzed. The Creepers had just realized the new paralyzing power of their claws, and they slowly crowded in on her and started filleting her body to pieces as she lay flat on her stomach in a whirlwind of pain that quickly dissipated as her life slipped away.

The first strike did not grab anyone's attention. She did not make much noise. People around the Highland district were congregating with each other, trying to figure out was happening west of town.

While the lady lay there, slashed to pieces by the highly evolved, monstrous people who had turned overnight, her fellow townsfolk gossiped in a small circle about the blasts they used to hear coming from the now defunct coal mine. They wondered if they were trying to reopen the mine for some reason, but that sounded ludicrous, to say the least.

Their discussion did not last long, though, as several Creepers descended upon them and ran their razor sharp nails across faces, stomachs, ears, legs, arms and scalps. Each one only got one slash from the Creepers' claws, and they all went down, instantly paralyzed.

The Creepers themselves hadn't been aware of this ability, but evidently, it was part of their evolution.

In total, eleven people from the Highland district were slashed apart while they were alive. Creepers tore off pieces of flesh and slid them down their throats in an enormous frenzy.

Others walked down Locust hill to the edge of Squaw Creek and the TC only to find the gaping hole left in the ground. It was just as their leader had predicted before he had sent them up to the Highland and told them the town was theirs.

People were gathered at the edge of the sinkhole, trying to find survivors of the TC collapse. They were spread out along the disaster line and the Creepers had to take them all one at a time.

Mike Brownsman dealt the first blow. While other Creepers were slashing people along the disaster line, one took a swipe at Mike and he saw it coming. He ducked out of its way and punched it with a side swing to the temple.

The Creeper's head came clean of its body and tumbled down the hole.

They might have had the advantage of extremely sharp nails and paralysis on their side, but one thing they didn't have was a physically strong body to defend themselves with. Their bodies had been broken down and were extremely vulnerable to even the slightest force. Their skin had become weak and easily broken. It had become apparent to them they were not quite as powerful as they might have thought in their bold attempt to feed off the town.

Mike came to the aid of a teenage girl who had been taken down by a Creeper's slash and he kicked its ribcage.

The Creeper's ribs splintered inside of it and it fell over and died almost instantly.

A few others fought back alongside Mike, but many had been slashed and paralyzed by the time Mike and his brave defenders got to them. The Creepers had already filleted parts of their flesh off and swallowed the chunks whole. When Mike came running, it tried to flee, but he had it boxed in at the side of the disaster line. The pain and fear in the Creeper's eyes turned to a snarl as it leaped into the hole and grasped the vertical wall with its nails. It scuttled along the wall and disappeared into the crashed mine below it.

Before the episode was over, the Creepers had taken out 26 people and left 11 others still alive, but paralyzed. They all started scurrying off at superhuman speeds, disappearing into the mine, scaling the walls with only the nails on their fingers and toes.

As soon as Mike turned around, a claw slashed directly across his face and dropped him like an insect that had just been spray bombed. It was Harry Keethers' hand that delivered the blow.

He squatted down to look Mike Browsman in the eyes. The teen could only stare back at the horrible monstrosity in front of him.

Mike's posse of heroes raced to his side, and before Harry took off over the edge, he slowly jabbed Mike's throat, running his nail from left to right. Blood poured out of Mike's neck and Harry's face turned into a painful visage before he disappeared into the mine.

Three men came to Mike's side to stop the bleeding. One man kneeled beside him and held his hand across his throat tightly, which also cut off Mike's air supply.

It was not meant to be. A second wave of Creepers came from behind and slashed all three men. The last of those who knew how to fight them, or who were at least brave enough to take swings at the menacing monsters, had been taken out.

The Creepers emerged from the mine pits and began feasting on the heroes, slicing off portions of their arms and legs first, then finishing off their stomachs and, finally, their throats.

The circumstances of their early evening feeding had differed quite rapidly from how they fed that morning, which was with disgusted and skeptical bites. Before, their guilt held them at bay, but not enough to turn away from the food. Now, they took pleasure in the pain their victims felt, almost as if they were delighted to see them experiencing the same pain as themselves.

They feasted with such ravenous voracity that they expelled their wastes on the spot. Their digestive tracts had adopted a cycling mechanism that allowed them to maintain a constant flow of nourishment.

Seventy-nine people lost their lives on the streets of Fogstow that evening before the party was interrupted by outside forces. The district of Alcatraz Beach was left mostly untouched.

3

Sheriff Marvin Kramer had tried to come into Fogstow through Derbie on Highway 66, but had found that the road had vanished from sight. He had called back into dispatch to have a Coast Guard boat meet him at the dock in Derbie and parked his cruiser at the Reservation with Carolyn. Then he'd called in support from the surrounding counties.

He registered a response from across the river in Loudon, Kentucky. Sheriff Harry Barnes said he was coming in with some deputies and his own locals, including Pete Little and the Broshears fella who'd played minor league ball in Macon, Georgia under the Atlanta Braves back in the '80s. They had been known around those parts to be a great asset to the local Red Cross efforts when the tornadoes swept through southwestern Indiana.

They all docked in Derbie and when the Coast Guard arrived, they took Sheriff Kramer into Fogstow with Barnes, Little and Broshears to get a read on the situation.

The duty officer navigated the boat into the Fogstow channel and the eerie scene was disconcerting to Kramer. Thick fog danced on the high bluff walls and floated across the surface of the water. The day was considerably darker after the cave-in and they all second-guessed the mission due to the creep factor alone. Once they reached the docks, it got even worse. There was no one in sight and the fog lifted only in the area that would allow them to dock and enter the town.

The duty officer slowly approached the dock and as he did, the water parted, revealing to Marvin Kramer the single most terrifying thing of his life.

The murky depths of the channel let loose the fruit of the River's loins. Bodies started surfacing from the dark water. Not one, but ten, twenty, maybe thirty bodies bubbled up from below and floated on the surface.

Kramer gasped as he held his heart and rubbed a hand through his hair. Barnes and Broshears had slowly pulled their service weapons from their holsters and quietly held them as they looked around for the ominous presence that undoubtedly had been responsible for this atrocity.

But the bodies did not come from Fogstow.

(The river will not kill people, but it will hide your bodies.)

The channel had brought these bodies in from the river, and instead of floating them for the Creepers, they floated them for men who had come there to save lives. The men who'd come to lend a hand to people in need. The channel floated these bodies to warn them of what it was capable of. It gave them a reason to leave the place alone. The town belonged to the river now. It belonged to the river and its Creepers.

* * *

Barnes and Broshears quickly raised their service weapons at the sight of three men running down the concrete steps that once served the town's thriving docks. They showed no sign of slowing down once they reached the dock, and Kramer lowered Barnes's and Broshears's arms with assurance once he saw who they were.

Linton Derr, Jeff Stark and the county fire inspector approached the boat, clearly in distress. Once they were dockside, instead of boarding, they just slumped over on their knees and stared at the ground while they caught their breath. The fog had already covered up the bodies in the water.

Kramer put a hand on Linton's back while he stood with one foot on the dock and the other in the boat.

"Linton? Tell me buddy. What's happened here?" Kramer

asked.

Linton regained his breath and leaned up to speak.

"They're all dead, Marv. Everyone is dead," Linton said.

"What do you mean? Did the sinkhole get *everyone*?"

"No, Marvin. You don't understand. They are all dead. As in, murdered."

"What?"

"Stark and I. We walked back up through the Jeffries plateau and circled around the lower bluffs behind the Beach. We came in through Squaw Creek and we found them, Marvin. It wasn't just some of them. The sinkhole only got the TC. It was someone, or something else that got the rest. They're all over the streets of Fogstow right now. Torn to pieces."

Kramer had a look on his face that almost seemed like he had tasted something disgusting and sour. He took his hand off Linton's back and stepped his one foot back on the boat. He turned to face the bluffs and noticed all the fog had strayed away from them and was floating over the channel, covering the floating bodies. As if it had just reminded him there were bodies floating in that channel, all around them. He looked back at Linton and Stark.

"Are you sure it's everyone?"

Linton nodded his head.

"All dead?" Kramer asked.

"Sheriff," Stark said, "Fogstow is gone. It's all over here."

"How would you like for us to proceed, Sheriff?" the duty officer asked him.

Kramer raised his hat and ran his hands through his hair for a moment, trying to absorb everything before he answered.

"Let's get these men back to Derbie," Kramer said. "They've been through hell today. We need to give the state boys a call and see what kind of help we can get down here."

"Would you like us to make any inquiries on your behalf, Sheriff?" the duty officer responded.

"I suppose it couldn't hurt. But for now, we need to get through to the governor's office and have them declare a state of emergency. I got a feeling we are going to need some federal dollars for this shit storm."

"Copy that, Sheriff," the duty officer replied. "Gentlemen, please climb aboard our vessel and we will get you back to Derbie."

"Wait! Wait!" voices from behind the Stow yelled at them. Barnes and Broshears pointed their sidearms.

Jack and Derri Emmons came running toward them, and Linton motioned for the men to lower their weapons. They both approached and didn't need to say a word.

Linton and Stark boarded and turned to help Jack and Derri onto the vessel. They slowly departed Fogstow through the channel. The fog parted for them to pass, and then repaired itself once they were through. When they were outside of the channel, they met boats clearing out from the Beach as well. Linton counted thirteen as they made their way into the currents of the Ohio.

He was relieved. *We're not the only ones who want out of this place. Thank God the Beach was cut off from the main district. It might have been the only thing that saved their lives.*

Fogstow, Indiana and all its ruins now belonged to the Creepers.

* * *

It would be another six hours before emergency crews would show up in Fogstow from the state. They went in through the channel armed with assault rifles and night vision equipment. They sported body armor and helmets, and when they encountered Creepers on the street feasting on dead bodies, they opened fire and took out at least forty of them.

Carrie LeBalte remained hidden inside the 'Bend, frozen in terror, and never came out.

Several Creepers had fled into the TC ruins, and they waited out the state and federal investigation before the town was permanently sealed off from the public. The only way in was through the channel.

Residents of the Beach got both state and federal funding for relocation, and the Bucky Cole barge came in and provided river transportation for the relocation efforts of the remaining townsfolk.

The Creeper's story would continue, at some point in the future. Cam Wright and Russ Morgan would make sure of that.

4

The duty officer pulled up to the Derbie dock in front of Carolyn's reservation and mounted. The day had been more than Linton could handle, and all he wanted to do was be with his family. He wanted to lie down beside Kelly and just close his eyes. He wanted to forget this day had ever happened.

They all got off the boat and Linton invited everyone inside. They had to wait there for the state boys anyway after Kramer made the call, and there was no need to make them wait on the boat.

But it was all the same to them and they stayed with their vessel. So did Barnes, Broshears and Little.

Linton, Stark, Kramer, Jack and Derri all made their way up to the main house and walked around the back to enter. They never used the front door because Carolyn kept a piano in front of it.

"Jack, you and Derri can stay here for the night. We'll suit up a cabin for you and you both can stay for as long as you like," Linton said.

"We appreciate it, Linton," Jack said. He led Derri out back toward the cabins.

Linton turned the corner to the back of the house. Just before he reached for the doorknob, he heard sobbing coming from inside the coal bin next to the house. Kramer and Stark both heard it too.

"What the hell?" Stark said.

Linton approached the coal bin, and when he opened the large wooden lid, a scream emerged. There lay Lucy, tucked into a corner and squirming like someone was about to hurt her.

"Dear God!" Linton said and reached for Lucy, who was weeping with her eyes closed. When Linton's hand touched her shoulder, she screamed bloody murder.

"Lucy! Lucy, it's Linton, sweetheart. It's Linton!"

Lucy opened her eyes and frantically crawled toward him. Linton scooped her up and held her. She locked onto him tightly, with surprising force.

"What's wrong, honey? It's okay. You can tell me," Linton said.

"Momma! You hafta help Momma!" Lucy said.

Linton took a look around and saw the back door was slightly ajar.

"Is your Momma inside, honey?"

Lucy nodded and mumbled "*uh-huh,*" still clinging to Linton.

Linton looked at Kramer and tried to hand her off to him, but Lucy resisted.

"It's okay, sweetie. Sheriff Kramer is going to take you to his car and he will lock it. No one can get you inside the police car," Linton said. "I'm gonna go help your momma."

Lucy leaned back and looked at him, and then grabbed Marvin Kramer. He took her to the car and sat inside with her while Linton and Stark took out their service weapons and entered the house.

Linton crept inside and peeked around the corner. He could see nothing in the kitchen except the knife block, which had been knocked over. He slowly crossed through the kitchen, and as he approached the living room, he saw Carolyn lying face down in a pool of blood. He quickly approached his mom and rolled her over. The shock of what he saw made him double back and stick his knuckle in his mouth.

"Oh, no. Oh, Momma. No, oh no," Linton said as he tried to shake his mother, uselessly. "Momma, no. Wake up, Momma. Wake up!"

She had been stabbed in both of her eyes repeatedly. Carolyn Weyerbacher-Derr had been dead for nearly an hour.

Stark put a hand on his shoulder, but Linton violently slung it away.

"Momma?"

Linton put his ear down to hear her heart, then put it to her nose.

"Come on, Momma. Take a breath."

"Linton, I'm sorry, buddy," Stark said.

Linton whipped around and scowled at Stark, and then tried again to get his mother to breathe.

"She's gone, man," Stark said as he pulled Linton back. He didn't fight him this time. "We still need to find Kelly."

Linton wiped the tears from his eyes with the back of his wrists. His hands had already been stained in his mother's blood. He stood up and positioned his gun in front of him to proceed. Stark followed him up the stairs slowly, and the boards creaked underfoot.

Linton stopped on one step and turned, holding a finger to his lips. He motioned for Stark to stay there.

Linton continued up the stairs alone. Stark watched him as he reached the top of the stairs and disappeared around a corner. He heard Linton open a door, and then nothing. After a few moments, Stark heard footsteps coming back to the corner as he stood there in the middle of the staircase, clueless.

Linton backed up, still leveling his gun in front of him. His face showed no expression. He lowered his gun and leaned against the rail of the stairs, and then slowly slid down the railing and sat on the floor, laying his gun down. He pulled his knees toward his chin and leaned over with his head between them.

Stark walked up the stairs with his gun pointed in front of him and gingerly made his way around Linton. He turned the corner and looked into the only room in sight. What he saw through the open door was too horrifying to register.

Kelly Doss lay naked over the rail of Carolyn's bed. Blood was splattered all over the room — on the walls, on the ceiling, over the open window, on the dresser, on the mirror, on the rug and flooring and all over the closet doors. Her lifeless body had been battered to horrible submission, and pieces of the lamps were scattered across the floor. Carolyn's jewelry box had been busted open and necklaces, earrings and various trinkets were scattered about, immersed in thick pools of blood. The mirror had been shattered to pieces. Kelly's body was covered in puncture wounds and her neck was stuck in a perpetual contortion, where the killer had finally shown her mercy and ended her suffering.

Stark looked back at Linton, wordless. Linton just looked at him with no expression on his face. Almost as if he weren't seeing Stark, or the horrible room behind him. No, Linton Derr was looking into oblivion, his own personal hell, one that he might not have been able to come back from.

Stark's only thought was to get Linton out of the house. He went back for him and raised him to his feet then led him outside. He sat Linton down on a bench beside the back door. The sign above it read "WELCOME TO OUR PEACEFUL HOME."

Kramer got out of his cruiser and shut the door so Lucy could stay inside of it and feel safe.

Stark approached him and spoke low in his ear.

"We need to get this entire Reservation locked down. We have two bodies inside, Sheriff," Stark said.

Kramer was obviously emotional. He started to walk past Stark and toward the door, but Stark grabbed his arm. Kramer thought it was either one of the boldest moves a young deputy had ever made, or that there was something so bad inside the house that his own deputy felt he had to protect him. He looked at Stark, who was showing respect for the sheriff by not looking him in the eyes.

"You're gonna have to trust me, sir. You don't want to go in there," Stark said.

Kramer looked away. He let go of it all for the moment, then took one look at Linton and realized that he appeared to be catatonic. He knew right away that if there was something so bad inside that house to put Linton Derr into that state, he had better heed his deputy's advice.

The men heard footsteps coming from the side of the house. Two people were approaching along in the gravel driveway. They were walking, not running.

Stark and Kramer both pulled out their guns and assumed defensive positions on the opposite side of the car. They realized it could have been the duty officers from the boat or those men from Loudon, but they also knew they had two murder victims inside the house, and they were on edge. They weren't going to take any chances.

The footsteps grew louder as two people, not speaking, approached near the side of the house, about to turn the corner. Stark had already taken his safety off.

Kramer was very much ready to blow holes in someone. But he knew that shooting first would leave no possibility for asking questions later.

The shadows of the two people were now breaching the side of the house. Just a few more steps and they would be within sight.

One step — and a slow trickle of sweat rolled down Stark's left temple, onto his cheek.

Two steps, and the foot of an old Converse sneaker, the kind Kramer hadn't seen in years, came forward. He could pull the trigger on it and someone would go down now and still be able to answer questions later.

But it was that third step that gave everyone a sense of how the future was going to change. It was that third step that would change their lives forever. It was that third step that brought Linton Derr out of his catatonia.

Linton stood. He could not utter a single word.

Standing in front of him was a man in a long-sleeved flannel shirt buttoned up to just below his neckline. He wore an unzipped vest. Beside him stood a woman, also in a flannel shirt, with her hair pulled back in a bandana, arranged like she had just finished dusting a house.

Jack and Derri Emmons came in behind the men. Their faces expressed total shock as they approached Stark and Linton, standing side-by-side.

Standing in front of them were Sammy Derr and Lorie Emmons. But it was not just them. It was them as they were the day they both went missing.

Sammy Derr had not aged one second since 1973, and he was still wearing the same red and white flannel shirt with the black stripes on it. Linton recognized it instantly.

Lorie Emmons still wore the same rag in her hair she had on that day she disappeared in 1979. Jack Emmons remembered it well. Derri had been too young to remember her, but she had seen pictures of her mother. There was no doubt in her mind who she was looking at.

"Excuse me, fellas," Sammy Derr said. "I'm looking for my wife. Her name is Carolyn, and we own this place."

* * *

ABOUT THE AUTHOR

Nick Younker has spent over fifteen years working in the local and national media. After transitioning from television to online journalism, he honed in on his lifelong love of horror entertainment and blended it with his unique abilities as a writer.

You can catch up with him on Twitter at @NYounker, or on his website, FogstowJamison.com, where he publishes his daily news articles about movement in the horror entertainment industry.